*Young Goodman Brown
and Other Stories*

Young Goodman Brown

and Other Stories

Nathaniel Hawthorne

ALMA CLASSICS

ALMA CLASSICS
an imprint of

ALMA BOOKS LTD
3 Castle Yard
Richmond
Surrey TW10 6TF
United Kingdom
www.almaclassics.com

This collection first published by Alma Classics in 2018

Edited text and notes © Alma Books Ltd
Extra Material © Richard Parker

Cover design: Will Dady

Printed in the United Kingdom by CPI Group (UK) Ltd, Croydon CR0 4YY

ISBN: 978-1-84749-652-2

Contents

Nathaniel Hawthorne (1804–64)

Captain Nathaniel "Hathorne",
Hawthorne's father

Sophia Hawthorne,
Hawthorne's wife

Henry Wadsworth Longfellow

Herman Melville

The Salem Custom House, where Hawthorne was employed

Hawthorne's grave in Concord

Manuscript by Hawthorne containing the
plot outline for an unpublished story

*Young Goodman Brown
and Other Stories*

The Gentle Boy

I N THE COURSE OF THE YEAR 1656, several of the people called Quakers, led, as they professed, by the inward movement of the spirit, made their appearance in New England. Their reputation, as holders of mystic and pernicious principles, having spread before them, the Puritans early endeavoured to banish, and to prevent the further intrusion of the rising sect. But the measures by which it was intended to purge the land of heresy, though more than sufficiently vigorous, were entirely unsuccessful. The Quakers, esteeming persecution as a divine call to the post of danger, laid claim to a holy courage, unknown to the Puritans themselves, who had shunned the cross, by providing for the peaceable exercise of their religion in a distant wilderness. Though it was the singular fact that every nation of the earth rejected the wandering enthusiasts who practised peace towards all men, the place of greatest uneasiness and peril, and therefore in their eyes the most eligible, was the province of Massachusetts Bay. The fines, imprisonments and stripes, liberally distributed by our pious forefathers, the popular antipathy, so strong that it endured nearly a hundred years after actual persecution had ceased, were attractions as powerful for the Quakers, as peace, honour and reward would have been for the worldly-minded. Every European vessel brought new cargoes of the sect, eager to testify against the oppression which they hoped to share; and, when shipmasters were restrained by heavy fines from affording them passage, they made long and circuitous journeys through the Indian country and appeared in the province as if conveyed by a supernatural power. Their enthusiasm, heightened almost to madness by the treatment which they received, produced actions contrary to the rules of decency, as well as of rational religion, and presented a singular contrast to the calm and staid deportment of their sectual successors of the present day. The command of the spirit, inaudible except to the soul, and not to be controverted on grounds of human wisdom, was made a plea for most indecorous exhibitions, which, abstractly considered, well deserved the moderate chastisement of the rod. These extravagances, and the persecution which was at once their cause and consequence, continued to increase, till, in the year 1659, the government of Massachusetts Bay indulged two members of the Quaker sect with the crown of martyrdom.*

That those who were active in or consenting to this measure made themselves responsible for innocent blood is not to be denied: yet the extenuating circumstances of their conduct are more numerous than can generally be pleaded by persecutors. The inhabitants of New England were a people whose original bond of union was their peculiar religious principles. For the peaceful exercise of their own mode of worship, an object, the very reverse of universal liberty of conscience, they had hewn themselves a home in the wilderness; they had made vast sacrifices of whatever is dear to man; they had exposed themselves to the peril of death, and to a life which rendered the accomplishment of that peril almost a blessing. They had found no city of refuge prepared for them, but, with Heaven's assistance, they had created one; and it would be hard to say whether justice did not authorize their determination to guard its gate against all who were destitute of the prescribed title to admittance. The principle of their foundation was such, that to destroy the unity of religion might have been to subvert the government and break up the colony, especially

at a period when the state of affairs in England had stopped
the tide of emigration and drawn back many of the pilgrims to
their native homes. The magistrates of Massachusetts Bay were,
moreover, most imperfectly informed respecting the real tenets
and character of the Quaker sect. They had heard of them, from
various parts of the earth, as opposers of every known opinion,
and enemies of all established governments; they had beheld
extravagances which seemed to justify these accusations; and the
idea suggested by their own wisdom may be gathered from the
fact that the persons of many individuals were searched, in the
expectation of discovering witch marks. But after all allowances,
it is to be feared that the death of the Quakers was principally
owing to the polemic fierceness, that distinct passion of human
nature, which has so often produced frightful guilt in the most
sincere and zealous advocates of virtue and religion. An indelible
stain of blood is upon the hands of all who consented to this act,
but a large share of the awful responsibility must rest upon the
person then at the head of the government.* He was a man of
narrow mind and imperfect education, and his uncompromis-
ing bigotry was made hot and mischievous by violent and hasty
passions; he exerted his influence indecorously and unjustifiably
to compass the death of the enthusiasts; and his whole conduct,
in respect to them, was marked by brutal cruelty. The Quakers,
whose revengeful feelings were not less deep because they were
inactive, remembered this man and his associates, in aftertimes.
The historian of the sect* affirms that, by the wrath of Heaven,
a blight fell upon the land in the vicinity of the "bloody town"
of Boston, so that no wheat would grow there, and he takes his
stand, as it were, among the graves of the ancient persecutors,
and triumphantly recounts the judgements that overtook them, in
old age or at the parting hour. He tells us that they died suddenly,
and violently, and in madness; but nothing can exceed the bitter

mockery with which he records the loathsome disease, and "death by rottenness", of the fierce and cruel governor.

* * *

On the evening of the autumn day that had witnessed the martyrdom of two men of the Quaker persuasion, a Puritan settler was returning from the metropolis to the neighbouring country town in which he resided. The air was cool, the sky clear and the lingering twilight was made brighter by the rays of a young moon, which had now nearly reached the verge of the horizon. The traveller, a man of middle age, wrapped in a grey frieze cloak, quickened his pace when he had reached the outskirts of the town, for a gloomy extent of nearly four miles lay between him and his house. The low, straw-thatched houses were scattered at considerable intervals along the road and, the country having been settled but about thirty years, the tracts of original forest still bore no small proportion to the cultivated ground. The autumn wind wandered among the branches, whirling away the leaves from all except the pine trees, and moaning as if it lamented the desolation of which it was the instrument. The road had penetrated the mass of woods that lay nearest to the town, and was just emerging into an open space, when the traveller's ears were saluted by a sound more mournful than even that of the wind. It was like the wailing of someone in distress, and it seemed to proceed from beneath a tall and lonely fir tree, in the centre of a cleared but unenclosed and uncultivated field. The Puritan could not but remember that this was the very spot which had been made accursed a few hours before by the execution of the Quakers, whose bodies had been thrown together into one hasty grave, beneath the tree on which they suffered. He struggled, however, against the superstitious fears which belonged to the age, and compelled himself to pause and listen.

"The voice is most likely mortal, nor have I cause to tremble if it be otherwise," thought he, straining his eyes through the dim moonlight. "Methinks it is like the wailing of a child; some infant, it may be, which has strayed from its mother and chanced upon this place of death. For the ease of mine own conscience, I must search this matter out."

He therefore left the path, and continued somewhat fearfully across the field. Though now so desolate, its soil was pressed down and trampled by the thousand footsteps of those who had witnessed the spectacle of that day, all of whom had now retired, leaving the dead to their loneliness. The traveller at length reached the fir tree, which from the middle upward was covered with living branches, although a scaffold had been erected beneath, and other preparations made for the work of death. Under this unhappy tree, which in aftertimes was believed to drop poison with its dew, sat the one solitary mourner for innocent blood. It was a slender and light-clad little boy, who leant his face upon a hillock of fresh-turned and half-frozen earth, and wailed bitterly, yet in a suppressed tone, as if his grief might receive the punishment of crime. The Puritan, whose approach had been unperceived, laid his hand upon the child's shoulder and addressed him compassionately.

"You have chosen a dreary lodging, my poor boy, and no wonder that you weep," said he. "But dry your eyes, and tell me where your mother dwells. I promise you, if the journey be not too far, I will leave you in her arms tonight."

The boy had hushed his wailing at once, and turned his face upward to the stranger. It was a pale, bright-eyed countenance, certainly not more than six years old, but sorrow, fear and want had destroyed much of its infantile expression. The Puritan, seeing the boy's frightened gaze, and feeling that he trembled under his hand, endeavoured to reassure him.

"Nay, if I intended to do you harm, little lad, the readiest way were to leave you here. What! You do not fear to sit beneath the gallows on a new-made grave, and yet you tremble at a friend's touch. Take heart, child, and tell me what is your name, and where is your home?"

"Friend," replied the little boy, in a sweet, though faltering voice, "they call me Ilbrahim, and my home is here."

The pale, spirited face, the eyes that seemed to mingle with the moonlight, the sweet, airy voice and the outlandish name almost made the Puritan believe that the boy was in truth a being which had sprung up out of the grave on which he sat. But perceiving that the apparition stood the test of a short mental prayer, and remembering that the arm which he had touched was lifelike, he adopted a more rational supposition.

"The poor child is stricken in his intellect," thought he, "but verily his words are fearful, in a place like this." He then spoke soothingly, intending to humour the boy's fantasy.

"Your home will scarce be comfortable, Ilbrahim, this cold autumn night, and I fear you are ill provided with food. I am hastening to a warm supper and bed, and if you will go with me, you shall share them!"

"I thank thee, friend, but though I be hungry and shivering with cold, thou wilt not give me food nor lodging," replied the boy, in the quiet tone which despair had taught him, even so young. "My father was of the people whom all men hate. They have laid him under this heap of earth, and here is my home."

The Puritan, who had laid hold of little Ilbrahim's hand, relinquished it as if he were touching a loathsome reptile. But he possessed a compassionate heart, which not even religious prejudice could harden into stone.

"God forbid that I should leave this child to perish, though he comes of the accursed sect," said he to himself. "Do we not all spring from an evil root? Are we not all in darkness till the light doth shine upon us? He shall not perish, neither in body nor, if prayer and instruction may avail for him, in soul." He then spoke aloud and kindly to Ilbrahim, who had again hid his face in the cold earth of the grave. "Was every door in the land shut against you, my child, that you have wandered to this unhallowed spot?"

"They drove me forth from the prison when they took my father thence," said the boy, "and I stood afar off, watching the crowd of people, and when they were gone, I came hither, and found only this grave. I knew that my father was sleeping here, and I said, 'This shall be my home.'"

"No, child, no – not while I have a roof over my head, or a morsel to share with you!" exclaimed the Puritan, whose sympathies were now fully excited. "Rise up and come with me, and fear not any harm."

The boy wept afresh, and clung to the heap of earth, as if the cold heart beneath it were warmer to him than any in a living breast. The traveller, however, continued to entreat him tenderly and, seeming to acquire some degree of confidence, he at length arose. But his slender limbs tottered with weakness, his little head grew dizzy and he leant against the tree of death for support.

"My poor boy, are you so feeble?" said the Puritan. "When did you taste food last?"

"I ate of bread and water with my father in the prison," replied Ilbrahim, "but they brought him none neither yesterday nor today, saying that he had eaten enough to bear him to his journey's end. Trouble not thyself for my hunger, kind friend, for I have lacked food many times ere now."

The traveller took the child in his arms and wrapped his cloak about him, while his heart stirred with shame and anger against the gratuitous cruelty of the instruments in this persecution. In the awakened warmth of his feelings, he resolved that, at whatever risk, he would not forsake the poor little defenceless being whom Heaven had confided to his care. With this determination, he left the accursed field, and resumed the homeward path from which the wailing of the boy had called him. The light and motionless burthen scarcely impeded his progress, and he soon beheld the fire rays from the windows of the cottage which he, a native of a distant clime, had built in the western wilderness. It was surrounded by a considerable extent of cultivated ground, and the dwelling was situated in the nook of a wood-covered hill, whither it seemed to have crept for protection.

"Look up, child," said the Puritan to Ilbrahim, whose faint head had sunk upon his shoulder, "there is our home."

At the word "home", a thrill passed through the child's frame, but he continued silent. A few moments brought them to the cottage door, at which the owner knocked; for at that early period, when savages were wandering everywhere among the settlers, bolt and bar were indispensable to the security of a dwelling. The summons was answered by a bondservant, a coarse-clad and dull-featured piece of humanity, who, after ascertaining that his master was the applicant, undid the door, and held a flaring pine-knot torch to light him in. Farther back in the passageway, the red blaze discovered a matronly woman, but no little crowd of children came bounding forth to greet their father's return. As the Puritan entered, he thrust aside his cloak and displayed Ilbrahim's face to the female.

"Dorothy, here is a little outcast whom Providence hath put into our hands," observed he. "Be kind to him, even as if he were of those dear ones who have departed from us."

The wife's eyes filled with tears; she enquired neither who little Ilbrahim was, nor whence he came, but kissed his cheek and led the way into the dwelling. The sitting room, which was also the kitchen, was lighted by a cheerful fire upon the large stone-laid hearth, and a confused variety of objects shone out and disappeared in the unsteady blaze. There were the household articles, the many wooden trenchers, the one large pewter dish and the copper kettle whose inner surface was glittering like gold. There were the lighter implements of husbandry, the spade, the sickle and the scythe, all hanging by the door, and the axe before which a thousand trees had bowed themselves. On another part of the wall were the steel cap and iron breastplate, the sword and the matchlock gun. There, in a corner, was a little chair, the memorial of a brood of children whose place by the fireside was vacant for ever. And there, on a table near the window, among all those tokens of labour, war and mourning, was the Holy Bible, the book of life, an emblem of the blessed comforts which it offers, to those who can receive them, amidst the toil, the strife and sorrow of this world. Dorothy hastened to bring the little chair from its corner; she placed it on the hearth and, seating the poor orphan there, addressed him in words of tenderness, such as only a mother's experience could have taught her. At length, when he had timidly begun to taste his warm bread and milk, she drew her husband apart.

"What pale and bright-eyed little boy is this, Tobias?" she enquired. "Is he one whom the wilderness folk have ravished from some Christian mother?"

"No, Dorothy, this poor child is no captive from the wilderness," he replied. "The heathen savage would have given him to eat of his scanty morsel, and to drink of his birchen cup; but Christian men – alas! – had cast him out to die."

Then he told her how he had found him beneath the gallows, upon his father's grave; and how his heart had prompted him, like the speaking of an inward voice, to take the little outcast home and be kind unto him. He acknowledged his resolution to feed and clothe him, as if he were his own child, and to afford him the instruction which should counteract the pernicious errors hitherto instilled into his infant mind. Dorothy was gifted with even a quicker tenderness than her husband, and she approved of all his doings and intentions. She drew near to Ilbrahim, who, having finished his repast, sat with the tears hanging upon his long eyelashes, but with a singular and unchildlike composure on his little face.

"Have you a mother, dear child?" she enquired.

The tears burst forth from his full heart, as he attempted to reply, but Dorothy at length understood that he had a mother, who, like the rest of her sect, was a persecuted wanderer. She had been taken from the prison a short time before, carried into the uninhabited wilderness, and left to perish there by hunger or wild beasts. This was no uncommon method of disposing of the Quakers, and they were accustomed to boast that the inhabitants of the desert were more hospitable to them than civilized man.

"Fear not, little boy, you shall not need a mother, and a kind one," said Dorothy, when she had gathered this information. "Dry your tears, Ilbrahim, and be my child, as I will be your mother."

The good woman prepared the little bed, from which her own children had successively been borne to another resting place. Before Ilbrahim would consent to occupy it, he knelt down, and as Dorothy listened to his simple and affecting prayer she marvelled how the parents that had taught it to him could have been judged worthy of death. When the boy had fallen asleep, she bent over his pale and spiritual countenance, pressed a kiss upon his white brow, drew the bedclothes up about his neck and went away with a pensive gladness in her heart.

Tobias Pearson was not among the earliest emigrants from the old country. He had remained in England during the first years of the Civil War, in which he had borne some share as a coronet of dragoons, under Cromwell. But when the ambitious designs of his leader began to develop themselves, he quitted the army of the parliament and sought a refuge from the strife, which was no longer holy among the people of his persuasion, in the colony of Massachusetts. A more worldly consideration had perhaps an influence in drawing him thither, for New England offered advantages to men of unprosperous fortunes as well as to dissatisfied religionists, and Pearson had hitherto found it difficult to provide for a wife and increasing family. To this supposed impurity of motive, the more bigoted Puritans were inclined to impute the removal by death of all the children, for whose earthly good the father had been over-thoughtful. They had left their native country blooming like roses, and like roses they had perished in a foreign soil. Those expounders of the ways of Providence, who had thus judged their brother, and attributed his domestic sorrows to his sin, were not more charitable when they saw him and Dorothy endeavouring to fill up the void in their hearts by the adoption of an infant of the accursed sect. Nor did they fail to communicate their disapprobation to Tobias; but the latter, in reply, merely pointed at the little quiet, lovely boy, whose appearance and deportment were indeed as powerful arguments as could possibly have been adduced in his own favour. Even his beauty, however, and his winning manners, sometimes produced an effect ultimately unfavourable; for the bigots, when the outer surfaces of their iron hearts had been softened and again grew hard, affirmed that no merely natural cause could have so worked upon them. Their antipathy to the poor infant was also increased by the ill success of divers theological discussions, in which it was attempted to convince him of the errors of his sect. Ilbrahim, it is true, was not a skilful controversialist, but the feeling of his religion was strong as instinct in him, and he could neither be enticed nor driven from the faith which his father had died for. The odium of this stubbornness was shared in a great measure by the child's protectors, insomuch that Tobias and Dorothy very shortly began to experience a most bitter species of persecution, in the cold regards of many a friend whom they had valued. The common people manifested their opinions more openly. Pearson was a man of some consideration, being a Representative to the General Court, and an approved lieutenant in the trainbands, yet, within a week after his adoption of Ilbrahim, he had been both hissed and hooted. Once, also, when walking through a solitary piece of woods, he heard a loud voice from some invisible speaker, and it cried, "What shall be done to the backslider? Lo! The scourge is knotted for him, even the whip of nine cords, and every cord three knots!" These insults irritated Pearson's temper for the moment; they entered also into his heart, and became imperceptible but powerful workers towards an end which his most secret thought had not yet whispered.

* * *

On the second Sabbath after Ilbrahim became a member of their family, Pearson and his wife deemed it proper that he should appear with them at public worship. They had anticipated some opposition to this measure from the boy, but he prepared himself in silence, and at the appointed hour was clad in the new mourning suit which Dorothy had wrought for him. As the parish was then, and during many subsequent years, unprovided with a bell, the signal for the commencement of religious exercises was the beat of a drum; in connection with which peculiarity it may be mentioned that an apartment of the meeting house served the purposes of a powder magazine and armoury. At the first sound of that martial call to the place of holy and quiet thoughts, Tobias and Dorothy set forth, each holding a hand of little Ilbrahim, like two parents linked together by the infant of their love. On their path through the leafless woods, they were overtaken by many persons of their acquaintance, all of whom avoided them and passed by on the other side; but a severer trial awaited their constancy when they had descended the hill, and drew near the pine-built and undecorated house of prayer. Around the door, from which the drummer still sent forth his thundering summons, was drawn up a formidable phalanx, including several of the oldest members of the congregation, many of the middle-aged, and nearly all the younger males. Pearson found it difficult to sustain their united and disapproving gaze, but Dorothy, whose mind was differently circumstanced, merely drew the boy closer to her, and faltered not in her approach. As they entered the door, they overheard the muttered sentiments of the assemblage, and when the reviling voices of the little children smote Ilbrahim's ear he wept.

The interior aspect of the meeting house was rude. The low ceiling, the unplastered walls, the naked woodwork and the undraperied pulpit offered nothing to excite the devotion, which, without such external aids, often remains latent in the heart. The floor of the building was occupied by rows of long, cushionless benches, supplying the place of pews, and the broad aisle formed a sexual division, impassable except by children beneath a certain age. On one side of the house sat the women, generally in sad-coloured and most unfanciful apparel, although there were a few high headdresses, on which the "Cobler of Aggawam"* would have lavished his empty wit of words. There was no veil to be seen among them all, and it must be allowed that the November sun, shining brightly through the windows, fell upon many a demure but pretty set of features, which no barbarity of art could spoil. The masculine department of the house presented somewhat more variety than that of the women. Most of the men, it is true, were clad in black or dark-grey broadcloth, and all coincided in the short, ungraceful and ear-displaying cut of their hair. But those who were in martial authority, having arrayed themselves in their embroidered buff coats, contrasted strikingly with the remainder of the congregation, and attracted many youthful thoughts which should have been otherwise employed. Pearson and Dorothy separated at the door of the meeting house, and Ilbrahim, being within the years of infancy, was retained under the care of the latter. The wrinkled beldams involved themselves in their rusty cloaks as he passed by; even the mild-featured maidens seemed to dread contamination; and many a stern old man arose and turned his repulsive and unheavenly countenance upon the gentle boy, as if the sanctuary were polluted by his presence. He was a sweet infant of the skies that had strayed away from his home, and all the inhabitants of this miserable world closed up their impure hearts against him, drew back their earth-soiled garments from his touch and said, "We are holier than thou."

Ilbrahim, seated by the side of his adopted mother, and retaining fast hold of her hand, assumed a grave and decorous demeanour, such as might befit a person of matured taste and understanding who should find himself in a temple dedicated to some worship which he did not recognize but felt himself bound to respect. The exercises had not yet commenced, however, when the boy's attention was arrested by an event, apparently of trifling interest. A woman, having her face muffled in a hood, and a cloak drawn completely about her form, advanced slowly up the broad aisle and took place upon the foremost bench. Ilbrahim's faint colour varied, his nerves fluttered, he was unable to turn his eyes from the muffled female.

When the preliminary prayer and hymn were over, the minister arose and, having turned the hourglass which stood by the great Bible, commenced his discourse. He was now well stricken in years, a man of pale, thin yet not intellectual countenance, and his grey hairs were closely covered by a black velvet skullcap. In his younger days he had practically learnt the meaning of persecution from Archbishop Laud,* and he was not now disposed to forget the lesson against which he had murmured them. Introducing the often discussed subject of the Quakers, he gave a history of that sect, and a description of their tenets, in which error predominated and prejudice distorted the aspect of what was true. He adverted to the recent measures in the province, and cautioned his hearers of weaker parts against calling in question the just severity which God-fearing magistrates had at length been compelled to exercise. He spoke of the danger of pity, in some cases a commendable and Christian virtue, but inapplicable to this pernicious sect. He observed that such was their devilish obstinacy in error that even the little children, the sucking babes, were hardened and desperate heretics. He affirmed that no man, without Heaven's especial warrant, should attempt their conversion, lest while he bent his hand to draw them from the slough he should himself be precipitated into its lowest depths. Into this discourse was worked much learning, both sacred and profane, which, however, came forth not digested into its original elements, but in short quotations, as if the preacher were unable to amalgamate his own mind with that of the author. His own language was generally plain, even to affectation, but there were frequent specimens of a dull man's efforts to be witty – little ripples fretting the surface of a stagnant pool.

The sands of the second hour were principally in the lower half of the glass, when the sermon concluded. An approving murmur followed, and the clergyman, having given out a hymn, took his seat with much self-congratulation and endeavoured to read the effect of his eloquence in the visages of the people. But while voices from all parts of the house were tuning themselves to sing, a scene occurred, which, though not very unusual at that period in the province, happened to be without precedent in this parish.

The muffled female, who had hitherto sat motionless in the front rank of the audience, now arose and, with slow, stately and unwavering step, ascended the pulpit stairs. The quaverings of incipient harmony were hushed, and the divine sat in speechless and almost terrified astonishment, while she undid the door and stood up in the sacred desk from which his maledictions had just been thundered. Having thus usurped a station to which her sex can plead no title, she divested herself of the cloak and hood, and appeared in a most singular array. A shapeless robe of sackcloth was girded about her waist with a knotted cord; her raven hair fell down upon her shoulders, and its blackness was defiled by pale streaks of ashes, which she had strewn upon her head. Her eyebrows, dark and strongly defined, added to the deathly white-ness of a countenance which, emaciated with want, and wild with enthusiasm and strange sorrows, retained no trace of earlier beauty. This figure stood gazing earnestly on the audience, and there was no sound, nor any movement, except a faint shudder-ing which every man observed in his neighbour, but was scarcely conscious of in himself. At length, when her fit of inspiration came, she spoke, for the first few moments, in a low voice, and not invariably distinct utterance. Her discourse gave evidence of an imagination hopelessly entangled with her reason; it was a vague and incomprehensible rhapsody, which, however, seemed to spread its own atmosphere round the hearer's soul, and to move his feelings by some influence unconnected with the words. As she proceeded, beautiful but shadowy images would sometimes be seen, like bright things moving in a turbid river; or a strong and singularly shaped idea leapt forth, and seized at once on the understanding or the heart. But the course of her unearthly eloquence soon led her to the persecutions of her sect, and from thence the step was short to her own peculiar sorrows. She was naturally a woman of mighty passions, and hatred and revenge now wrapped themselves in the garb of piety; the character of her speech was changed, her images became distinct though wild and her denunciations had an almost hellish bitterness.

"The Governor and his mighty men," she said, "have gathered together, taking counsel among themselves and saying, 'What shall we do unto this people – even unto the people that have come into this land to put our iniquity to the blush?' And lo! The Devil entereth into the council chamber, like a lame man of low stature and gravely apparelled, with a dark and twisted countenance and a bright, downcast eye. And he standeth up among the rulers; yea, he goeth to and fro, whispering to each; and every man lends his ear, for his word is 'slay, slay!' But I say unto ye: woe to them that slay! Woe to them that shed the blood of saints! Woe to them that have slain the husband, and cast forth the child, the tender infant, to wander homeless, and hungry, and cold, till he die; and have saved the mother alive, in the cruelty of their tender mercies! Woe to them in their lifetime, cursed are they in the delight and pleasure of their hearts! Woe to them in their death hour, whether it come swiftly with blood and violence, or after long and lingering pain! Woe, in the dark house, in the rottenness of the grave, when the children's children shall revile the ashes of the fathers! Woe, woe, woe, at the judgement, when all the persecuted and all the slain in this bloody land, and the father, the mother and the child shall await them in a day that they cannot escape! Seed of the faith, seed of the faith, ye whose hearts are moving with a power that ye know not, arise, wash your hands of this innocent blood! Lift your voices, chosen ones, cry aloud, and call down a woe and a judgement with me!"

Having thus given vent to the flood of malignity which she mistook for inspiration, the speaker was silent. Her voice was succeeded by the hysteric shrieks of several women, but the feelings of the audience generally had not been drawn onward in the current with her own. They remained stupefied, stranded as it were, in the midst of a torrent, which deafened them by its roaring, but might not move them by its violence. The clergyman, who could not hitherto have ejected the usurper of his pulpit otherwise than by bodily force, now addressed her in the tone of just indignation and legitimate authority.

"Get you down, woman, from the holy place which you profane," he said. "Is it to the Lord's house that you come to pour forth the foulness of your heart, and the inspiration of the Devil? Get you down, and remember that the sentence of death is on you – yea, and shall be executed, were it but for this day's work."

"I go, friend, I go, for the voice hath had its utterance," replied she, in a depressed and even mild tone. "I have done my mission unto thee and to thy people. Reward me with stripes, imprisonment or death, as ye shall be permitted."

The weakness of exhausted passion caused her steps to totter as she descended the pulpit stairs. The people, in the meanwhile, were stirring to and fro on the floor of the house, whispering among themselves, and glancing towards the intruder. Many of them now recognized her as a woman who had assaulted the Governor with frightful language, as he passed by the window of her prison; they knew, also, that she was adjudged to suffer death, and had been preserved only by an involuntary banishment into the wilderness. The new outrage, by which she had provoked her fate, seemed to render further lenity impossible; and a gentleman in military dress, with a stout man of inferior rank, drew towards the door of the meeting house and awaited her approach. Scarcely did her feet press the floor, however, when an unexpected scene occurred. In that moment of her peril, when every eye frowned with death, a little timid boy pressed forth and threw his arms round his mother.

"I am here, Mother, it is I, and I will go with thee to prison," he exclaimed.

She gazed at him with a doubtful and almost frightened expression, for she knew that the boy had been cast out to perish, and she had not hoped to see his face again. She feared, perhaps, that it was but one of the happy visions with which her excited fancy had often deceived her, in the solitude of the desert, or in prison. But when she felt his hand warm within her own, and heard his little eloquence of childish love, she began to know that she was yet a mother.

"Blessed art thou, my son," she sobbed. "My heart was withered – yea, dead with thee and with thy father – and now it leaps as in the first moment when I pressed thee to my bosom."

She knelt down, and embraced him again and again, while the joy that could find no words expressed itself in broken accents, like the bubbles gushing up to vanish at the surface of a deep fountain. The sorrows of past years, and the darker peril that was nigh, cast not a shadow on the brightness of that fleeting moment. Soon, however, the spectators saw a change upon her face, as the consciousness of her sad estate returned and grief supplied the fount of tears which joy had opened. By the words she uttered, it would seem that the indulgence of natural love had given her mind a momentary sense of its errors, and made her know how far she had strayed from duty in following the dictates of a wild fanaticism.

"In a doleful hour art thou returned to me, poor boy," she said, "for thy mother's path has gone darkening onward, till now the end is death. Son, son, I have borne thee in my arms when my limbs were tottering, and I have fed thee with the food that I was fainting for; yet I have ill performed a mother's part by thee in life, and now I leave thee no inheritance but woe and shame. Thou wilt go seeking through the world, and find all hearts closed against thee, and their sweet affections turned to bitterness for my sake. My child, my child, how many a pang awaits thy gentle spirit, and I the cause of all!"

She hid her face on Ilbrahim's head, and her long, raven hair, discoloured with the ashes of her mourning, fell down about him like a veil. A low and interrupted moan was the voice of her heart's anguish, and it did not fail to move the sympathies of many who mistook their involuntary virtue for a sin. Sobs were audible in the female section of the house, and every man who was a father drew his hand across his eyes. Tobias Pearson was agitated and uneasy, but a certain feeling like the consciousness of guilt oppressed him, so that he could not go forth and offer himself as the protector of the child. Dorothy, however, had watched her husband's eye. Her mind was free from the influence that had begun to work on his, and she drew near the Quaker woman, and addressed her in the hearing of all the congregation.

"Stranger, trust this boy to me, and I will be his mother," she said, taking Ilbrahim's hand. "Providence has signally marked out my husband to protect him, and he has fed at our table and lodged under our roof, now many days, till our hearts have grown very strongly unto him. Leave the tender child with us, and be at ease concerning his welfare."

The Quaker rose from the ground, but drew the boy closer to her, while she gazed earnestly in Dorothy's face. Her mild but saddened features and neat, matronly attire harmonized together, and were like a verse of fireside poetry. Her very aspect proved that she was blameless, so far as mortal could be so, in respect to God and man; while the enthusiast, in her robe of sackcloth and girdle of knotted cord, had as evidently violated the duties of the present life and the future, by fixing her attention wholly on the latter. The two females, as they held each a hand of Ilbrahim, formed a practical allegory; it was rational piety and unbridled fanaticism, contending for the empire of a young heart.

"Thou art not of our people," said the Quaker mournfully.

"No, we are not of your people," replied Dorothy, with mildness, "but we are Christians, looking upward to the same heaven with you. Doubt not that your boy shall meet you there, if there be a blessing on our tender and prayerful guidance of him. Thither, I trust, my own children have gone before me, for I also have been a mother – I am no longer so," she added, in a faltering tone, "and your son will have all my care."

"But will ye lead him in the path which his parents have trodden?" demanded the Quaker. "Can ye teach him the enlightened faith which his father has died for, and for which I, even I, am soon to become an unworthy martyr? The boy has been baptized in blood; will ye keep the mark fresh and ruddy upon his forehead?"

"I will not deceive you," answered Dorothy. "If your child become our child, we must breed him up in the instruction which Heaven has imparted to us; we must pray for him the prayers of our own faith; we must do towards him according to the dictates of our own consciences, and not of yours. Were we to act otherwise, we should abuse your trust, even in complying with your wishes."

The mother looked down upon her boy with a troubled countenance, and then turned her eyes upward to heaven. She seemed to pray internally, and the contention of her soul was evident.

"Friend," she said at length to Dorothy, "I doubt not that my son shall receive all earthly tenderness at thy hands. Nay, I will believe that thy imperfect lights may guide him to a better world, for surely thou art on the path thither. But thou hast spoken of a husband. Doth he stand here among this multitude of people? Let him come forth, for I must know to whom I commit this most precious trust."

She turned her face upon the male auditors, and after a momentary delay Tobias Pearson came forth from among them. The Quaker saw the dress which marked his military rank, and shook her head; but then she noted the hesitating air, the eyes that struggled with her own and were vanquished; the colour that went and came, and could find no resting place. As she gazed, an unmirthful smile spread over her features, like sunshine that grows melancholy in some desolate spot. Her lips moved inaudibly, but at length she spake.

"I hear it, I hear it. The voice speaketh within me and saith, 'Leave thy child, Catharine, for his place is here, and go hence, for I have other work for thee. Break the bonds of natural affection, martyr thy love, and know that in all these things eternal wisdom hath its ends.' I go, friends, I go. Take ye my boy, my precious jewel. I go hence, trusting that all shall be well, and that even for his infant hands there is a labour in the vineyard."

She knelt down and whispered to Ilbrahim, who at first struggled and clung to his mother, with sobs and tears, but remained passive when she had kissed his cheek and arisen from the ground. Having held her hands over his head in mental prayer, she was ready to depart.

"Farewell, friends, in mine extremity," she said to Pearson and his wife. "The good deed ye have done me is a treasure laid up in heaven, to be returned a thousandfold hereafter. And farewell ye, mine enemies, to whom it is not permitted to harm so much as a hair of my head, nor to stay my footsteps even for a moment. The day is coming when ye shall call upon me to witness for ye to this one sin committed, and I will rise up and answer."

She turned her steps towards the door, and the men, who had stationed themselves to guard it, withdrew, and suffered her to pass. A general sentiment of pity overcame the virulence of religious hatred. Sanctified by her love, and her affliction, she went forth, and all the people gazed after her till she had journeyed up the hill, and was lost behind its brow. She went, the apostle of her own unquiet heart, to renew the wanderings of past years. For her voice had been already heard in many lands of Christendom, and she had pined in the cells of a Catholic Inquisition, before she felt the lash and ate the bread of the Puritans. Her mission had extended also to the followers of the Prophet, and from them she had received the courtesy and kindness which all the contending sects of our purer religion united to deny her. Her husband and herself had resided many months in Turkey, where even the Sultan's countenance was gracious to them; in that pagan land, too, was Ilbrahim's birthplace, and his oriental name was a mark of gratitude for the good deeds of an unbeliever.

* * *

When Pearson and his wife had thus acquired all the rights over Ilbrahim that could be delegated, their affection for him became, like the memory of their native land, or their mild sorrow for the dead, a piece of the immovable furniture of their hearts. The boy, also, after a week or two of mental disquiet, began to gratify his protectors, by many inadvertent proofs that he considered them as parents, and their house as home. Before the winter snows were melted, the persecuted infant, the little wanderer from a remote and heathen country, seemed native in the New England cottage, and inseparable from the warmth and security of its hearth. Under the influence of kind treatment, and in the consciousness that he was loved, Ilbrahim's demeanour lost a premature manliness, which had resulted from his earlier situation; he became more childlike, and his natural character displayed itself with freedom. It was in many respects a beautiful one, yet the disordered imaginations of both his father and mother had perhaps propagated a certain unhealthiness in the mind of the boy. In his general state, Ilbrahim would derive enjoyment from the most trifling events, and from every object about him; he seemed to discover precious views of happiness, by a faculty analogous to that of the witch hazel, which points to hidden treasure where all is barren to the eye.

His airy gaiety, coming to him from a thousand sources, communicated itself to the family, and Ilbrahim was like a domesticated sunbeam, brightening moody countenances and chasing away the gloom from the dark corners of the cottage. On the other hand, as the susceptibility of pleasure is also that of pain, the exuberant cheerfulness of the boy's prevailing temper sometimes yielded to moments of deep depression. His sorrows could not always be followed up to their original source, but most frequently they appeared to flow, though Ilbrahim was young to be sad for such a cause, from wounded love. The flightiness of his mirth rendered him often guilty of offences against the decorum of a Puritan household, and on these occasions he did not invariably escape rebuke. But the slightest word of real bitterness, which he was infallible in distinguishing from pretended anger, seemed to sink into his heart and poison all his enjoyments, till he became sensible that he was entirely forgiven. Of the malice which generally accompanies a superfluity of sensitiveness Ilbrahim was altogether destitute; when trodden upon, he would not turn; when wounded, he could but die. His mind was wanting in the stamina for self-support; it was a plant that would twine beautifully round something stronger than itself, but if repulsed, or torn away, it had no choice but to wither on the ground. Dorothy's acuteness taught her that severity would crush the spirit of the child, and she nurtured him with the gentle care of one who handles a butterfly. Her husband manifested an equal affection, although it grew daily less productive of familiar caresses.

The feelings of the neighbouring people, in regard to the Quaker infant and his protectors, had not undergone a favourable change, in spite of the momentary triumph which the desolate mother had obtained over their sympathies. The scorn and bitterness of which he was the object were very grievous to Ilbrahim, especially when any circumstance made him sensible that the children, his equals in age, partook of the enmity of their parents. His tender and social nature had already overflowed in attachments to everything about him, and still there was a residue of unappropriate love, which he yearned to bestow upon the little ones who were taught to hate him. As the warm days of spring came on, Ilbrahim was accustomed to remain for hours, silent and inactive, within hearing of the children's voices at their play; yet, with his usual delicacy of feeling, he avoided their notice, and would flee and hide himself from the smallest individual among them. Chance, however, at length seemed to open a medium of communication between his heart and theirs; it was by means of a boy about two years older than Ilbrahim, who was injured by a fall from a tree in the vicinity of Pearson's habitation. As the sufferer's own home was at some distance, Dorothy willingly received him under her roof, and became his tender and careful nurse.

Ilbrahim was the unconscious possessor of much skill in physiognomy, and it would have deterred him, in other circumstances, from attempting to make a friend of this boy. The countenance of the latter immediately impressed a beholder disagreeably, but it required some examination to discover that the cause was a very slight distortion of the mouth, and the irregular, broken line and near approach of the eyebrows. Analogous, perhaps, to these trifling deformities was an almost imperceptible twist of every joint, and the uneven prominence of the breast; forming a body, regular in its general outline, but faulty in almost all its details. The disposition of the boy was sullen and reserved, and the village schoolmaster stigmatized him as obtuse in intellect; although, at a later period of life, he evinced ambition and very peculiar talents. But whatever might be his personal or moral irregularities, Ilbrahim's heart seized upon, and clung to him, from the moment that he was brought wounded into the cottage; the child of persecution seemed to compare his own fate with that of the sufferer, and to feel that even different modes of misfortune had created a sort of relationship between them. Food, rest and the fresh air for which he languished were neglected; he nestled continually by the bedside of the little stranger and, with a fond jealousy, endeavoured to be the medium of all the cares that were bestowed upon him. As the boy became convalescent, Ilbrahim contrived games suitable to his situation, or amused him by a faculty which he had perhaps breathed in with the air of his barbaric birthplace. It was that of reciting imaginary adventures, on the spur of the moment, and apparently in inexhaustible succession. His tales were of course monstrous, disjointed and without aim, but they were curious on account of a vein of human tenderness which ran through them all and was like a sweet, familiar face encountered in the midst of wild and unearthly scenery. The auditor paid much attention to these romances, and sometimes interrupted them by brief remarks upon the incidents, displaying shrewdness above his years, mingled with a moral obliquity which grated very harshly against Ilbrahim's instinctive rectitude. Nothing, however, could arrest the progress of the latter's affection, and there were many proofs that it met with a response from the dark and stubborn nature on which it was lavished. The boy's parents at length removed him, to complete his cure under their own roof.

Ilbrahim did not visit his new friend after his departure, but he made anxious and continual enquiries respecting him, and informed himself of the day when he was to reappear among his playmates. On a pleasant summer afternoon, the children of the neighbourhood had assembled in the little forest-crowned amphitheatre behind the meeting house, and the recovering invalid was there, leaning on a staff. The glee of a score of untainted bosoms was heard in light and airy voices, which danced among the trees like sunshine become audible; the grown men of this weary world, as they journeyed by the spot, marvelled why life, beginning in such brightness, should proceed in gloom; and their hearts, or their imaginations, answered them and said that the bliss of childhood gushes from its innocence. But it happened that an unexpected addition was made to the heavenly little band. It was Ilbrahim, who came towards the children with a look of sweet confidence on his fair and spiritual face, as if, having manifested his love to one of them, he had no longer to fear a repulse from their society. A hush came over their mirth, the moment they beheld him, and they stood whispering to each other while he drew nigh; but, all at once, the devil of their fathers entered into the unbreeched fanatics and, sending up a fierce, shrill cry, they rushed upon the poor Quaker child. In an instant, he was the centre of a brood of baby fiends, who lifted sticks against him, pelted him with stones and displayed an instinct of destruction far more loathsome than the bloodthirstiness of manhood. The invalid, in the meanwhile, stood apart from the tumult, crying out with a loud voice, "Fear not, Ilbrahim: come hither and take my hand" – and his unhappy friend endeavoured to obey him. Having watched the victim's struggling approach with a calm smile and unabashed eye, the foul-hearted little villain lifted his staff and struck Ilbrahim on the mouth so forcibly that the blood issued in a stream. The poor child's arms had been raised to guard his head from the storm of blows, but now he dropped them at once, for he was stricken in a tender part. His persecutors beat him down, trampled upon him, dragged him by his long, fair locks, and Ilbrahim was on the point of becoming as veritable a martyr as ever entered bleeding into heaven. The uproar, however, attracted the notice of a few neighbours, who put themselves to the trouble of rescuing the little heretic, and of conveying him to Pearson's door.

Ilbrahim's bodily harm was severe, but long and careful nursing accomplished his recovery; the injury done to his sensitive spirit was more serious, though not so visible. Its signs were principally of a negative character, and to be discovered only by those who had previously known him. His gait was thenceforth slow, even and unvaried by the sudden bursts of sprightlier motion which had once corresponded to his overflowing gladness; his countenance was heavier, and its former play of expression, the dance of sunshine reflected from moving water, was destroyed by the cloud over his existence; his notice was attracted in a far less degree by passing events, and he appeared to find greater difficulty in comprehending what was new to him than at a happier period. A stranger, founding his judgement upon these circumstances, would have said that the dullness of the child's intellect widely contradicted the promise of his features, but the secret was in the direction of Ilbrahim's thoughts, which were brooding within him when they should naturally have been wandering abroad. An attempt of Dorothy to revive his former sportiveness was the single occasion on which his quiet demeanour yielded to a violent display of grief; he burst into passionate weeping, and ran and hid himself, for his heart had become so miserably sore that even the hand of kindness tortured it like fire. Sometimes, at night and probably in his dreams, he was heard to cry, "Mother! Mother!" as if her place, which a stranger had supplied while Ilbrahim was happy, admitted of no substitute in his extreme affliction. Perhaps, among the many life-weary wretches then upon the earth, there was not one who combined innocence and misery like this poor, broken-hearted infant, so soon the victim of his own heavenly nature.

While this melancholy change had taken place in Ilbrahim, one of an earlier origin and of different character had come to its perfection in his adopted father. The incident with which this tale commences found Pearson in a state of religious dullness, yet mentally disquieted and longing for a more fervid faith than he possessed. The first effect of his kindness to Ilbrahim was to produce a softened feeling, an incipient love for the child's whole sect; but joined to this, and resulting perhaps from self-suspicion, was a proud and ostentatious contempt of their tenets and practical extravagances. In the course of much thought, however, for the subject struggled irresistibly into his mind, the foolishness of the doctrine began to be less evident, and the points which had particularly offended his reason assumed another aspect or vanished entirely away. The work within him appeared to go on even while he slept, and that which had been a doubt, when he laid down to rest, would often hold the place of a truth, confirmed by some forgotten demonstration, when he recalled his thoughts in the morning. But while he was thus becoming assimilated to the enthusiasts, his contempt, in nowise decreasing towards them, grew very fierce against himself; he imagined, also, that every face of his acquaintance wore a sneer, and that every word addressed to him was a gibe. At length, when the change in his belief was fully accomplished, the contest grew very terrible between the love of the world, in its thousand shapes, and the power which moved him to sacrifice all for the one pure faith; to quote his own words, subsequently uttered at a meeting of Friends, it was as if "Earth and Hell had garrisoned the fortress of his miserable soul, and Heaven came battering against it to storm the walls". Such was his state of warfare at the period of Ilbrahim's misfortune; and the emotions consequent upon that event enlisted with the besieging army, and decided the victory. There was a triumphant shout within him, and from that moment all was peace. Dorothy had not been the subject of a similar process, for her reason was as clear as her heart was tender.

In the mean time neither the fierceness of the persecutors nor the infatuation of their victims had decreased. The dungeons were never empty; the streets of almost every village echoed daily with the lash; the life of a woman, whose mild and Christian spirit no cruelty could embitter, had been sacrificed; and more innocent blood was yet to pollute the hands that were so often raised in prayer. Early after the Restoration, the English Quakers represented to Charles II that a "vein of blood was opened in his dominions", but though the displeasure of the voluptuous king was roused, his interference was not prompt.* And now the tale must stride forward over many months, leaving Pearson to exult in the midst of ignominy and misfortune; his wife to a firm endurance of a thousand sorrows; poor Ilbrahim to pine and droop like a cankered rosebud; his mother to wander on a mistaken errand, neglectful of the holiest trust which can be committed to a woman.

* * *

A winter evening, a night of storm, had darkened over Pearson's habitation, and there were no cheerful faces to drive the gloom from his broad hearth. The fire, it is true, sent forth a glowing heat and a ruddy light, and large logs, dripping with half-melted snow, lay ready to be cast upon the embers. But the apartment was saddened in its aspect by the absence of much of the homely wealth which had once adorned it; for the exaction of repeated fines and his own neglect of temporal affairs had greatly impoverished the owner. And with the furniture of peace, the implements of war had likewise disappeared; the sword was broken, the helm and cuirass were cast away for ever; the soldier had done with battles, and might not lift so much as his naked hand to guard his head. But the Holy Book remained, and the table on which it rested was drawn before the fire, while two of the persecuted sect sought comfort from its pages. He who listened, while the other read, was the master of the house, now emaciated in form and altered as to the expression and healthiness of his countenance; for his mind had dwelt too long among visionary thoughts, and his body had been worn by imprisonment and stripes. The hale and weather-beaten old man who sat beside him had sustained less injury from a far longer course of the same mode of life. His features were strong and well connected, and seemed to express firmness of purpose and sober understanding, although his actions had frequently been at variance with this last attribute. In person he was tall and dignified, and, which alone would have made him hateful to the Puritans, his grey locks fell from beneath the broad-brimmed hat and rested on his shoulders. As the old man read the sacred page, the snow drifted against the windows or eddied in at the crevices of the door, while a blast kept laughing in the chimney, and the blaze leaped fiercely up to seek it. And sometimes, when the wind struck the hill at a certain angle, and swept down by the cottage across the wintry plain, its voice was the most doleful that can be conceived; it came as if the Past were speaking, as if the Dead had contributed each a whisper, as if the Desolation of Ages were breathed in that one lamenting sound.

The Quaker at length closed the book, retaining however his hand between the pages which he had been reading, while he looked steadfastly at Pearson. The attitude and features of the latter might have indicated the endurance of bodily pain; he leant his forehead on his hands, his teeth were firmly closed and his frame was tremulous at intervals with a nervous agitation.

"Friend Tobias," enquired the old man compassionately, "hast thou found no comfort in these many blessed passages of Scripture?"

"Thy voice has fallen on my ear like a sound afar off and indistinct," replied Pearson, without lifting his eyes. "Yea, and when I have hearkened carefully, the words seemed cold and lifeless, and intended for another and a lesser grief than mine. Remove the book," he added, in a tone of sullen bitterness. "I have no part in its consolations, and they do but fret my sorrow the more."

"Nay, feeble brother, be not as one who hath never known the light," said the elder Quaker, earnestly, but with mildness. "Art thou he that wouldst be content to give all, and endure all, for conscience sake, desiring even peculiar trials, that thy faith might be purified, and thy heart weaned from worldly desires? And wilt thou sink beneath an affliction which happens alike to them that have their portion here below, and to them that lay up treasure in heaven? Faint not, for thy burthen is yet light."

"It is heavy! It is heavier than I can bear!" exclaimed Pearson, with the impatience of a variable spirit. "From my youth upward I have been a man marked out for wrath; and year by year, yea, day after day, I have endured sorrows such as others know not in their lifetime. And now I speak not of the love that has been turned to hatred, the honour to ignominy, the ease and plentifulness of all things to danger, want and nakedness. All this I could have borne, and counted myself blessed. But when my heart was desolate with many losses, I fixed it upon the child of a stranger, and he became dearer to me than all my buried ones; and now he too must die, as if my love were poison. Verily, I am an accursed man, and I will lay me down in the dust and lift up my head no more."

"Thou sinnest, brother, but it is not for me to rebuke thee; for I also have had my hours of darkness, wherein I have murmured against the cross," said the old Quaker. He continued, perhaps in the hope of distracting his companion's thoughts from his own sorrows. "Even of late was the light obscured within me, when the men of blood had banished me on pain of death, and the constables led me onward from village to village, towards the wilderness. A strong and cruel hand was wielding the knotted cords; they sunk deep into the flesh, and thou might have tracked every reel and totter of my footsteps by the blood that followed. As we went on—"

"Have I not borne all this, and have I murmured?" interrupted Pearson impatiently.

"Nay, friend, but hear me," continued the other. "As we journeyed on, night darkened on our path, so that no man could see the rage of the persecutors, or the constancy of my endurance, though Heaven forbid that I should glory therein. The lights began to glimmer in the cottage windows, and I could discern the inmates as they gathered, in comfort and security, every man with his wife and children by their own evening hearth. At length we came to a tract of fertile land; in the dim light, the forest was not visible around it; and behold! there was a straw-thatched dwelling, which bore the very aspect of my home, far over the wild ocean, far in our own England. Then came bitter thoughts upon me – yea, remembrances that were like death to my soul. The happiness of my early days was painted to me, the disquiet of my manhood, the altered faith of my declining years. I remembered how I had been moved to go forth a wanderer, when my daughter, the youngest, the dearest of my flock, lay on her dying bed, and—"

"Couldst thou obey the command at such a moment?" exclaimed Pearson, shuddering.

"Yea, yea," replied the old man hurriedly. "I was kneeling by her bedside when the voice spoke loud within me, but immediately I rose, and took my staff, and gat me gone. Oh, that it were permitted me to forget her woeful look, when I thus withdrew my arm, and left her journeying through the dark valley alone! For her soul was faint, and she had leant upon my prayers. Now in that night of horror I was assailed by the thought that I had been an erring Christian, and a cruel parent; yea, even my daughter, with her pale, dying features, seemed to stand by me and whisper, 'Father, you are deceived; go home and shelter your grey head.' Oh! Thou, to whom I have looked in my farthest wanderings," continued the Quaker, raising his agitated eyes to heaven, "inflict not upon the bloodiest of our persecutors the unmitigated agony of my soul, when I believed that all I had done and suffered for

Thee was at the instigation of a mocking fiend! But I yielded not: I knelt down and wrestled with the tempter, while the scourge bit more fiercely into the flesh. My prayer was heard, and I went on in peace and joy towards the wilderness."

The old man, though his fanaticism had generally all the calmness of reason, was deeply moved while reciting this tale, and his unwonted emotion seemed to rebuke and keep down that of his companion. They sat in silence, with their faces to the fire, imaging, perhaps, in its red embers, new scenes of persecution yet to be encountered. The snow still drifted hard against the windows, and sometimes, as the blaze of the logs had gradually sunk, came down the spacious chimney and hissed upon the hearth. A cautious footstep might now and then be heard in a neighbouring apartment, and the sound invariably drew the eyes of both Quakers to the door which led thither. When a fierce and riotous gust of wind had led his thoughts, by a natural association, to homeless travellers on such a night, Pearson resumed the conversation.

"I have well nigh sunk under my own share of this trial," observed he, sighing heavily, "yet I would that it might be doubled to me, if so the child's mother could be spared. Her wounds have been deep and many, but this will be the sorest of all."

"Fear not for Catharine," replied the old Quaker, "for I know that valiant woman, and have seen how she can bear the cross. A mother's heart, indeed, is strong in her, and may seem to contend mightily with her faith, but soon she will stand up and give thanks that her son has been thus early an accepted sacrifice. The boy hath done his work, and she will feel that he is taken hence in kindness both to him and her. Blessed, blessed are they, that with so little suffering can enter into peace!"

The fitful rush of the wind was now disturbed by a portentous sound: it was a quick and heavy knocking at the outer door. Pearson's wan countenance grew paler, for many a visit of persecution had taught him what to dread; the old man, on the other hand, stood up erect, and his glance was firm as that of the tried soldier who awaits his enemy.

"The men of blood have come to seek me," he observed, with calmness. "They have heard how I was moved to return from banishment, and now am I to be led to prison, and thence to death. It is an end I have long looked for. I will open unto them, lest they say, 'Lo, he feareth!'"

"Nay, I will present myself before them," said Pearson, with recovered fortitude. "It may be that they seek me alone, and know not that thou abidest with me."

"Let us go boldly, both one and the other," rejoined his companion. "It is not fitting that thou or I should shrink."

They therefore proceeded through the entry to the door, which they opened, bidding the applicant "Come in, in God's name!" A furious blast of wind drove the storm into their faces, and extinguished the lamp; they had barely time to discern a figure, so white from head to foot with the drifted snow that it seemed like Winter's self, come in human shape to seek refuge from its own desolation.

"Enter, friend, and do thy errand, be it what it may," said Pearson. "It must needs be pressing, since thou comest on such a bitter night."

"Peace be with this household," said the stranger, when they stood on the floor of the inner apartment.

Pearson started; the elder Quaker stirred the slumbering embers of the fire, till they sent up a clear and lofty blaze; it was a female voice that had spoken; it was a female form that shone out, cold and wintry, in that comfortable light.

"Catharine, blessed woman," exclaimed the old man, "art thou come to this darkened land again? Art thou come to bear a valiant testimony as in former years? The scourge hath not prevailed against thee, and from the dungeon hast thou come forth triumphant; but strengthen, strengthen now thy heart, Catharine, for Heaven will prove thee yet this once, ere thou go to thy reward."

"Rejoice, friends!" she replied. "Thou who hast long been of our people, and thou whom a little child hath led to us, rejoice! Lo! I come, the messenger of glad tidings, for the day of persecution is overpast. The heart of the King, even Charles, hath been moved in gentleness towards us, and he hath sent forth his letters to stay the hands of the men of blood. A ship's company of our friends hath arrived at yonder town, and I also sailed joyfully among them."

As Catharine spoke, her eyes were roaming about the room, in search of him for whose sake security was dear to her. Pearson made a silent appeal to the old man, nor did the latter shrink from the painful task assigned him.

"Sister," he began, in a softened yet perfectly calm tone, "thou tellest us of His Love, manifested in temporal good; and now must we speak to thee of that selfsame love, displayed in chastenings. Hitherto, Catharine, thou hast been as one journeying in a darksome and difficult path, and leading an infant by the hand; fain wouldst thou have looked heavenward continually, but still the cares of that little child have drawn thine eyes, and thy affections, to the earth. Favourite sister! Go on rejoicing, for his tottering footsteps shall impede thine own no more."

But the unhappy mother was not thus to be consoled: she shook like a leaf, she turned white as the very snow that hung drifted into her hair. The firm old man extended his hand and held her up, keeping his eye upon hers, as if to repress any outbreak of passion.

"I am a woman, I am but a woman – will He try me above my strength?" said Catharine, very quickly, and almost in a whisper. "I have been wounded sore; I have suffered much; many things in the body; many in the mind; crucified in myself, and in them that were dearest to me. Surely," added she, with a long shudder, "He hath spared me in this one thing." She broke forth with sudden and irrepressible violence. "Tell me, man of cold heart, what has God done to me? Hath He cast me down never to rise again? Hath He crushed my very heart in his hand? And thou, to whom I committed my child, how hast thou fulfilled thy trust? Give me back the boy, well, sound, alive, alive; or earth and heaven shall avenge me!"

The agonized shriek of Catharine was answered by the faint, the very faint voice of a child.

On this day it had become evident to Pearson, to his aged guest and to Dorothy, that Ilbrahim's brief and troubled pilgrimage drew near its close. The two former would willingly have remained by him, to make use of the prayers and pious discourses which they deemed appropriate to the time, and which, if they be impotent as to the departing traveller's reception in the world whither he goes, may at least sustain him in bidding adieu to earth. But though Ilbrahim uttered no complaint, he was disturbed by the faces that looked upon him; so that Dorothy's entreaties, and their own conviction that the child's feet might tread heaven's pavement and not soil it, had induced the two Quakers to remove. Ilbrahim then closed his eyes and grew calm, and, except for now and then a kind and low word to his nurse, might have been thought to slumber. As nightfall came on, however, and the storm began to rise, something seemed to trouble the repose of the boy's mind, and to render his sense of hearing active and acute. If a passing wind lingered to shake the casement, he strove to turn his head towards it; if the door jarred to and fro upon its hinges, he looked long and anxiously thitherward; if the heavy voice of the old man, as he read the Scriptures, rose but a little higher, the child almost held his dying breath to listen; if a snowdrift swept by the cottage, with a sound like the trailing of a garment, Ilbrahim seemed to watch that some visitant should enter. But, after a little time, he relinquished whatever secret hope had agitated him, and, with one low, complaining whisper, turned his cheek upon the pillow. He then addressed Dorothy with his usual sweetness, and besought her to draw near him; she did so, and Ilbrahim took her hand in both of his, grasping it with a gentle pressure, as if to assure himself that he retained it. At intervals, and without disturbing the repose of his countenance, a very faint trembling passed over him from head to foot, as if a mild but somewhat cool wind had breathed upon him, and made him shiver. As the boy thus led her by the hand, in his quiet progress over the borders of eternity, Dorothy almost imagined that she could discern the near, though dim delightfulness of the home he was about to reach; she would not have enticed the little wanderer back, though she bemoaned herself that she must leave him and return. But just when Ilbrahim's feet were pressing on the soil of Paradise, he heard a voice behind him, and it recalled him a few, few paces of the weary path which he had travelled. As Dorothy looked upon his features, she perceived that their placid expression was again disturbed; her own thoughts had been so wrapt in him that all sounds of the storm, and of human speech, were lost to her; but when Catharine's shriek pierced through the room, the boy strove to raise himself.

"Friend, she is come! Open unto her!" cried he.

In a moment, his mother was kneeling by the bedside; she drew Ilbrahim to her bosom, and he nestled there, with no violence of joy, but contentedly as if he were hushing himself to sleep. He looked into her face, and reading its agony, said, with feeble earnestness:

"Mourn not, dearest mother. I am happy now." And with these words, the gentle boy was dead.

* * *

The King's mandate to stay the New England persecutors was effectual in preventing further martyrdoms; but the colonial authorities, trusting in the remoteness of their situation, and perhaps in the supposed instability of the royal government, shortly renewed their severities in all other respects. Catharine's fanaticism had become wilder by the sundering of all human ties; and wherever a scourge was lifted, there was she to receive the blow; and whenever a dungeon was unbarred, thither she came, to cast herself upon the floor. But in process of time, a more Christian spirit – a spirit of forbearance, though not of cordiality or approbation, began to pervade the land in regard to the persecuted sect. And then, when the rigid old Pilgrims eyed her rather in pity than in wrath; when the matrons fed her with the fragments of their children's food, and offered her a lodging on a hard and lowly bed; when no little crowd of schoolboys left their sports to cast stones after the roving enthusiast – then did Catherine return to Pearson's dwelling, and made that her home. As if Ilbrahim's sweetness yet lingered round his ashes, as if his gentle spirit came down from heaven to teach his parent a true religion, her fierce and vindictive nature was softened by the same griefs which had once irritated it. When the course of years had made the features of the unobtrusive mourner familiar in the set- tlement, she became a subject of not deep, but general interest, a being on whom the otherwise superfluous sympathies of all might be bestowed. Everyone spoke of her with that degree of pity which it is pleasant to experience; everyone was ready to do her the little kindnesses which are not costly, yet manifest goodwill; and when at last she died, a long train of her once bitter persecutors followed her, with decent sadness and tears that were not painful, to her place by Ilbrahim's green and sunken grave. My heart is glad of this triumph of our better nature – it gives me a kindlier feeling for the fathers of my native land – and with it I will close the tale.

My Kinsman, Major Molineux

A FTER THE KINGS OF GREAT BRITAIN had assumed the right of appointing the colonial governors,* the measures of the latter seldom met with the ready and general approbation which had been paid to those of their predecessors, under the original charters. The people looked with most jealous scrutiny to the exercise of power which did not emanate from themselves, and they usually rewarded their rulers with slender gratitude for the compliances by which, in softening their instructions from beyond the sea, they had incurred the reprehension of those who gave them. The annals of Massachusetts Bay will inform us that of six governors in the space of about forty years from the surrender of the old charter, under James II, two were imprisoned by a popular insurrection; a third, as Hutchinson inclines to believe, was driven from the province by the whizzing of a musket ball; a fourth, in the opinion of the same historian, was hastened to his grave by continual bickerings with the House of Representatives; and the remaining two, as well as their successors, till the Revolution, were favoured with few and brief intervals of peaceful sway.* The inferior members of the court party, in times of high political excitement, led scarcely a more desirable life. These remarks may serve as a preface to the following adventures, which chanced upon a summer night, not far from a hundred years ago. The reader, in order to avoid a long and dry detail of colonial affairs, is requested to dispense with an account of the train of circumstances that had caused much temporary inflammation of the popular mind.

It was near nine o'clock of a moonlight evening, when a boat crossed the ferry with a single passenger, who had obtained his conveyance at that unusual hour by the promise of an extra fare. While he stood on the landing place, searching in either pocket for the means of fulfilling his agreement, the ferryman lifted a lantern, by the aid of which, and the newly risen moon, he took a very accurate survey of the stranger's figure. He was a youth of barely eighteen years, evidently country-bred, and now, as it should seem, upon his first visit to town. He was clad in a coarse grey coat, well worn, but in excellent repair; his undergarments were durably constructed of leather, and fitted tight to a pair of serviceable and well-shaped limbs; his stockings of blue yarn were the incontrovertible work of a mother or a sister; and on his head was a three-cornered hat, which in its better days had perhaps sheltered the graver brow of the lad's father. Under his left arm was a heavy cudgel, formed of an oak sapling and retaining a part of the hardened root; and his equipment was completed by a wallet, not so abundantly stocked as to incommode the vigorous shoulders on which it hung. Brown, curly hair, well-shaped features and bright, cheerful eyes were nature's gifts, and worth all that art could have done for his adornment.

The youth, one of whose names was Robin, finally drew from his pocket the half of a little province bill of five shillings, which, in the depreciation of that sort of currency, did but satisfy the ferryman's demand, with the surplus of a sexangular piece of parchment, valued at three pence. He then walked forward into the town, with as light a step as if his day's journey had not already exceeded thirty miles, and with as eager an eye as if he were entering London city, instead of the little metropolis of a New England colony. Before Robin had proceeded far, however, it occurred to him that he knew not whither to direct his steps; so he paused and looked up and down the narrow street, scrutinizing the small and mean wooden buildings that were scattered on either side.

"This low hovel cannot be my kinsman's dwelling," thought he, "not yonder old house, where the moonlight enters at the broken casement; and truly I see none hereabouts that might be worthy of him. It would have been wise to enquire my way of the ferryman, and doubtless he would have gone with me, and earned a shilling from the Major for his pains. But the next man I meet will do as well."

He resumed his walk, and was glad to perceive that the street now became wider, and the houses more respectable in their appearance. He soon discerned a figure moving on moderately in advance, and hastened his steps to overtake it. As Robin drew nigh, he saw that the passenger was a man in years, with a full periwig of grey hair, a wide-skirted coat of dark cloth and silk stockings rolled above his knees. He carried a long and polished cane, which he struck down perpendicularly before him, at every step; and at regular intervals he uttered two successive hems, of a peculiarly solemn and sepulchral intonation. Having made these observations, Robin laid hold of the skirt of the old man's coat, just when the light from the open door and windows of a barber's shop fell upon both their figures.

"Good evening to you, honoured sir," said he, making a low bow, and still retaining his hold of the skirt. "I pray you tell me whereabouts is the dwelling of my kinsman, Major Molineux."

The youth's question was uttered very loudly, and one of the barbers, whose razor was descending on a well-soaped chin, and another who was dressing a Ramillies wig,* left their occupations, and came to the door. The citizen, in the mean time, turned a long-favoured countenance upon Robin, and answered him in a tone of excessive anger and annoyance. His two sepulchral hems, however, broke into the very centre of his rebuke, with most singular effect, like a thought of the cold grave obtruding among wrathful passions.

"Let go my garment, fellow! I tell you, I know not the man you speak of. What! I have authority, I have... hem, hem... authority; and if this be the respect you show for your betters, your feet shall be brought acquainted with the stocks by daylight, tomorrow morning!"

Robin released the old man's skirt, and hastened away, pursued by an ill-mannered roar of laughter from the barber's shop. He was at first considerably surprised by the result of his question, but, being a shrewd youth, soon thought himself able to account for the mystery.

"This is some country representative," was his conclusion, "who has never seen the inside of my kinsman's door, and lacks the breeding to answer a stranger civilly. The man is old, or verily – I might be tempted to turn back and smite him on the nose. Ah, Robin, Robin! Even the barber's boys laugh at you for choosing such a guide! You will be wiser in time, friend Robin."

He now became entangled in a succession of crooked and narrow streets, which crossed each other, and meandered at no great distance from the waterside. The smell of tar was obvious to his nostrils, the masts of vessels pierced the moonlight above the tops of the buildings, and the numerous signs, which Robin paused to read, informed him that he was near the centre of business. But the streets were empty, the shops were closed, and lights were visible only in the second stories of a few dwelling houses. At length, on the corner of a narrow lane, through which he was passing, he beheld the broad countenance of a British hero swinging before the door of an inn, whence proceeded the voices of many guests. The casement of one of the lower windows was thrown back, and a very thin curtain permitted Robin to distinguish a party at supper, round a well-furnished table. The fragrance of the good cheer steamed forth into the outer air, and the youth could not fail to recollect that the last remnant of his travelling stock of provision had yielded to his morning appetite, and that noon had found and left him dinnerless.

"Oh, that a parchment threepenny might give me a right to sit at yonder table!" said Robin, with a sigh. "But the Major will make me welcome to the best of his victuals, so I will even step boldly in, and enquire my way to his dwelling."

He entered the tavern, and was guided by the murmur of voices and the fumes of tobacco to the public room. It was a long and low apartment, with oaken walls, grown dark in the continual smoke, and a floor which was thickly sanded, but of no immaculate purity. A number of persons – the larger part of whom appeared to be mariners, or in some way connected with the sea – occupied the wooden benches, or leather-bottomed chairs, conversing on various matters and occasionally lending their attention to some topic of general interest. Three or four little groups were draining as many bowls of punch, which the West India trade had long since made a familiar drink in the colony. Others, who had the appearance of men who lived by regular and laborious handicraft, preferred the insulated bliss of an unshared potation, and became more taciturn under its influence. Nearly all, in short, evinced a predilection for the Good Creature in some of its various shapes, for this is a vice to which, as Fast Day sermons of a hundred years ago will testify, we have a long hereditary claim. The only guests to whom Robin's sympathies inclined him were two or three sheepish countrymen, who were using the inn somewhat after the fashion of a Turkish caravanserai; they had gotten themselves into the darkest corner of the room and, heedless of the nicotian atmosphere, were supping on the bread of their own ovens and the bacon cured in their own chimney smoke. But though Robin felt a sort of brotherhood with these strangers, his eyes were attracted from them to a person who stood near the door, holding whispered conversation with a group of ill-dressed associates. His features were separately striking almost to grotesqueness, and the whole face left a deep impression on the memory. The forehead bulged out into a double prominence, with a vale between; the nose came boldly forth in an irregular curve, and its bridge was of more than a finger's breadth; the eyebrows were deep and shaggy, and the eyes glowed beneath them like fire in a cave.

While Robin deliberated of whom to enquire respecting his kinsman's dwelling, he was accosted by the innkeeper, a little man in a stained white apron, who had come to pay his professional welcome to the stranger. Being in the second generation from a French Protestant, he seemed to have inherited the courtesy of his parent nation; but no variety of circumstances was ever known to change his voice from the one shrill note in which he now addressed Robin.

"From the country, I presume, sir?" said he, with a profound bow. "Beg leave to congratulate you on your arrival, and trust you intend a long stay with us. Fine town here, sir, beautiful buildings, and much that may interest a stranger. May I hope for the honour of your commands in respect to supper?"

"The man sees a family likeness! The rogue has guessed that I am related to the Major!" thought Robin, who had hitherto experienced little superfluous civility.

All eyes were now turned on the country lad standing at the door, in his worn three-cornered hat, grey coat, leather breeches and blue yarn stockings, leaning on an oaken cudgel and bearing a wallet on his back.

Robin replied to the courteous innkeeper, with such an assumption of confidence as befitted the Major's relative. "My honest friend," he said, "I shall make it a point to patronize your house on some occasion, when" – here he could not help lowering his voice – "when I may have more than a parchment threepence in my pocket. My present business," continued he, speaking with lofty confidence, "is merely to enquire my way to the dwelling of my kinsman, Major Molineux."

There was a sudden and general movement in the room, which Robin interpreted as expressing the eagerness of each individual to become his guide. But the innkeeper turned his eyes to a written paper on the wall, which he read, or seemed to read, with occasional recurrences to the young man's figure.

"What have we here?" said he, breaking his speech into little dry fragments. "'Left the house of the subscriber, bounden servant, Hezekiah Mudge – had on, when he went away, grey coat, leather breeches, master's third-best hat. One pound currency reward to whosoever shall lodge him in any jail of the province.' Better trudge, boy, better trudge!"

Robin had begun to draw his hand towards the lighter end of the oak cudgel, but a strange hostility in every countenance induced him to relinquish his purpose of breaking the courteous innkeeper's head. As he turned to leave the room, he encountered a sneering glance from the bold-featured personage whom he had before noticed; and no sooner was he beyond the door than he heard a general laugh, in which the innkeeper's voice might be distinguished, like the dropping of small stones into a kettle.

"Now, is it not strange," thought Robin, with his usual shrewdness, "is it not strange that the confession of an empty pocket should outweigh the name of my kinsman, Major Molineux? Oh, if I had one of those grinning rascals in the woods, where I and my oak sapling grew up together, I would teach him that my arm is heavy, though my purse be light!"

On turning the corner of the narrow lane, Robin found himself in a spacious street, with an unbroken line of lofty houses on each side, and a steepled building at the upper end, whence the ringing of a bell announced the hour of nine. The light of the moon and the lamps from the numerous shop windows discovered people promenading on the pavement, and amongst them Robin hoped to recognize his hitherto inscrutable relative. The result of his former enquiries made him unwilling to hazard another, in a scene of such publicity, and he determined to walk slowly and silently up the street, thrusting his face close to that of every elderly gentleman, in search of the Major's lineaments. In his progress, Robin encountered many gay and gallant figures. Embroidered garments of showy colours, enormous periwigs, gold-laced hats and silver-hilted swords glided past him and dazzled his optics. Travelled youths, imitators of the European fine gentlemen of the period, trod jauntily along, half-dancing to the fashionable tunes which they hummed, and making poor Robin ashamed of his quiet and natural gait. At length, after many pauses to examine the gorgeous display of goods in the shop windows, and after suffering some rebukes for the impertinence of his scrutiny into people's faces, the Major's kinsman found himself near the steepled building, still unsuccessful in his search. As yet, however he had seen only one side of the thronged street; so Robin crossed, and continued the same sort of inquisition down the opposite pavement, with stronger hopes than the philosopher seeking an honest man, but with no better fortune. He had arrived about midway towards the lower end, from which his course began, when he overheard the approach of someone who struck down a cane on the flagstones at every step, uttering, at regular intervals, two sepulchral hems.

"Mercy on us!" quoth Robin, recognizing the sound.

Turning a corner, which chanced to be close at his right hand, he hastened to pursue his researches in some other part of the town. His patience now was wearing low, and he seemed to feel more fatigue from his rambles since he crossed the ferry than from his journey of several days on the other side. Hunger also pleaded loudly within him, and Robin began to balance the propriety of demanding violently and with lifted cudgel, the necessary guidance from the first solitary passenger whom he should meet. While a resolution to this effect was gaining strength, he entered a street of mean appearance, on either side of which a row of ill-built houses was straggling towards the harbour. The moonlight fell upon no passenger along the whole extent, but in the third domicile which Robin passed there was a half-opened door, and his keen glance detected a woman's garment within.

"My luck may be better here," said he to himself.

Accordingly, he approached the door, and beheld it shut closer as he did so; yet an open space remained, sufficing for the fair occupant to observe the stranger, without a corresponding display on her part. All that Robin could discern was a strip of scarlet petticoat, and the occasional sparkle of an eye, as if the moonbeams were trembling on some bright thing.

"Pretty mistress" – for I may call her so with a good conscience, thought the shrewd youth, since I know nothing to the contrary – "my sweet pretty mistress, will you be kind enough to tell me whereabouts I must seek the dwelling of my kinsman, Major Molineux?"

Robin's voice was plaintive and winning, and the female, seeing nothing to be shunned in the handsome country youth, thrust open the door, and came forth into the moonlight. She was a dainty little figure, with a white neck, round arms and a slender waist, at the extremity of which her scarlet petticoat jutted out over a hoop, as if she were standing in a balloon. Moreover, her face was oval and pretty, her hair dark beneath the little cap and her bright eyes possessed a sly freedom, which triumphed over those of Robin.

"Major Molineux dwells here," said this fair woman.

Now, her voice was the sweetest Robin had heard that night, the airy counterpart of a stream of melted silver, yet he could not help doubting whether that sweet voice spoke Gospel truth. He looked up and down the mean street, and then surveyed the house before which they stood. It was a small, dark edifice of two stories, the second of which projected over the lower floor, and the front apartment had the aspect of a shop for petty commodities.

"Now, truly, I am in luck," replied Robin, cunningly, "and so indeed is my kinsman, the Major, in having so pretty a house-keeper. But I prithee trouble him to step to the door; I will deliver him a message from his friends in the country, and then go back to my lodgings at the inn."

"Nay, the Major has been abed this hour or more," said the lady of the scarlet petticoat, "and it would be to little purpose to disturb him tonight, seeing his evening draught was of the strongest. But he is a kind-hearted man, and it would be as much as my life's worth to let a kinsman of his turn away from the door. You are the good old gentleman's very picture, and I could swear that was his rainy-weather hat. Also he has garments very much resembling those leather small clothes. But come in, I pray, for I bid you hearty welcome in his name."

So saying, the fair and hospitable dame took our hero by the hand, and the touch was light, and the force was gentleness, and though Robin read in her eyes what he did not hear in her words, yet the slender-waisted woman in the scarlet petticoat proved stronger than the athletic country youth. She had drawn his half-willing footsteps nearly to the threshold, when the opening of a door in the neighbourhood startled the Major's housekeeper and, leaving the Major's kinsman, she vanished speedily into her own domicile. A heavy yawn preceded the appearance of a man, who, like the Moonshine of *Pyramus and Thisbe*,* carried a lantern, needlessly aiding his sister luminary in the heavens. As he walked sleepily up the street, he turned his broad, dull face on Robin and displayed a long staff, spiked at the end.

"Home, vagabond, home!" said the watchman, in accents that seemed to fall asleep as soon as they were uttered. "Home, or we'll set you in the stocks, by peep of day!"

"This is the second hint of the kind," thought Robin. "I wish they would end my difficulties, by setting me there tonight."

Nevertheless, the youth felt an instinctive antipathy towards the guardian of midnight order, which at first prevented him from asking his usual question. But just when the man was about to vanish behind the corner, Robin resolved not to lose the opportunity, and shouted lustily after him:

"I say, friend! Will you guide me to the house of my kinsman, Major Molineux?"

The watchman made no reply, but turned the corner and was gone; yet Robin seemed to hear the sound of drowsy laughter stealing along the solitary street. At that moment, also, a pleasant titter saluted him from the open window above his head; he looked up, and caught the sparkle of a saucy eye; a round arm beckoned to him, and next he heard light footsteps descending the staircase within. But Robin, being of the household of a New England clergyman, was a good youth, as well as a shrewd one; so he resisted temptation, and fled away.

He now roamed desperately, and at random, through the town, almost ready to believe that a spell was on him, like that by which a wizard of his country had once kept three pursuers wandering, a whole winter night, within twenty paces of the cottage which they sought. The streets lay before him, strange and desolate, and the lights were extinguished in almost every house. Twice, however, little parties of men, among whom Robin distinguished individuals in outlandish attire, came hurrying along; but though on both occasions they paused to address him, such intercourse did not at all enlighten his perplexity. They did but utter a few words in some language of which Robin knew nothing and, perceiving his inability to answer, bestowed a curse upon him in plain English, and hastened away. Finally, the lad determined to knock at the door of every mansion that might appear worthy to be occupied by his kinsman, trusting that perseverance would overcome the fatality that had hitherto thwarted him. Firm in this resolve, he was passing beneath the walls of a church, which formed the corner of two streets, when, as he turned into the shade of its steeple, he encountered a bulky stranger, muffled in a cloak. The man was proceeding with the speed of earnest business, but Robin planted himself full before him, holding the oak cudgel with both hands across his body as a bar to further passage.

"Halt, honest man, and answer me a question," said he, very resolutely. "Tell me, this instant, whereabouts is the dwelling of my kinsman, Major Molineux!"

"Keep your tongue between your teeth, fool, and let me pass!" said a deep, gruff voice, which Robin partly remembered. "Let me pass, I say, or I'll strike you to the earth!"

"No, no, neighbour!" cried Robin, flourishing his cudgel, and then thrusting its larger end close to the man's muffled face.

"No, no, I'm not the fool you take me for, nor do you pass till I have an answer to my question. Whereabouts is the dwelling of my kinsman, Major Molineux?"

The stranger, instead of attempting to force his passage, stepped back into the moonlight, unmuffled his face and stared full into that of Robin.

"Watch here an hour, and Major Molineux will pass by," said he.

Robin gazed with dismay and astonishment on the unprecedented physiognomy of the speaker. The forehead with its double prominence, the broad hooked nose, the shaggy eyebrows and fiery eyes were those which he had noticed at the inn, but the man's complexion had undergone a singular or, more properly, a twofold change. One side of the face blazed an intense red, while the other was black as midnight, the division line being in the broad bridge of the nose; and a mouth which seemed to extend from ear to ear was black or red, in contrast to the colour of the cheek. The effect was as if two individual devils, a fiend of fire and a fiend of darkness, had united themselves to form this infernal visage. The stranger grinned in Robin's face, muffled his particoloured features and was out of sight in a moment.

"Strange things we travellers see!" ejaculated Robin.

He seated himself, however, upon the steps of the church door, resolving to wait the appointed time for his kinsman. A few moments were consumed in philosophical speculations upon the species of man who had just left him; but having settled this point shrewdly, rationally and satisfactorily, he was compelled to look elsewhere for his amusement. And first he threw his eyes along the street. It was of more respectable appearance than most of those into which he had wandered, and the moon, creating, like the imaginative power, a beautiful strangeness in familiar objects, gave something of romance to a scene that might not have possessed it in the light of day. The irregular and often quaint architecture of the houses – some of whose roofs were broken into numerous little peaks, while others ascended, steep and narrow, into a single point, and others again were square – the pure snow-white of some of their complexions, the aged darkness of others and the thousand sparklings reflected from bright substances in the walls of many; these matters engaged Robin's attention for a while, and then began to grow wearisome. Next he endeavoured to define the forms of distant objects, starting away, with almost ghostly indistinctness, just as his eye appeared to grasp them; and finally he took a minute survey of an edifice which stood on the opposite side of the street, directly in front of the church door, where he was stationed. It was a large, square mansion, distinguished from its neighbours by a balcony, which rested on tall pillars, and by an elaborate Gothic window, communicating therewith.

"Perhaps this is the very house I have been seeking," thought Robin.

Then he strove to speed away the time, by listening to a murmur which swept continually along the street, yet was scarcely audible, except to an unaccustomed ear like his; it was a low, dull, dreamy sound, compounded of many noises, each of which was at too great a distance to be separately heard. Robin marvelled at this snore of a sleeping town, and marvelled more whenever its continuity was broken by now and then a distant shout, apparently loud where it originated. But altogether it was a sleep-inspiring sound, and to shake off its drowsy influence Robin arose and climbed a window frame, that he might view the interior of the church. There the moonbeams came trembling in, and fell down upon the deserted pews and extended along the quiet aisles. A fainter yet more awful radiance was hovering around the pulpit, and one solitary ray had dared to rest upon the open page of the great Bible. Had nature, in that deep hour, become a worshipper in the house which man had built? Or was that heavenly light the visible sanctity of the place – visible because no earthly and impure feet were within the walls? The scene made Robin's heart shiver with a sensation of loneliness stronger than he had ever felt in the remotest depths of his native woods; so he turned away and sat down again before the door. There were graves around the church, and now an uneasy thought obtruded into Robin's breast. What if the object of his search, which had been so often and so strangely thwarted, were all the time mouldering in his shroud? What if his kinsman should glide through yonder gate, and nod and smile to him in dimly passing by?

"Oh, that any breathing thing were here with me!" said Robin.

Recalling his thoughts from this uncomfortable track, he sent them over forest, hill and stream, and attempted to imagine how that evening of ambiguity and weariness had been spent by his father's household. He pictured them assembled at the door, beneath the tree, the great old tree, which had been spared for its huge twisted trunk and venerable shade, when a thousand leafy brethren fell. There, at the going down of the summer sun, it was his father's custom to perform domestic worship, that the neighbours might come and join with him like brothers of the family, and that the wayfaring man might pause to drink at that fountain, and keep his heart pure by freshening the memory of home. Robin distinguished the seat of every individual of the little audience; he saw the good man in the midst, holding the Scriptures in the golden light that fell from the western clouds; he beheld him close the book and all rise up to pray. He heard the old thanksgivings for daily mercies, the old supplications for their continuance, to which he had so often listened in weariness, but which were now among his dear remembrances. He perceived the slight inequality of his father's voice when he came to speak of the absent one; he noted how his mother turned her face to the broad and knotted trunk; how his elder brother scorned, because the beard was rough upon his upper lip, to permit his features to be moved; how the younger sister drew down a low hanging branch before her eyes; and how the little one of all, whose sports had hitherto broken the decorum of the scene, understood the prayer for her playmate and burst into clamorous grief. Then he saw them go in at the door, and when Robin would have entered also, the latch tinkled into its place, and he was excluded from his home.

"Am I here, or there?" cried Robin, starting; for all at once, when his thoughts had become visible and audible in a dream, the long, wide, solitary street shone out before him.

He aroused himself, and endeavoured to fix his attention steadily upon the large edifice which he had surveyed before. But still his mind kept vibrating between fancy and reality; by turns, the pillars of the balcony lengthened into the tall, bare stems of pines, dwindled down to human figures, settled again into their true shape and size and then commenced a new succession of changes. For a single moment, when he deemed himself awake, he could have sworn that a visage – one which he seemed to remember, yet could not absolutely name as his kinsman's – was looking towards him from the Gothic window. A deeper sleep wrestled with and nearly overcame him, but fled at the sound of footsteps along the opposite pavement. Robin rubbed his eyes, discerned a man passing at the foot of the balcony and addressed him in a loud, peevish and lamentable cry.

"Hallo, friend! Must I wait here all night for my kinsman, Major Molineux?"

The sleeping echoes awoke, and answered the voice; and the passenger, barely able to discern a figure sitting in the oblique shade of the steeple, traversed the street to obtain a nearer view. He was himself a gentleman in his prime, of open, intelligent, cheerful and altogether prepossessing countenance. Perceiving a country youth, apparently homeless and without friends, he accosted him in a tone of real kindness, which had become strange to Robin's ears.

"Well, my good lad, why are you sitting here?" enquired he. "Can I be of service to you in any way?"

"I am afraid not, sir," replied Robin, despondingly, "yet I shall take it kindly if you'll answer me a single question. I've been searching, half the night, for one Major Molineux; now, sir, is there really such a person in these parts, or am I dreaming?"

"Major Molineux! The name is not altogether strange to me," said the gentleman, smiling. "Have you any objection to telling me the nature of your business with him?"

Then Robin briefly related that his father was a clergyman, settled on a small salary, at a long distance back in the country, and that he and Major Molineux were brothers' children. The Major, having inherited riches and acquired civil and military rank, had visited his cousin, in great pomp, a year or two before, had manifested much interest in Robin and an elder brother, and, being childless himself, had thrown out hints respecting the future establishment of one of them in life. The elder brother was destined to succeed to the farm which his father cultivated in the interval of sacred duties: it was therefore determined that Robin should profit by his kinsman's generous intentions, especially as he seemed to be rather the favourite, and was thought to possess other necessary endowments.

"For I have the name of being a shrewd youth," observed Robin, in this part of his story.

"I doubt not you deserve it," replied his new friend, good-naturedly, "but pray proceed."

"Well, sir, being nearly eighteen years old, and well grown, as you see," continued Robin, drawing himself up to his full height, "I thought it high time to begin the world. So my mother and sister put me in handsome trim, and my father gave me half the remnant of his last year's salary, and five days ago I started for this place, to pay the Major a visit. But – would you believe it, sir! – I crossed the ferry a little after dark, and have yet found nobody that would show me the way to his dwelling; only, an hour or two since, I was told to wait here, and Major Molineux would pass by."

"Can you describe the man who told you this?" enquired the gentleman.

"Oh, he was a very ill-favoured fellow, sir," replied Robin, "with two great bumps on his forehead, a hook nose, fiery eyes – and, what struck me as the strangest, his face was of two different colours. Do you happen to know such a man, sir?"

"Not intimately," answered the stranger, "but I chanced to meet him a little time previous to your stopping me. I believe you may trust his word, and that the Major will very shortly pass through this street. In the mean time, as I have a singular curiosity to witness your meeting, I will sit down here upon the steps and bear you company."

He seated himself accordingly, and soon engaged his companion in animated discourse. It was but of brief continuance, however, for a noise of shouting, which had long been remotely audible, drew so much nearer that Robin enquired its cause.

"What may be the meaning of this uproar?" asked he. "Truly, if your town be always as noisy, I shall find little sleep while I am an inhabitant."

"Why, indeed, friend Robin, there do appear to be three or four riotous fellows abroad tonight," replied the gentleman. "You must not expect all the stillness of your native woods here in our streets. But the watch will shortly be at the heels of these lads, and—"

"Ay, and set them in the stocks by peep of day," interrupted Robin, recollecting his own encounter with the drowsy lantern-bearer. "But, dear sir, if I may trust my ears, an army of watchmen would never make head against such a multitude of rioters. There were at least a thousand voices went up to make that one shout."

"May not a man have several voices, Robin, as well as two complexions?" said his friend.

"Perhaps a man may, but Heaven forbid that a woman should!" responded the shrewd youth, thinking of the seductive tones of the Major's housekeeper.

The sounds of a trumpet in some neighbouring street now became so evident and continual that Robin's curiosity was strongly excited. In addition to the shouts, he heard frequent bursts from many instruments of discord, and a wild and confused laughter filled up the intervals. Robin rose from the steps and looked wistfully towards a point whither several people seemed to be hastening.

"Surely some prodigious merry-making is going on," exclaimed he. "I have laughed very little since I left home, sir, and should be sorry to lose an opportunity. Shall we step round the corner by that darkish house and take our share of the fun?"

"Sit down again, sit down, good Robin," replied the gentleman, laying his hand on the skirt of the grey coat. "You forget that we must wait here for your kinsman, and there is reason to believe that he will pass by in the course of a very few moments."

The near approach of the uproar had now disturbed the neighbourhood: windows flew open on all sides, and many heads, in the attire of the pillow and confused by sleep suddenly broken, were protruded to the gaze of whoever had leisure to observe them. Eager voices hailed each other from house to house, all demanding the explanation, which not a soul could give. Half-dressed men hurried towards the unknown commotion, stumbling as they went over the stone steps that thrust themselves into the narrow footwalk. The shouts, the laughter and the tuneless bray, the antipodes of music, came onwards with increasing din, till scattered individuals, and then denser bodies, began to appear round a corner at the distance of a hundred yards.

"Will you recognize your kinsman, if he passes in this crowd?" enquired the gentleman.

"Indeed, I can't warrant it, sir, but I'll take my stand here and keep a bright lookout," answered Robin, descending to the outer edge of the pavement.

A mighty stream of people now emptied into the street and came rolling slowly towards the church. A single horseman wheeled the corner in the midst of them, and close behind him came a band of fearful wind instruments, sending forth a fresher discord, now that no intervening buildings kept it from the ear. Then a redder light disturbed the moonbeams, and a dense multitude of torches shone along the street, concealing, by their glare, whatever object they illuminated. The single horseman, clad in a military dress and bearing a drawn sword, rode onward as the leader and, by his fierce and variegated countenance, appeared like war personified; the red of one cheek was an emblem of fire and sword; the blackness of the other betokened the mourning that attends them. In his train were wild figures in the Indian dress, and many fantastic shapes without a model, giving the whole march a visionary air, as if a dream had broken forth from some feverish brain and were sweeping visibly through the midnight streets. A mass of people, inactive, except as applauding spectators, hemmed the procession in; and several women ran along the sidewalk, piercing the confusion of heavier sounds with their shrill voices of mirth or terror.

"The double-faced fellow has his eye upon me," muttered Robin, with an indefinite but an uncomfortable idea that he was himself to bear a part in the pageantry.

The leader turned himself in the saddle and fixed his glance full upon the country youth, as the steed went slowly by. When Robin had freed his eyes from those fiery ones, the musicians were passing before him, and the torches were close at hand; but the unsteady brightness of the latter formed a veil which he could not penetrate. The rattling of wheels over the stones sometimes found its way to his ears, and confused traces of a human form appeared at intervals, and then melted into the vivid light. A moment more, and the leader thundered a command to halt: the trumpets vomited a horrid breath, and then held their peace; the shouts and laughter of the people died away, and there remained only a universal hum, allied to silence. Right before Robin's eyes was an uncovered cart. There the torches blazed the brightest, there the moon shone out like day and there, in tar-and-feathery dignity, sat his kinsman, Major Molineux!

He was an elderly man, of large and majestic person and strong, square features, betokening a steady soul; but steady as it was, his enemies had found means to shake it. His face was pale as death, and far more ghastly; the broad forehead was contracted in his agony, so that his eyebrows formed one grizzled line; his eyes were red and wild, and the foam hung white upon his quivering lip. His whole frame was agitated by a quick and continual tremor, which his pride strove to quell, even in those circumstances of overwhelming humiliation. But perhaps the bitterest pang of all was when his eyes met those of Robin; for he evidently knew him on the instant, as the youth stood witnessing the foul disgrace of a head grown grey in honour. They stared at each other in silence, and Robin's knees shook, and his hair bristled, with a mixture of pity and terror. Soon, however, a bewildering excitement began to seize upon his mind; the preceding adventures of the night, the unexpected appearance of the crowd, the torches, the confused din and the hush that followed, the spectre of his kinsman reviled by that great multitude – all this and, more than all, a perception of tremendous ridicule in the whole scene, affected him with a sort of mental inebriety. At that moment a voice of sluggish merriment saluted Robin's ears; he turned instinctively, and just behind the corner of the church stood the lantern-bearer, rubbing his eyes and drowsily enjoying the lad's amazement. Then he heard a peal of laughter like the ringing of silvery bells; a woman twitched his arm, a saucy eye met his and he saw the lady of the scarlet petticoat. A sharp, dry cachinnation appealed to his memory, and, standing on tiptoe in the crowd, with his white apron over his head, he beheld the courteous little innkeeper. And lastly, there sailed over the heads of the multitude a great, broad laugh, broken in the midst by two sepulchral hems; thus: "Haw, haw, haw – hem, hem – haw, haw, haw, haw!"

The sound proceeded from the balcony of the opposite edifice, and thither Robin turned his eyes. In front of the Gothic window stood the old citizen, wrapped in a wide gown, his grey periwig exchanged for a nightcap, which was thrust back from his forehead, and his silk stockings hanging about his legs. He supported himself on his polished cane in a fit of convulsive merriment, which manifested itself on his solemn old features like a funny inscription on a tombstone. Then Robin seemed to hear the voices of the barbers, of the guests of the inn and of all who had made sport of him that night. The contagion was spreading among the multitude, when, all at once, it seized upon Robin, and he sent forth a shout of laughter that echoed through the street – every man shook his sides, every man emptied his lungs, but Robin's shout was the loudest there. The cloud spirits peeped from their silvery islands, as the congregated mirth went roaring up the sky! The Man in the Moon heard the far bellow. "Oho," quoth he, "the old earth is frolicsome tonight!"

When there was a momentary calm in that tempestuous sea of sound, the leader gave the sign, the procession resumed its march. On they went, like fiends that throng in mockery around some dead potentate, mighty no more, but majestic still in his agony. On they went, in counterfeited pomp, in senseless uproar, in frenzied merriment, trampling all on an old man's heart. On swept the tumult and left a silent street behind.

* * *

"Well, Robin, are you dreaming?" enquired the gentleman, laying his hand on the youth's shoulder.

Robin started, and withdrew his arm from the stone post to which he had instinctively clung, as the living stream rolled by him. His cheek was somewhat pale, and his eye not quite as lively as in the earlier part of the evening.

"Will you be kind enough to show me the way to the ferry?" said he, after a moment's pause.

"You have, then, adopted a new subject of enquiry?" observed his companion, with a smile.

"Why, yes, sir," replied Robin, rather drily. "Thanks to you, and to my other friends, I have at last met my kinsman, and he will scarce desire to see my face again. I begin to grow weary of a town life, sir. Will you show me the way to the ferry?"

"No, my good friend Robin – not tonight, at least," said the gentleman. "Some few days hence, if you wish it, I will speed you on your journey. Or, if you prefer to remain with us, perhaps, as you are a shrewd youth, you may rise in the world without the help of your kinsman, Major Molineux."

Roger Malvin's Burial

O NE OF THE FEW INCIDENTS of Indian warfare naturally susceptible of the moonlight of romance was that expedition undertaken for the defence of the frontiers in the year 1725, which resulted in the well-remembered "Lovell's Fight".* Imagination, by casting certain circumstances judicially into the shade, may see much to admire in the heroism of a little band who gave battle to twice their number in the heart of the enemy's country. The open bravery displayed by both parties was in accordance with civilized ideas of valour, and Chivalry itself might not blush to record the deeds of one or two individuals. The battle, though so fatal to those who fought, was not unfortunate in its consequences to the country; for it broke the strength of a tribe and conduced to the peace which subsisted during several ensuing years. History and tradition are unusually minute in their memorials of this affair, and the captain of a scouting party of frontier men has acquired as actual a military renown as many a victorious leader of thousands. Some of the incidents contained in the following pages will be recognized, notwithstanding the substitution of fictitious names, by such as have heard, from old men's lips, the fate of the few combatants who were in a condition to retreat after "Lovell's Fight".

* * *

The early sunbeams hovered cheerfully upon the treetops, beneath which two weary and wounded men had stretched their limbs the night before. Their bed of withered oak leaves was strewn upon the small level space, at the foot of a rock, situated near the summit of one of the gentle swells by which the face of the country is there diversified. The mass of granite, rearing its smooth flat surface fifteen or twenty feet above their heads, was not unlike a gigantic gravestone, upon which the veins seemed to form an inscription in forgotten characters. On a tract of several acres around this rock, oaks and other hardwood trees had supplied the place of the pines, which were the usual growth of the land, and a young and vigorous sapling stood close beside the travellers.

The severe wound of the elder man had probably deprived him of sleep; for, as soon as the first ray of sunshine rested on the top of the highest tree, he reared himself painfully from his recumbent posture and sat erect. The deep lines of his countenance and the scattered grey of his hair marked him as past the middle age, but his muscular frame would, but for the effects of his wound, have been as capable of sustaining fatigue as in the early vigour of life. Languor and exhaustion now sat upon his haggard features, and the despairing glance which he sent forward through the depths of the forest proved his own conviction that his pilgrimage was at an end. He next turned his eyes to the companion who reclined by his side. The youth – for he had scarcely attained the years of manhood – lay, with his head upon his arm, in the embrace of an unquiet sleep, which a thrill of pain from his wounds seemed each moment on the point of breaking. His right hand grasped a musket; and, to judge from the violent action of his features, his slumbers were bringing back a vision of the conflict of which he was one of the few survivors. A shout – deep and loud in his dreaming fancy – found its way in an imperfect murmur to his lips; and, starting even at the slight sound of his own voice, he suddenly awoke. The first act of reviving recollection was to make anxious enquiries respecting the condition of his wounded fellow traveller. The latter shook his head.

"Reuben, my boy," said he, "this rock beneath which we sit will serve for an old hunter's gravestone. There is many and many a long mile of howling wilderness before us yet; nor would it avail me anything if the smoke of my own chimney were but on the other side of that swell of land. The Indian bullet was deadlier than I thought."

"You are weary with our three days' travel," replied the youth, "and a little longer rest will recruit you. Sit you here while I search the woods for the herbs and roots that must be our sustenance; and, having eaten, you shall lean on me, and we will turn our faces homeward. I doubt not that, with my help, you can attain to some one of the frontier garrisons."

"There is not two days' life in me, Reuben," said the other calmly, "and I will no longer burden you with my useless body, when you can scarcely support your own. Your wounds are deep and your strength is failing fast; yet, if you hasten onward alone, you may be preserved. For me there is no hope, and I will await death here."

"If it must be so, I will remain and watch by you," said Reuben resolutely.

"No, my son, no," rejoined his companion. "Let the wish of a dying man have weight with you; give me one grasp of your hand, and get you hence. Think you that my last moments will be eased by the thought that I leave you to die a more lingering death? I have loved you like a father, Reuben; and at a time like this I should have something of a father's authority. I charge you to be gone, that I may die in peace."

"And because you have been a father to me, should I therefore leave you to perish and to lie unburied in the wilderness?" exclaimed the youth. "No: if your end be in truth approaching, I will watch by you and receive your parting words. I will dig a grave here by the rock, in which, if my weakness overcome me, we will rest together or, if Heaven gives me strength, I will seek my way home."

"In the cities and wherever men dwell," replied the other, "they bury their dead in the earth; they hide them from the sight of the living; but here, where no step may pass perhaps for a hundred years, wherefore should I not rest beneath the open sky, covered only by the oak leaves when the autumn winds shall strew them? And for a monument here is this grey rock, on which my dying hand shall carve the name of Roger Malvin; and the traveller in days to come will know that here sleeps a hunter and a warrior. Tarry not, then, for a folly like this, but hasten away, if not for your own sake, for hers who will else be desolate."

Malvin spoke the last few words in a faltering voice, and their effect upon his companion was strongly visible. They reminded him that there were other and less questionable duties than that of sharing the fate of a man whom his death could not benefit. Nor can it be affirmed that no selfish feeling strove to enter Reuben's heart, though the consciousness made him more earnestly resist his companion's entreaties.

"How terrible to wait the slow approach of death in this solitude!" exclaimed he. "A brave man does not shrink in the battle; and, when friends stand round the bed, even women may die composedly – but here—"

"I shall not shrink even here, Reuben Bourne," interrupted Malvin. "I am a man of no weak heart – and, if I were, there is a surer support than that of earthly friends. You are young, and life is dear to you. Your last moments will need comfort far more than mine, and when you have laid me in the earth, and are alone, and night is settling on the forest, you will feel all the bitterness of the death that may now be escaped. But I will urge no selfish motive to your generous nature. Leave me for my sake, that, having said a prayer for your safety, I may have space to settle my account undisturbed by worldly sorrows."

"And your daughter – how shall I dare to meet her eye?" exclaimed Reuben. "She will ask the fate of her father, whose life I vowed to defend with my own. Must I tell her that he travelled three days' march with me from the field of battle, and that then I left him to perish in the wilderness? Were it not better to lie down and die by your side than to return safe and say this to Dorcas?"

"Tell my daughter," said Roger Malvin, "that, though yourself sore wounded, and weak, and weary, you led my tottering footsteps many a mile, and left me only at my earnest entreaty, because I would not have your blood upon my soul. Tell her that through pain and danger you were faithful, and that, if your lifeblood could have saved me, it would have flowed to its last drop; and tell her that you will be something dearer than a father, and that my blessing is with you both, and that my dying eyes can see a long and pleasant path in which you will journey together."

As Malvin spoke, he almost raised himself from the ground, and the energy of his concluding words seemed to fill the wild and lonely forest with a vision of happiness; but, when he sank exhausted upon his bed of oak leaves, the light which had kindled in Reuben's eye was quenched. He felt as if it were both sin and folly to think of happiness at such a moment. His companion watched his changing countenance, and sought with generous art to wile him to his own good.

"Perhaps I deceive myself in regard to the time I have to live," he resumed. "It may be that, with speedy assistance, I might recover of my wound. The foremost fugitives must, ere this, have carried tidings of our fatal battle to the frontier, and parties will be out to succour those in like condition with ourselves. Should you meet one of these and guide them hither, who can tell but that I may sit by my own fireside again?"

A mournful smile strayed across the features of the dying man as he insinuated that unfounded hope – which, however, was not without its effect on Reuben. No merely selfish motive, nor even the desolate condition of Dorcas, could have induced him to desert his companion at such a moment, but his wishes seized upon the thought that Malvin's life might be preserved, and his sanguine nature heightened almost to certainty the remote possibility of procuring human aid.

"Surely there is reason, weighty reason, to hope that friends are not far distant," he said, half aloud. "There fled one coward, unwounded, in the beginning of the fight, and most probably he made good speed. Every true man on the frontier would shoulder his musket at the news, and, though no party may range so far into the woods as this, I shall perhaps encounter them in one day's march. Counsel me faithfully," he added, turning to Malvin, in distrust of his own motives. "Were your situation mine, would you desert me while life remained?"

"It is now twenty years," replied Roger Malvin, sighing, however, as he secretly acknowledged the wide dissimilarity between the two cases, "it is now twenty years since I escaped with one dear friend from Indian captivity near Montreal. We journeyed many days through the woods, till at length, overcome with hunger and weariness, my friend lay down and besought me to leave him; for he knew that, if I remained, we both must perish; and, with but little hope of obtaining succour, I heaped a pillow of dry leaves beneath his head and hastened on."

"And did you return in time to save him?" asked Reuben, hanging on Malvin's words as if they were to be prophetic of his own success.

"I did," answered the other. "I came upon the camp of a hunting party before sunset of the same day. I guided them to the spot where my comrade was expecting death – and he is now a hale and hearty man upon his own farm, far within the frontiers, while I lie wounded here in the depths of the wilderness."

This example, powerful in effecting Reuben's decision, was aided, unconsciously to himself, by the hidden strength of many another motive. Roger Malvin perceived that the victory was nearly won.

"Now, go, my son, and Heaven prosper you!" he said. "Turn not back with your friends when you meet them, lest your wounds and weariness overcome you, but send hitherward two or three that may be spared to search for me – and believe me, Reuben, my heart will be lighter with every step you take towards home." Yet there was, perhaps, a change both in his countenance and voice as he spoke thus; for, after all, it was a ghastly fate to be left expiring in the wilderness.

Reuben Bourne, but half convinced that he was acting rightly, at length raised himself from the ground and prepared himself for his departure. And first, though contrary to Malvin's wishes, he collected a stock of roots and herbs, which had been their only food during the last two days. This useless supply he placed within reach of the dying man, for whom, also, he swept together a fresh bed of dry oak leaves. Then climbing to the summit of the rock, which on one side was rough and broken, he bent the oak sapling downward, and bound his handkerchief to the topmost branch. This precaution was not unnecessary to direct any who might come in search of Malvin; for every part of the rock, except its broad smooth front, was concealed at a little distance by the dense undergrowth of the forest. The handkerchief had been the bandage of a wound upon Reuben's arm, and, as he bound it to the tree he vowed by the blood that stained it that he would return either to save his companion's life, or to lay his body in the grave. He then descended, and stood, with downcast eyes, to receive Roger Malvin's parting words.

The experience of the latter suggested much and minute advice respecting the youth's journey through the trackless forest. Upon this subject he spoke with calm earnestness, as if he were sending Reuben to the battle or the chase while he himself remained secure at home, and not as if the human countenance that was about to leave him were the last he would ever behold. But his firmness was shaken before he concluded.

"Carry my blessing to Dorcas, and say that my last prayer shall be for her and you. Bid her to have no hard thoughts because you left me here" – Reuben's heart smote him – "for that your life would not have weighed with you if its sacrifice could have done me good. She will marry you after she has mourned a little while for her father, and Heaven grant you long and happy days, and may your children's children stand round your deathbed! And, Reuben," added he, as the weakness of mortality made its way at last, "return – when your wounds are healed and your weariness refreshed – return to this wild rock and lay my bones in the grave, and say a prayer over them."

An almost superstitious regard, arising perhaps from the customs of the Indians, whose war was with the dead as well as the living, was paid by the frontier inhabitants to the rites of sepulture, and there are many instances of the sacrifice of life in the attempt to bury those who had fallen by the "sword of the wilderness". Reuben, therefore, felt the full importance of the promise which he most solemnly made to return and perform Roger Malvin's obsequies. It was remarkable that the latter, speaking his whole heart in his parting words, no longer endeavoured to persuade the youth that even the speediest succour might avail to the preservation of his life. Reuben was internally convinced that he should see Malvin's living face no more. His generous nature would fain have delayed him, at whatever risk, till the dying scene were past, but the desire of existence and the hope of happiness had strengthened in his heart, and he was unable to resist them.

"It is enough," said Roger Malvin, having listened to Reuben's promise. "Go, and God speed you!"

The youth pressed his hand in silence, turned and was departing. His slow and faltering steps, however, had borne him but a little way before Malvin's voice recalled him.

"Reuben, Reuben," said he faintly, and Reuben returned and knelt down by the dying man.

"Raise me, and let me lean against the rock," was his last request. "My face will be turned towards home, and I shall see you a moment longer as you pass among the trees." Reuben, having made the desired alteration in his companion's posture, again began his solitary pilgrimage. He walked more hastily at first than was consistent with his strength; for a sort of guilty feeling, which sometimes torments men in their most justifiable acts, caused him to seek concealment from Malvin's eyes; but after he had trodden far upon the rustling forest leaves he crept back, impelled by a wild and painful curiosity, and, sheltered by the earthy roots of an uptorn tree, gazed earnestly at the desolate man. The morning sun was unclouded, and the trees and shrubs imbibed the sweet air of the month of May; yet there seemed a gloom on Nature's face, as if she sympathized with mortal pain and sorrow. Roger Malvin's hands were uplifted in a fervent prayer, some of the words of which stole through the stillness of the woods and entered Reuben's heart, torturing it with an unutterable pang. They were the broken accents of a petition for his own happiness and that of Dorcas; and, as the youth listened, conscience, or something in its similitude, pleaded strongly with him to return and lie down again by the rock. He felt how hard was the doom of the kind and generous being whom he had deserted in his extremity. Death would come like the slow approach of a corpse, stealing gradually towards him through the forest and showing its ghastly and motionless features from behind a nearer and yet a nearer tree. But such must have been Reuben's own fate had he tarried another sunset – and who shall impute blame to him if he shrank from so useless a sacrifice? As he gave a parting look, a breeze waved the little banner upon the sapling oak and reminded Reuben of his vow.

*　*　*

Many circumstances contributed to retard the wounded traveller in his way to the frontiers. On the second day the clouds, gathering densely over the sky, precluded the possibility of regulating his course by the position of the sun, and he knew not but that every effort of his almost exhausted strength was removing him farther from the home he sought. His scanty sustenance was supplied by the berries and other spontaneous products of the forest. Herds of deer, it is true, sometimes bounded past him, and partridges frequently whirred up before his footsteps, but his ammunition had been expended in the fight and he had no means of slaying them. His wounds, irritated by the constant exertion in which lay the only hope of life, wore away his strength and at intervals confused his reason. But, even in the wanderings of intellect, Reuben's young heart clung strongly to existence, and it was only through absolute incapacity of motion that he at last sank down beneath a tree, compelled there to await death.

In this situation he was discovered by a party who, upon the first intelligence of the fight, had been dispatched to the relief of the survivors. They conveyed him to the nearest settlement, which chanced to be that of his own residence.

Dorcas, in the simplicity of the olden time, watched by the bedside of her wounded lover, and administered all those comforts that are in the sole gift of woman's heart and hand. During several days Reuben's recollection strayed drowsily among the perils and hardships through which he had passed, and he was incapable of returning definite answers to the enquiries with which many were eager to harass him. No authentic particulars of the battle had yet been circulated; nor could mothers, wives and children tell whether their loved ones were detained by captivity or by the stronger chain of death. Dorcas nourished her apprehensions in silence till one afternoon when Reuben awoke from an unquiet sleep, and seemed to recognize her more perfectly than at any previous time. She saw that his intellect had become composed, and she could no longer restrain her filial anxiety.

"My father, Reuben?" she began – but the change in her lover's countenance made her pause.

The youth shrank as if with a bitter pain, and the blood gushed vividly into his wan and hollow cheeks. His first impulse was to cover his face, but, apparently with a desperate effort, he half raised himself and spoke vehemently, defending himself against an imaginary accusation.

"Your father was sore wounded in the battle, Dorcas, and he bade me not burden myself with him, but only to lead him to the lakeside, that he might quench his thirst and die. But I would not desert the old man in his extremity, and, though bleeding myself, I supported him; I gave him half my strength, and led him away with me. For three days we journeyed on together, and your father was sustained beyond my hopes; but, awaking at sunrise on the fourth day, I found him faint and exhausted; he was unable to proceed; his life had ebbed away fast, and—"

"He died!" exclaimed Dorcas faintly.

Reuben felt it impossible to acknowledge that his selfish love of life had hurried him away before her father's fate was decided. He spoke not; he only bowed his head; and, between shame and exhaustion, sank back and hid his face in the pillow. Dorcas wept when her fears were thus confirmed, but the shock, as it had been long anticipated, was on that account the less violent.

"You dug a grave for my poor father in the wilderness, Reuben?" was the question by which her filial piety manifested itself.

"My hands were weak, but I did what I could," replied the youth in a smothered tone. "There stands a noble tombstone above his head, and I would to Heaven I slept as soundly as he!"

Dorcas, perceiving the wildness of his latter words, enquired no further at the time, but her heart found ease in the thought that Roger Malvin had not lacked such funeral rites as it was possible to bestow. The tale of Reuben's courage and fidelity lost nothing when she communicated it to her friends, and the poor youth, tottering from his sick chamber to breathe the sunny air, experienced from every tongue the miserable and humiliating torture of unmerited praise. All acknowledged that he might worthily demand the hand of the fair maiden to whose father he had been "faithful unto death" – and, as my tale is not of love, it shall suffice to say that in the space of a few months Reuben became the husband of Dorcas Malvin. During the marriage ceremony the bride was covered with blushes, but the bridegroom's face was pale.

There was now in the breast of Reuben Bourne an incommunicable thought – something which he was to conceal most heedfully from her whom he most loved and trusted. He regretted, deeply and bitterly, the moral cowardice that had restrained his words when he was about to disclose the truth to Dorcas; but pride, the fear of losing her affection, the dread of universal scorn forbade him to rectify this falsehood. He felt that for leaving Roger Malvin he deserved no censure. His presence, the gratuitous sacrifice of his own life, would have added only another and a needless agony to the last moments of the dying man, but concealment had imparted to a justifiable act much of the secret effect of guilt, and Reuben, while reason told him that he had done right, experienced in no small degree the mental horrors which punish the perpetrator of undiscovered crime. By a certain association of ideas he at times almost imagined himself a murderer. For years, also, a thought would occasionally recur, which, though he perceived all its folly and extravagance, he had not power to banish from his mind. It was a haunting and torturing fancy that his father-in-law was yet sitting at the foot of the rock, on the withered forest leaves, alive and awaiting his pledged assistance. These mental deceptions, however, came and went, nor did he ever mistake them for realities; but in the calmest and clearest moods of his mind he was conscious that he had a deep vow unredeemed, and that an unburied corpse was calling to him out of the wilderness. Yet such was the consequence of his prevarication that he could not obey the call. It was now too late to require the assistance of Roger Malvin's friends in performing his long-deferred sepulture, and superstitious fears, of which none were more susceptible than the people of the outward settlements, forbade Reuben to go alone. Neither did he know where in the pathless and illimitable forest to seek that smooth and lettered rock at the base of which the body lay; his remembrance of every portion of his travel thence was indistinct, and the latter part had left no impression upon his mind. There was, however, a continual impulse, a voice audible only to himself, commanding him to go forth and redeem his vow, and he had a strange impression that, were he to make the trial, he would be led straight to Malvin's bones. But year after year that summons, unheard but felt, was disobeyed. His one secret thought became like a chain binding down his spirit and like a serpent gnawing into his heart, and he was transformed into a sad and downcast yet irritable man.

In the course of a few years after their marriage changes began to be visible in the external prosperity of Reuben and Dorcas. The only riches of the former had been his stout heart and strong arm, but the latter, her father's sole heiress, had made her husband master of a farm, under older cultivation, larger and better stocked than most of the frontier establishments. Reuben Bourne, however, was a neglectful husbandman, and while the lands of the other settlers became annually more fruitful, his deteriorated in the same proportion. The discouragements to agriculture were greatly lessened by the cessation of Indian war, during which men held the plough in one hand and the musket in the other, and were fortunate if the products of their dangerous labour were not destroyed, either in the field or in the barn, by the savage enemy. But Reuben did not profit by the altered condition of the country, nor can it be denied that his intervals of industrious attention to his affairs were but scantily rewarded with success. The irritability by which he had recently become distinguished was another cause of his declining prosperity, as it occasioned frequent quarrels in his unavoidable intercourse with the neighbouring settlers. The results of these were innumerable lawsuits, for the people of New England, in the earliest stages and wildest circumstances of the country, adopted, whenever attainable, the legal mode of deciding their differences. To be brief, the world did not go well with Reuben Bourne, and, though not till many years after his marriage, he was finally a ruined man, with but one remaining expedient against the evil fate that had pursued him. He was to throw sunlight into some deep recess of the forest, and seek subsistence from the virgin bosom of the wilderness.

The only child of Reuben and Dorcas was a son, now arrived at the age of fifteen years, beautiful in youth and giving promise of a glorious manhood. He was peculiarly qualified for, and already began to excel in, the wild accomplishments of frontier life. His foot was fleet, his aim true, his apprehension quick, his heart glad and high, and all who anticipated the return of Indian war spoke of Cyrus Bourne as a future leader in the land. The boy was loved by his father with a deep and silent strength, as if whatever was good and happy in his own nature had been transferred to his child, carrying his affections with it. Even Dorcas, though loving and beloved, was far less dear to him, for Reuben's secret thoughts and insulated emotions had gradually made him a selfish man, and he could no longer love deeply except where he saw or imagined some reflection or likeness of his own mind. In Cyrus he recognized what he had himself been in other days, and at intervals he seemed to partake of the boy's spirit and to be revived with a fresh and happy life. Reuben was accompanied by his son in the expedition, for the purpose of selecting a tract of land and felling and burning the timber, which necessarily preceded the removal of the household gods. Two months of autumn were thus occupied, after which Reuben Bourne and his young hunter returned to spend their last winter in the settlements.

* * *

It was early in the month of May that the little family snapped asunder whatever tendrils of affection had clung to inanimate objects, and bade farewell to the few who, in the blight of fortune, called themselves their friends. The sadness of the parting moment had, to each of the pilgrims, its peculiar alleviations. Reuben, a moody man, and misanthropic because unhappy, strode onward with his usual stern brow and downcast eye, feeling few regrets and disdaining to acknowledge any. Dorcas, while she wept abundantly over the broken ties by which her simple and affectionate nature had bound itself to everything, felt that the inhabitants of her inmost heart moved on with her, and that all else would be supplied wherever she might go. And the boy dashed one teardrop from his eye, and thought of the adventurous pleasures of the untrodden forest.

Oh, who, in the enthusiasm of a daydream, has not wished that he were a wanderer in a world of summer wilderness, with one fair and gentle being hanging lightly on his arm? In youth his free and exulting step would know no barrier but the rolling ocean or the snow-topped mountains; calmer manhood would choose a home where Nature had strewn a double wealth in the vale of some transparent stream; and when hoary age, after long years of that pure life, stole on and found him there, it would find him the father of a race, the patriarch of a people, the founder of a mighty nation yet to be. When death, like the sweet sleep which we welcome after a day of happiness, came over him, his far descendants would mourn over the venerated dust. Enveloped by tradition in mysterious attributes, the men of future generations would call him godlike, and remote posterity would see him standing, dimly glorious, far up the valley of a hundred centuries.

The tangled and gloomy forest through which the personages of my tale were wandering differed widely from the dreamer's land of fantasy; yet there was something in their way of life that Nature asserted as her own, and the gnawing cares which went with them from the world were all that now obstructed their happiness. One stout and shaggy steed, the bearer of all their wealth, did not shrink from the added weight of Dorcas; although her hardy breeding sustained her, during the latter part of each day's journey, by her husband's side. Reuben and his son, their muskets on their shoulders and their axes slung behind them, kept an unwearied pace, each watching with a hunter's eye for the game that supplied their food. When hunger bade, they halted and prepared their meal on the bank of some unpolluted forest brook, which, as they knelt down with thirsty lips to drink, murmured a sweet unwillingness, like a maiden at love's first kiss. They slept beneath a hut of branches, and awoke at peep of light refreshed for the toils of another day. Dorcas and the boy went on joyously, and even Reuben's spirit shone at intervals with an outward gladness; but inwardly there was a cold, cold sorrow, which he compared to the snowdrifts lying deep in the glens and hollows of the rivulets while the leaves were brightly green above.

Cyrus Bourne was sufficiently skilled in the travel of the woods to observe that his father did not adhere to the course they had pursued in their expedition of the preceding autumn. They were now keeping farther to the north, striking out more directly from the settlements and into a region of which savage beasts and savage men were as yet the sole possessors. The boy sometimes hinted his opinions upon the subject, and Reuben listened attentively, and once or twice altered the direction of their march in accordance with his son's counsel – but, having done so, he seemed ill at ease. His quick and wandering glances were sent forward, apparently in search of enemies lurking behind the tree trunks – and, seeing nothing there, he would cast his eyes backwards as if in fear of some pursuer. Cyrus, perceiving that his father gradually resumed the old direction, forbore to interfere; nor, though something began to weigh upon his heart, did his adventurous nature permit him to regret the increased length and the mystery of their way.

On the afternoon of the fifth day they halted, and made their simple encampment nearly an hour before sunset. The face of the country, for the last few miles, had been diversified by swells of land resembling huge waves of a petrified sea, and in one of the corresponding hollows, a wild and romantic spot, had the family reared their hut and kindled their fire. There is something chilling, and yet heart-warming, in the thought of these three, united by strong bands of love and insulated from all that breathe beside. The dark and gloomy pines looked down upon them, and as the wind swept through their tops a pitying sound was heard in the forest – or did those old trees groan in fear that men were come to lay the axe to their roots at last? Reuben and his son, while Dorcas made ready their meal, proposed to wander out in search of game, of which that day's march had afforded no supply. The boy, promising not to quit the vicinity of the encampment, bounded off with a step as light and elastic as that of the deer he hoped to slay; while his father, feeling a transient happiness as he gazed after him, was about to pursue an opposite direction. Dorcas, in the meanwhile, had seated herself near their fire of fallen branches, upon the moss-grown and mouldering trunk of a tree uprooted years before. Her employment, diversified by an occasional glance at the pot now beginning to simmer over the blaze, was the perusal of the current year's *Massachusetts Almanac*, which, with the exception of an old black-letter Bible, comprised all the literary wealth of the family. None pay a greater regard to arbitrary divisions of time than those who are excluded from society, and Dorcas mentioned, as if the information were of importance, that it was now the twelfth of May. Her husband started.

"The twelfth of May! I should remember it well," muttered he, while many thoughts occasioned a momentary confusion in his mind. "Where am I? Whither am I wandering? Where did I leave him?"

Dorcas, too well accustomed to her husband's wayward moods to note any peculiarity of demeanour, now laid aside the almanac and addressed him in that mournful tone which the tender-hearted appropriate to griefs long cold and dead.

"It was near this time of the month, eighteen years ago, that my poor father left this world for a better. He had a kind arm to hold his head and a kind voice to cheer him, Reuben, in his last moments; and the thought of the faithful care you took of him has comforted me many a time since. Oh, death would have been awful to a solitary man in a wild place like this!"

"Pray Heaven, Dorcas," said Reuben, in a broken voice, "pray Heaven that neither of us three dies solitary and lies unburied in this howling wilderness!" And he hastened away, leaving her to watch the fire beneath the gloomy pines.

Reuben Bourne's rapid pace gradually slackened as the pang unintentionally inflicted by the words of Dorcas became less acute. Many strange reflections, however, thronged upon him; and, straying onward rather like a sleepwalker than a hunter, it was attributable to no care of his own that his devious course kept him in the vicinity of the encampment. His steps were imperceptibly led almost in a circle; nor did he observe that he was on the verge of a tract of land heavily timbered, but not with pine trees. The place of the latter was here supplied by oaks and other of the harder woods, and around their roots clustered a dense and bushy undergrowth, leaving, however, barren spaces between the trees, thick strewn with withered leaves. Whenever the rustling of the branches or the creaking of the trunks made a sound, as if the forest were waking from slumber, Reuben instinctively raised the musket that rested on his arm, and cast a quick, sharp glance on every side; but, convinced by a partial observation that no animal was near, he would again give himself up to his thoughts. He was musing on the strange influence that had led him away from his premeditated course and so far into the depths of the wilderness. Unable to penetrate to the secret place of his soul where his motives lay hidden, he believed that a supernatural voice had called him onward and that a supernatural power had obstructed his retreat. He trusted that it was Heaven's intent to afford him an opportunity of expiating his sin; he hoped that he might find the bones so long unburied; and that having laid the earth over them, peace would throw its sunlight into the sepulchre of his heart. From these thoughts he was aroused by a rustling in the forest at some distance from the spot to which he had wandered. Perceiving the motion of some object behind a thick veil of undergrowth, he fired, with the instinct of a hunter and the aim of a practised marksman. A low moan, which told his success, and by which even animals can express their dying agony, was unheeded by Reuben Bourne. What were the recollections now breaking upon him?

The thicket into which Reuben had fired was near the summit of a swell of land, and was clustered around the base of a rock, which, in the shape and smoothness of one of its surfaces, was not unlike a gigantic gravestone. As if reflected in a mirror, its likeness was in Reuben's memory. He even recognized the veins which seemed to form an inscription in forgotten characters: everything remained the same, except that a thick covert of bushes shrouded the lower part of the rock, and would have hidden Roger Malvin had he still been sitting there. Yet in the next moment Reuben's eye was caught by another change that time had effected since he last stood where he was now standing again behind the earthy roots of the uptorn tree. The sapling to which he had bound the bloodstained symbol of his vow had increased and strengthened into an oak, far indeed from its maturity, but with no mean spread of shadowy branches. There was one singularity observable in this tree which made Reuben tremble. The middle and lower branches were in luxuriant life, and an excess of vegetation had fringed the trunk almost to the ground, but a blight had apparently stricken the upper part of the oak, and the very topmost bough was withered, sapless and utterly dead. Reuben remembered how the little banner had fluttered on that topmost bough, when it was green and lovely, eighteen years before. Whose guilt had blasted it?

* * *

Dorcas, after the departure of the two hunters, continued her preparations for the evening repast. Her sylvan table was the moss-covered trunk of a large fallen tree, on the broadest part of which she had spread a snow-white cloth and arranged what were left of the bright pewter vessels that had been her pride in the settlements. It had a strange aspect, that one little spot of homely comfort in the desolate heart of Nature. The sunshine yet lingered upon the higher branches of the trees that grew on rising ground, but the shadows of evening had deepened into the hollow where the encampment was made, and the firelight began to redden as it gleamed up the tall trunks of the pines or hovered on the dense and obscure mass of foliage that circled round the spot. The heart of Dorcas was not sad; for she felt that it was better to journey in the wilderness with two whom she loved than to be a lonely woman in a crowd that cared not for her. As she busied herself in arranging seats of mouldering wood covered with leaves, for Reuben and her son, her voice danced through the gloomy forest in the measure of a song that she had learnt in youth. The rude melody, the production of a bard who won no name, was descriptive of a winter evening in a frontier cottage, when, secured from savage inroad by the high-piled snowdrifts, the family rejoiced by their own fireside. The whole song possessed the nameless charm peculiar to unborrowed thought, but four continually recurring lines shone out from the rest like the blaze of the hearth whose joys they celebrated. Into them, working magic with a few simple words, the poet had instilled the very essence of domestic love and household happiness, and they were poetry and picture joined in one. As Dorcas sang, the walls of her forsaken home seemed to encircle her; she no longer saw the gloomy pines, nor heard the wind, which still, as she began each verse, sent a heavy breath through the branches and died away in a hollow moan from the burden of the song. She was aroused by the report of a gun in the vicinity of the encampment, and either the sudden sound or her loneliness by the glowing fire caused her to tremble violently. The next moment she laughed in the pride of a mother's heart.

"My beautiful young hunter! My boy has slain a deer!" she exclaimed, recollecting that in the direction whence the shot proceeded Cyrus had gone to the chase.

She waited a reasonable time to hear her son's light step bounding over the rustling leaves to tell of his success. But he did not immediately appear, and she sent her cheerful voice among the trees in search of him.

"Cyrus! Cyrus!"

His coming was still delayed, and she determined, as the report had apparently been very near, to seek for him in person. Her assistance, also, might be necessary in bringing home the venison which she flattered herself he had obtained. She therefore set forward, directing her steps by the long-past sound and singing as she went, in order that the boy might be aware of her approach and run to meet her. From behind the trunk of every tree and from every hiding place in the thick foliage of the undergrowth she hoped to discover the countenance of her son, laughing with the sportive mischief that is born of affection. The sun was now beneath the horizon, and the light that came down among the trees was sufficiently dim to create many illusions in her expecting fancy. Several times she seemed indistinctly to see his face gazing out from among the leaves, and once she imagined that he stood beckoning to her at the base of a craggy rock. Keeping her eyes on this object, however, it proved to be no more than the trunk of an oak, fringed to the very ground with little branches, one of which, thrust out farther than the rest, was shaken by the breeze. Making her way round to the foot of the rock, she suddenly found herself close to her husband, who had approached in another direction. Leaning upon the butt of his gun, the muzzle of which rested upon the withered leaves, he was apparently absorbed in the contemplation of some object at his feet.

"How is this, Reuben? Have you slain the deer and fallen asleep over him?" exclaimed Dorcas, laughing cheerfully, on her first slight observation of his posture and appearance.

He stirred not, neither did he turn his eyes towards her, and a cold shuddering fear, indefinite in its source and object, began to creep into her blood. She now perceived that her husband's face was ghastly pale, and his features were rigid, as if incapable of assuming any other expression than the strong despair which had hardened upon them. He gave not the slightest evidence that he was aware of her approach.

"For the love of Heaven, Reuben, speak to me!" cried Dorcas, and the strange sound of her own voice affrighted her even more than the dead silence.

Her husband started, stared into her face, drew her to the front of the rock and pointed with his finger.

Oh, there lay the boy, asleep but dreamless, upon the fallen forest leaves! His cheek rested upon his arm – his curled locks were thrown back from his brow – his limbs were slightly relaxed. Had a sudden weariness overcome the youthful hunter? Would his mother's voice arouse him? She knew that it was death.

"This broad rock is the gravestone of your near kindred, Dorcas," said her husband. "Your tears will fall at once over your father and your son."

She heard him not. With one wild shriek, that seemed to force its way from the sufferer's inmost soul, she sank insensible by the side of her dead boy. At that moment the withered topmost bough of the oak loosened itself in the stilly air, and fell in soft, light fragments upon the rock, upon the leaves, upon Reuben, upon his wife and child and upon Roger Malvin's bones. Then Reuben's heart was stricken, and the tears gushed out like water from a rock. The vow that the wounded youth had made, the blighted man had come to redeem. His sin was expiated – the curse was gone from him – and in the hour when he had shed blood dearer to him than his own, a prayer, the first for years, went up to heaven from the lips of Reuben Bourne.

The Canterbury Pilgrims

THE SUMMER MOON, which shines in so many a tale, was beaming over a broad extent of uneven country. Some of its brightest rays were flung into a spring of water, where no traveller, toiling, as the writer has, up the hilly road beside which it gushes, ever failed to quench his thirst. The work of neat hands and considerate art was visible about this blessed fountain. An open cistern, hewn and hollowed out of solid stone, was placed above the waters, which filled it to the brim, but, by some invisible outlet, were conveyed away without dripping down its sides. Though the basin had not room for another drop, and the continual gush of water made a tremor on the surface, there was a secret charm that forbade it to overflow. I remember, that when I had slaked my summer thirst, and sat panting by the cistern, it was my fanciful theory that Nature could not afford to lavish so pure a liquid, as she does the waters of all meaner fountains.

While the moon was hanging almost perpendicularly over this spot, two figures appeared on the summit of the hill, and came with noiseless footsteps down towards the spring. They were then in the first freshness of youth; nor is there a wrinkle now on either of their brows, and yet they wore a strange, old-fashioned garb. One, a young man with ruddy cheeks, walked beneath the canopy of a broad-brimmed grey hat; he seemed to have inherited his great-grandsire's square-skirted coat, and a waistcoat that extended its immense flaps to his knees; his brown locks, also, hung down behind, in a mode unknown to our times. By his side was a sweet young damsel, her fair features sheltered by a prim little bonnet, within which appeared the vestal muslin of a cap; her close, long-waisted gown, and indeed her whole attire, might have been worn by some rustic beauty who had faded half a century before. But that there was something too warm and lifelike in them, I would here have compared this couple to the ghosts of two young lovers, who had died long since in the glow of passion, and now were straying out of their graves to renew the old vows, and shadow forth the unforgotten kiss of their earthly lips, beside the moonlit spring.

"Thee and I will rest here a moment, Miriam," said the young man, as they drew near the stone cistern, "for there is no fear that the elders know what we have done, and this may be the last time we shall ever taste this water."

Thus speaking, with a little sadness in his face, which was also visible in that of his companion, he made her sit down on a stone, and was about to place himself very close to her side; she, however, repelled him, though not unkindly.

"Nay, Josiah," said she, giving him a timid push with her maiden hand, "thee must sit farther off, on that other stone, with the spring between us. What would the sisters say, if thee were to sit so close to me?"

"But we are of the world's people now, Miriam," answered Josiah.

The girl persisted in her prudery, nor did the youth, in fact, seem altogether free from a similar sort of shyness; so they sat apart from each other, gazing up the hill, where the moonlight discovered the tops of a group of buildings. While their attention was thus occupied, a party of travellers, who had come wearily upon the long ascent, made a halt to refresh themselves at the spring. There were three men, a woman and a little girl and boy.

Their attire was mean, covered with the dust of the summer's day, and damp with the night dew; they all looked woebegone, as if the cares and sorrows of the world had made their steps heavier as they climbed the hill; even the two little children appeared older in evil days than the young man and maiden who had first approached the spring.

"Good evening to you, young folks," was the salutation of the travellers – and "Good evening, friends," replied the youth and damsel.

"Is that white building the Shaker meeting house?" asked one of the strangers. "And are those the red roofs of the Shaker village?"

"Friend, it is the Shaker village," answered Josiah, after some hesitation.

The travellers, who, from the first, had looked suspiciously at the garb of these young people, now taxed them with an intention which all the circumstances, indeed, rendered too obvious to be mistaken.

"It is true, friends," replied the young man, summoning up his courage. "Miriam and I have a gift to love each other, and we are going among the world's people, to live after their fashion. And ye know that we do not transgress the law of the land – and neither ye, nor the elders themselves, have a right to hinder us."

"Yet you think it expedient to depart without leave-taking," remarked one of the travellers.

"Yea, ye-a," said Josiah, reluctantly, "because father Job is a very awful man to speak with, and being aged himself he has but little charity for what he calls the iniquities of the flesh."

"Well," said the stranger, "we will neither use force to bring you back to the village, nor will we betray you to the elders. But sit you here awhile, and when you have heard what we shall tell you of the world which we have left, and into which you are going, perhaps you will turn back with us of your own accord. What say you?" added he, turning to his companions. "We have travelled thus far without becoming known to each other. Shall we tell our stories, here by this pleasant spring, for our own pastime, and the benefit of these misguided young lovers?"

In accordance with this proposal, the whole party stationed themselves round the stone cistern; the two children, being very weary, fell asleep upon the damp earth, and the pretty Shaker girl, whose feelings were those of a nun or a Turkish lady, crept as close as possible to the female traveller, and as far as she well could from the unknown men. The same person who had hitherto been the chief spokesman now stood up, waving his hat in his hand, and suffered the moonlight to fall full upon his front.

"In me," said he, with a certain majesty of utterance, "in me, you behold a poet."

Though a lithographic print of this gentleman is extant, it may be well to notice that he was now nearly forty, a thin and stooping figure, in a black coat, out at elbows; notwithstanding the ill condition of his attire, there were about him several tokens of a peculiar sort of foppery, unworthy of a mature man, particularly in the arrangement of his hair, which was so disposed as to give all possible loftiness and breadth to his forehead. However, he had an intelligent eye and, on the whole, a marked countenance.

"A poet!" repeated the young Shaker, a little puzzled how to understand such a designation, seldom heard in the utilitarian community where he had spent his life. "Oh, ay, Miriam, he means a varse-maker, thee must know."

This remark jarred upon the susceptible nerves of the poet; nor could he help wondering what strange fatality had put into this young man's mouth an epithet which ill-natured people had affirmed to be more proper to his merit than the one assumed by himself.

"True, I am a verse-maker," he resumed, "but my verse is no more than the material body into which I breathe the celestial soul of thought. Alas! How many a pang has it cost me, this same insensibility to the ethereal essence of poetry, with which you have here tortured me again, at the moment when I am to relinquish my profession for ever! O Fate! Why hast thou warred with Nature, turning all her higher and more perfect gifts to the ruin of me, their possessor? What is the voice of song, when the world lacks the ear of taste? How can I rejoice in my strength and delicacy of feeling, when they have but made great sorrows out of little ones? Have I dreaded scorn like death, and yearned for fame as others pant for vital air, only to find myself in a middle state between obscurity and infamy? But I have my revenge! I could have given existence to a thousand bright creations. I crush them into my heart, and there let them putrefy! I shake off the dust of my feet against my countrymen! But posterity, tracing my footsteps up this weary hill, will cry shame upon the unworthy age that drove one of the fathers of American song to end his days in a Shaker village!"

During this harangue, the speaker gesticulated with great energy, and, as poetry is the natural language of passion, there appeared reason to apprehend his final explosion into an ode extempore. The reader must understand that, for all these bitter words, he was a kind, gentle, harmless, poor fellow enough, whom Nature, tossing her ingredients together without looking at her recipe, had sent into the world with too much of one sort of brain, and hardly any of another.

"Friend," said the young Shaker, in some perplexity, "thee seemest to have met with great troubles – and doubtless I should pity them, if... if I could but understand what they were."

"Happy in your ignorance!" replied the poet, with an air of sublime superiority. "To your coarser mind, perhaps, I may seem to speak of more important griefs, when I add, what I had well nigh forgotten, that I am out at elbows, and almost starved to death. At any rate, you have the advice and example of one individual to warn you back; for I am come hither, a disappointed man, flinging aside the fragments of my hopes and seeking shelter in the calm retreat which you are so anxious to leave."

"I thank thee, friend," rejoined the youth, "but I do not mean to be a poet, nor – Heaven be praised! – do I think Miriam ever made a varse in her life. So we need not fear thy disappointments. But, Miriam," he added, with real concern, "thee knowest that the elders admit nobody that has not a gift to be useful. Now, what under the sun can they do with this poor varse-maker?"

"Nay, Josiah, do not thee discourage the poor man," said the girl, in all simplicity and kindness. "Our hymns are very rough, and perhaps they may trust him to smooth them."

Without noticing this hint of professional employment, the poet turned away, and gave himself up to a sort of vague reverie, which he called thought. Sometimes he watched the moon pouring a silvery liquid on the clouds, through which it slowly melted till they became all bright; then he saw the same sweet radiance dancing on the leafy trees which rustled as if to shake it off, or sleeping on the high tops of hills, or hovering down in distant valleys, like the material of unshaped dreams; lastly, he looked into the spring, and there the light was mingling with the water. In its crystal bosom, too, beholding all heaven reflected there, he found an emblem of a pure and tranquil breast. He listened to that most ethereal of all sounds, the song of crickets, coming in full choir upon the wind, and fancied that, if moonlight could be heard, it would sound just like that. Finally, he took a draught at the Shaker spring and, as if it were true Castalia,* was forthwith moved to compose a lyric, a Farewell to his Harp, which he swore should be its closing strain, the last verse that an ungrateful world should have from him. This effusion, with two or three other little pieces, subsequently written, he took the first opportunity to send, by one of the Shaker brethren, to Concord, where they were published in the *New Hampshire Patriot*.

Meantime, another of the Canterbury pilgrims, one so different from the poet that the delicate fancy of the latter could hardly have conceived of him, began to relate his sad experience. He was a small man, of quick and unquiet gestures, about fifty years old, with a narrow forehead, all wrinkled and drawn together. He held in his hand a pencil, and a card of some commission merchant in foreign parts, on the back of which, for there was light enough to read or write by, he seemed ready to figure out a calculation.

"Young man," said he abruptly, "what quantity of land do the Shakers own here, in Canterbury?"

"That is more than I can tell thee, friend," answered Josiah, "but it is a very rich establishment, and for a long way by the roadside thee may guess the land to be ours, by the neatness of the fences."

"And what may be the value of the whole," continued the stranger, "with all the buildings and improvements, pretty nearly, in round numbers?"

"Oh, a monstrous sum – more than I can reckon," replied the young Shaker.

"Well, sir," said the pilgrim, "there was a day, and not very long ago, neither, when I stood at my counting-room window and watched the signal flags of three of my own ships entering the harbour, from the East Indies, from Liverpool and from up the Straits, and I would not have given the invoice of the least of them for the title deeds of this whole Shaker settlement. You stare. Perhaps, now, you won't believe that I could have put more value on a little slip of paper, no bigger than the palm of your hand, than all these solid acres of grain, grass and pastureland would sell for?"

"I won't dispute it, friend," answered Josiah, "but I know I had rather have fifty acres of this good land than a whole sheet of thy paper."

"You may say so now," said the ruined merchant bitterly, "for my name would not be worth the paper I should write it on. Of course, you must have heard of my failure?"

And the stranger mentioned his name, which, however mighty it might have been in the commercial world, the young Shaker had never heard of among the Canterbury hills.

"Not heard of my failure!" exclaimed the merchant, considerably piqued. "Why, it was spoken of on 'Change in London, and from Boston to New Orleans men trembled in their shoes. At all events, I did fail, and you see me here on my road to the Shaker village, where, doubtless (for the Shakers are a shrewd sect), they will have a due respect for my experience, and give me the management of the trading part of the concern, in which case I think I can pledge myself to double their capital in four or five years. Turn back with me, young man, for though you will never meet with my good luck, you can hardly escape my bad."

"I will not turn back for this," replied Josiah calmly, "any more than for the advice of the varse-maker, between whom and thee, friend, I see a sort of likeness, though I can't justly say where it lies. But Miriam and I can earn our daily bread among the world's people, as well as in the Shaker village. And do we want anything more, Miriam?"

"Nothing more, Josiah," said the girl quietly.

"Yea, Miriam, and daily bread for some other little mouths, if God send them," observed the simple Shaker lad.

Miriam did not reply, but looked down into the spring, where she encountered the image of her own pretty face, blushing within the prim little bonnet. The third pilgrim now took up the conversation. He was a sunburnt countryman, of tall frame and bony strength, on whose rude and manly face there appeared a darker, more sullen and obstinate despondency than on those of either the poet or the merchant.

"Well, now, youngster," he began, "these folks have had their say, so I'll take my turn. My story will cut but a poor figure by the side of theirs, for I never supposed that I could have a right to meat and drink, and great praise besides, only for tagging rhymes together, as it seems this man does – nor ever tried to get the substance of hundreds into my own hands, like the trader there. When I was about your years, I married me a wife – just such a neat and pretty young woman as Miriam, if that's her name – and all I asked of Providence was an ordinary blessing on the sweat of my brow, so that we might be decent and comfortable, and have daily bread for ourselves, and for some other little mouths that we soon had to feed. We had no very great prospects before us, but I never wanted to be idle, and I thought it a matter of course that the Lord would help me, because I was willing to help myself."

"And didn't He help thee, friend?" demanded Josiah, with some eagerness.

"No," said the yeoman, sullenly, "for then you would not have seen me here. I have laboured hard for years, and my means have been growing narrower, and my living poorer, and my heart colder and heavier, all the time – till at last I could bear it no longer. I set myself down to calculate whether I had best go on the Oregon expedition,* or come here to the Shaker village, but I had not hope enough left in me to begin the world over again – and, to make my story short, here I am. And now, youngster, take my advice, and turn back – or else, some few years hence, you'll have to climb this hill, with as heavy a heart as mine."

This simple story had a strong effect on the young fugitives. The misfortunes of the poet and merchant had won little sympathy for their plain good sense and unworldly feelings, qualities which made them such unprejudiced and inflexible judges, that few men would have chosen to take the opinion of this youth and maiden as to the wisdom or folly of their pursuits. But here was one whose simple wishes had resembled their own, and who, after efforts which almost gave him a right to claim success from fate, had failed in accomplishing them.

"But thy wife, friend?" exclaimed the young man. "What became of the pretty girl, like Miriam? Oh, I am afraid she is dead!"

"Yea, poor man, she must be dead – she and the children too," sobbed Miriam.

The female pilgrim had been leaning over the spring, wherein latterly a tear or two might have been seen to fall, and form its little circle on the surface of the water. She now looked up, disclosing features still comely, but which had acquired an expression of fretfulness, in the same long course of evil fortune that had thrown a sullen gloom over the temper of the unprosperous yeoman.

"I am his wife," said she, a shade of irritability just perceptible in the sadness of her tone. "These poor little things, asleep on the ground, are two of our children. We had two more, but God has provided better for them than we could, by taking them to Himself."

"And what would thee advise Josiah and me to do?" asked Miriam, this being the first question which she had put to either of the strangers.

"'Tis a thing almost against nature for a woman to try to part true lovers," answered the yeoman's wife, after a pause, "but I'll speak as truly to you as if these were my dying words. Though my husband told you some of our troubles, he didn't mention the greatest, and that which makes all the rest so hard to bear. If you and your sweetheart marry, you'll be kind and pleasant to each other for a year or two, and while that's the case you never will repent; but, by and by, he'll grow gloomy, rough and hard to please, and you'll be peevish, and full of little angry fits, and apt to be complaining by the fireside, when he comes to rest himself from his troubles out of doors; so your love will wear away by little and little, and leave you miserable at last. It has been so with us – and yet my husband and I were true lovers once, if ever two young folks were."

As she ceased, the yeoman and his wife exchanged a glance, in which there was more and warmer affection than they had supposed to have escaped the frost of a wintry fate in either of their breasts. At that moment, when they stood on the utmost verge of married life, one word fitly spoken, or perhaps one peculiar look, had they had mutual confidence enough to reciprocate it, might have renewed all their old feelings, and sent them back, resolved to sustain each other amid the struggles of the world. But the crisis passed, and never came again. Just then, also, the children, roused by their mother's voice, looked up and added their wailing accents to the testimony borne by all the Canterbury pilgrims against the world from which they fled.

"We are tired and hungry!" cried they. "Is it far to the Shaker village?"

The Shaker youth and maiden looked mournfully into each other's eyes. They had but stepped across the threshold of their homes, when lo! – the dark array of cares and sorrows that rose up to warn them back. The varied narratives of the strangers had arranged themselves into a parable; they seemed not merely instances of woeful fate that had befallen others, but shadowy omens of disappointed hope and unavailing toil, domestic grief and estranged affection, that would cloud the onward path of these poor fugitives. But after one instant's hesitation they opened their arms, and sealed their resolve with as pure and fond an embrace as ever youthful love had hallowed.

"We will not go back," said they. "The world never can be dark to us, for we will always love one another."

Then the Canterbury pilgrims went up the hill, while the poet chanted a drear and desperate stanza of the 'Farewell to His Harp', fitting music for that melancholy band. They sought a home where all former ties of nature or society would be sundered, and all old distinctions levelled, and a cold and passionless security be substituted for mortal hope and fear, as in that other refuge of the world's weary outcasts, the grave. The lovers drank at the Shaker spring, and then, with chastened hopes, but more confiding affections, went on to mingle in an untried life.

The Seven Vagabonds

R AMBLING ON FOOT IN THE SPRING of my life and the summer of the year, I came one afternoon to a point which gave me the choice of three directions. Straight before me, the main road extended its dusty length to Boston; on the left a branch went towards the sea, and would have lengthened my journey a trifle of twenty or thirty miles; while by the right-hand path I might have gone over hills and lakes to Canada, visiting in my way the celebrated town of Stamford. On a level spot of grass, at the foot of the guidepost, appeared an object which, though locomotive on a different principle, reminded me of Gulliver's portable mansion among the Brobdingnags.* It was a huge covered wagon, or, more properly, a small house on wheels, with a door on one side and a window shaded by green blinds on the other. Two horses, munching provender out of the baskets which muzzled them, were fastened near the vehicle: a delectable sound of music proceeded from the interior, and I immediately conjectured that this was some itinerant show, halting at the confluence of the roads to intercept such idle travellers as myself. A shower had long been climbing up the western sky, and now hung so blackly over my onward path that it was a point of wisdom to seek shelter here.

"Halloo! Who stands guard here? Is the doorkeeper asleep?" cried I, approaching a ladder of two or three steps which was let down from the wagon.

The music ceased at my summons, and there appeared at the door, not the sort of figure that I had mentally assigned to the wandering showman, but a most respectable old personage, whom I was sorry to have addressed in so free a style. He wore a snuff-coloured coat and small clothes, with white-top boots, and exhibited the mild dignity of aspect and manner which may often be noticed in aged schoolmasters, and sometimes in deacons, selectmen or other potentates of that kind. A small piece of silver was my passport within his premises, where I found only one other person, hereafter to be described.

"This is a dull day for business," said the old gentleman, as he ushered me in, "but I merely tarry here to refresh the cattle, being bound for the camp meeting at Stamford."

Perhaps the movable scene of this narrative is still peregrinating New England, and may enable the reader to test the accuracy of my description. The spectacle – for I will not use the unworthy term of puppet show – consisted of a multitude of little people assembled on a miniature stage. Among them were artisans of every kind, in the attitudes of their toil, and a group of fair ladies and gay gentlemen standing ready for the dance; a company of foot soldiers formed a line across the stage, looking stern, grim and terrible enough to make it a pleasant consideration that they were but three inches high; and conspicuous above the whole was seen a merry andrew, in the pointed cap and motley coat of his profession. All the inhabitants of this mimic world were motionless, like the figures in a picture, or like that people who one moment were alive in the midst of their business and delights, and the next were transformed to statues, preserving an eternal semblance of labour that was ended and pleasure that could be felt no more. Anon, however, the old gentleman turned the handle of a barrel organ, the first note of which produced a most enlivening effect upon the figures, and awoke them all to their proper occupations and amusements. By the selfsame impulse the tailor plied his needle, the blacksmith's hammer descended upon the anvil and the dancers whirled away on feathery tiptoes; the company of soldiers broke into platoons, retreated from the stage and were succeeded by a troop of horse, who came prancing onward with such a sound of trumpets and trampling of hoofs as might have startled Don Quixote* himself; while an old toper, of inveterate ill habits, uplifted his black bottle and took off a hearty swig. Meantime the Merry Andrew began to caper and turn somersaults, shaking his sides, nodding his head and winking his eyes in as life-like a manner as if he were ridiculing the nonsense of all human affairs, and making fun of the whole multitude beneath him. At length the old magician (for I compared the showman to Prospero, entertaining his guests with a mask of shadows) paused that I might give utterance to my wonder.

"What an admirable piece of work is this!" exclaimed I, lifting up my hands in astonishment.

Indeed, I liked the spectacle, and was tickled with the old man's gravity as he presided at it, for I had none of that foolish wisdom which reproves every occupation that is not useful in this world of vanities. If there be a faculty which I possess more perfectly than most men, it is that of throwing myself mentally into situations foreign to my own, and detecting, with a cheerful eye, the desirable circumstances of each. I could have envied the life of this grey-headed showman, spent as it had been in a course of safe and pleasurable adventure, in driving his huge vehicle sometimes through the sands of Cape Cod, and sometimes over the rough forest roads of the north and east, and halting now on the green before a village meeting house, and now in a paved square of the metropolis. How often must his heart have been gladdened by the delight of children, as they viewed these animated figures! or his pride indulged, by haranguing learnedly to grown men on the mechanical powers which produced such wonderful effects! or his gallantry brought into play (for this is an attribute which such grave men do not lack) by the visits of pretty maidens!

And then with how fresh a feeling must he return, at intervals, to his own peculiar home!

"I would I were assured of as happy a life as his," thought I.

Though the showman's wagon might have accommodated fifteen or twenty spectators, it now contained only himself and me, and a third person at whom I threw a glance on entering. He was a neat and trim young man of two or three and twenty; his drab hat and green frock coat with velvet collar were smart, though no longer new; while a pair of green spectacles, that seemed needless to his brisk little eyes, gave him something of a scholar-like and literary air. After allowing me a sufficient time to inspect the puppets, he advanced with a bow, and drew my attention to some books in a corner of the wagon. These he forthwith began to extol, with an amazing volubility of well-sounding words, and an ingenuity of praise that won him my heart, as being myself one of the most merciful of critics. Indeed, his stock required some considerable powers of commendation in the salesman; there were several ancient friends of mine, the novels of those happy days when my affections wavered between the Scottish Chiefs and Thomas Thumb,* besides a few of later date, whose merits had not been acknowledged by the public. I was glad to find that dear little venerable volume, the *New England Primer*,* looking as antique as ever, though in its thousandth new edition; a bundle of superannuated gilt picture books made such a child of me that, partly for the glittering covers, and partly for the fairy tales within, I bought the whole; and an assortment of ballads and popular theatrical songs drew largely on my purse. To balance these expenditures, I meddled neither with sermons, nor science, nor morality, though volumes of each were there; nor with a *Life of Franklin** in the coarsest of paper, but so showily bound that it was emblematical of the Doctor himself, in the court dress which he refused to wear at Paris; nor with Webster's spelling book,* nor some of Byron's minor poems, nor half a dozen little Testaments at twenty-five cents each.

Thus far the collection might have been swept from some great bookstore, or picked up at an evening auction room; but there was one small blue-covered pamphlet, which the pedlar handed me with so peculiar an air that I purchased it immediately at his own price; and then, for the first time, the thought struck me that I had spoken face to face with the veritable author of a printed book. The literary man now evinced a great kindness for me, and I ventured to enquire which way he was travelling.

"Oh," said he, "I keep company with this old gentleman here, and we are moving now towards the camp meeting at Stamford!"

He then explained to me, that for the present season he had rented a corner of the wagon as a bookstore, which, as he wittily observed, was a true circulating library, since there were few parts of the country where it had not gone its rounds. I approved of the plan exceedingly, and began to sum up within my mind the many uncommon felicities in the life of a book pedlar, especially when his character resembled that of the individual before me. At a high rate was to be reckoned the daily and hourly enjoyment of such interviews as the present, in which he seized upon the admiration of a passing stranger and made him aware that a man of literary taste, and even of literary achievement, was travelling the country in a showman's wagon. A more valuable, yet not infrequent triumph might be won in his conversation with some elderly clergyman, long vegetating in a rocky, woody, watery back settlement of New England, who, as he recruited his library from the pedlar's stock of sermons, would exhort him to seek a college education and become the first scholar in his class. Sweeter and prouder yet would be his sensations, when, talking

poetry while he sold spelling books, he should charm the mind
and haply touch the heart of a fair country schoolmistress, herself
an unhonoured poetess, a wearer of blue stockings which none
but himself took pains to look at. But the scene of his completest
glory would be when the wagon had halted for the night, and his
stock of books was transferred to some crowded barroom. Then
would he recommend to the multifarious company, whether
traveller from the city, or teamster from the hills, or neighbouring
squire, or the landlord himself, or his loutish ostler, works suited
to each particular taste and capacity – proving, all the while, by
acute criticism and profound remark, that the lore in his books
was even exceeded by that in his brain.

Thus happily would he traverse the land; sometimes a herald
before the march of Mind; sometimes walking arm in arm with
awful Literature; and reaping everywhere a harvest of real and
sensible popularity, which the secluded bookworms, by whose toil
he lived, could never hope for. "If ever I meddle with literature,"
thought I, fixing myself in adamantine resolution, "it shall be as
a travelling bookseller."

Though it was still mid-afternoon, the air had now grown dark
about us, and a few drops of rain came down upon the roof of
our vehicle, pattering like the feet of birds that had flown thither
to rest. A sound of pleasant voices made us listen, and there soon
appeared halfway up the ladder the pretty person of a young
damsel, whose rosy face was so cheerful that even amid the gloomy
light it seemed as if the sunbeams were peeping under her bonnet.
We next saw the dark and handsome features of a young man,
who, with easier gallantry than might have been expected in the
heart of Yankee land, was assisting her into the wagon. It became
immediately evident to us, when the two strangers stood within
the door, that they were of a profession kindred to those of my
companions, and I was delighted with the more than hospitable,

the even paternal kindness of the old showman's manner as he welcomed them; while the man of literature hastened to lead the merry-eyed girl to a seat on the long bench.

"You are housed but just in time, my young friends," said the master of the wagon. "The sky would have been down upon you within five minutes."

The young man's reply marked him as a foreigner, not by any variation from the idiom and accent of good English, but because he spoke with more caution and accuracy than if perfectly familiar with the language.

"We knew that a shower was hanging over us," said he, "and consulted whether it were best to enter the house on the top of yonder hill, but seeing your wagon in the road—"

"We agreed to come hither," interrupted the girl, with a smile, "because we should be more at home in a wandering house like this."

I, meanwhile, with many a wild and undetermined fantasy, was narrowly inspecting these two doves that had flown into our ark. The young man, tall, agile and athletic, wore a mass of black shining curls clustering round a dark and vivacious countenance, which, if it had not greater expression, was at least more active, and attracted readier notice, than the quiet faces of our countrymen. At his first appearance, he had been laden with a neat mahogany box, of about two feet square, but very light in proportion to its size, which he had immediately unstrapped from his shoulders and deposited on the floor of the wagon.

The girl had nearly as fair a complexion as our own beauties, and a brighter one than most of them; the lightness of her figure, which seemed calculated to traverse the whole world without weariness, suited well with the glowing cheerfulness of her face; and her gay attire, combining the rainbow hues of crimson, green, and a deep orange, was as proper to her lightsome aspect as if she had been born in it. This gay stranger was appropriately burdened with that mirth-inspiring instrument, the fiddle, which her companion took from her hands, and shortly began the process of tuning. Neither of us – the previous company of the wagon – needed to enquire their trade, for this could be no mystery to frequenters of brigade musters, ordinations, cattle shows, commencements and other festal meetings in our sober land; and there is a dear friend of mine who will smile when this page recalls to his memory a chivalrous deed performed by us, in rescuing the show box of such a couple from a mob of great double-fisted countrymen.

"Come," said I to the damsel of gay attire, "shall we visit all the wonders of the world together?"

She understood the metaphor at once, though indeed it would not much have troubled me if she had assented to the literal meaning of my words. The mahogany box was placed in a proper position, and I peeped in through its small round magnifying window, while the girl sat by my side, and gave short descriptive sketches, as one after another the pictures were unfolded to my view. We visited together, at least our imaginations did, full many a famous city, in the streets of which I had long yearned to tread; once, I remember, we were in the harbour of Barcelona, gazing townwards; next, she bore me through the air to Sicily, and bade me look up at blazing Etna; then we took wing to Venice, and sat in a gondola beneath the arch of the Rialto; and anon she sat me down among the thronged spectators at the coronation of Napoleon. But there was one scene – its locality she could not tell – which charmed my attention longer than all those gorgeous palaces and churches, because the fancy haunted me, that I myself, the preceding summer, had beheld just such a humble meeting house, in just such a pine-surrounded nook, among our own green mountains. All these pictures were tolerably executed though far inferior to the girl's touches of description; nor was it easy to comprehend, how in so few sentences, and these, as I supposed, in a language foreign to her, she contrived to present in airy copy of each varied scene. When we had travelled through the vast extent of the mahogany box, I looked into my guide's face.

"Where are you going, my pretty maid?" enquired I, in the words of an old song.*

"Ah," said the gay damsel, "you might as well ask where the summer wind is going. We are wanderers here, and there, and everywhere. Wherever there is mirth, our merry hearts are drawn to it. Today, indeed, the people have told us of a great frolic and festival in these parts; so perhaps we may be needed at what you call the camp meeting at Stamford."

Then in my happy youth, and while her pleasant voice yet sounded in my ears, I sighed; for none but myself, I thought, should have been her companion in a life which seemed to realize my own wild fancies, cherished all through visionary boyhood to that hour. To these two strangers the world was in its golden age, not that indeed it was less dark and sad than ever, but because its weariness and sorrow had no community with their ethereal nature. Wherever they might appear in their pilgrimage of bliss, Youth would echo back their gladness, care-stricken Maturity would rest a moment from its toil, and Age, tottering among the graves, would smile in withered joy for their sakes. The lonely cot, the narrow and gloomy street, the sombre shade, would catch a passing gleam like that now shining on ourselves, as these bright spirits wandered by. Blessed pair, whose happy home was throughout all the earth! I looked at my shoulders, and thought them broad enough to sustain those pictured towns and mountains; mine, too, was an elastic foot, as tireless as the wing of the bird of paradise; mine was then an untroubled heart that would have gone singing on its delightful way.

"O maiden!" said I aloud. "Why did you not come hither alone?"

While the merry girl and myself were busy with the show box, the unceasing rain had driven another wayfarer into the wagon. He seemed pretty nearly of the old showman's age, but much smaller, leaner and more withered than he, and less respectably clad in a patched suit of grey; withal, he had a thin, shrewd countenance and a pair of diminutive grey eyes, which peeped rather too keenly out of their puckered sockets. This old fellow had been joking with the showman, in a manner which intimated previous acquaintance; but perceiving that the damsel and I had terminated our affairs, he drew forth a folded document, and presented it to me. As I had anticipated, it proved to be a circular, written in a very fair and legible hand, and signed by several distinguished gentlemen whom I had never heard of, stating that the bearer had encountered every variety of misfortune, and recommending him to the notice of all charitable people. Previous disbursements had left me no more than a five-dollar bill, out of which, however, I offered to make the beggar a donation, provided he would give me change for it. The object of my beneficence looked keenly in my face, and discerned that I had none of that abominable spirit, characteristic though it be, of a full-blooded Yankee, which takes pleasure in detecting every little harmless piece of knavery.

"Why, perhaps," said the ragged old mendicant, "if the bank is in good standing, I can't say but I may have enough about me to change your bill."

"It is a bill of the Suffolk Bank," said I, "and better than the specie."

As the beggar had nothing to object, he now produced a small buff-leather bag, tied up carefully with a shoestring. When this was opened, there appeared a very comfortable treasure of silver coins of all sorts and sizes, and I even fancied that I saw, gleaming among them, the golden plumage of that rare bird in our currency, the American Eagle. In this precious heap was my banknote deposited, the rate of exchange being considerably against me. His wants being thus relieved, the destitute man pulled out of his pocket an old pack of greasy cards, which had probably contributed to fill the buff-leather bag in more ways than one.

"Come," said he, "I spy a rare fortune in your face, and for twenty-five cents more I'll tell you what it is."

I never refuse to take a glimpse into futurity; so, after shuffling the cards, and when the fair damsel had cut them, I dealt a portion to the prophetic beggar. Like others of his profession, before predicting the shadowy events that were moving on to meet me, he gave proof of his preternatural science by describing scenes through which I had already passed. Here let me have credit for a sober fact. When the old man had read a page in his book of fate, he bent his keen grey eyes on mine, and proceeded to relate, in all its minute particulars, what was then the most singular event of my life. It was one which I had no purpose to disclose, till the general unfolding of all secrets; nor would it be a much stranger instance of inscrutable knowledge, or fortunate conjecture, if the beggar were to meet me in the street today, and repeat, word for word, the page which I have here written. The fortune-teller, after predicting a destiny which time seems loath to make good, put up his cards, secreted his treasure bag and began to converse with the other occupants of the wagon.

"Well, old friend," said the showman, "you have not yet told us which way your face is turned this afternoon."

"I am taking a trip northward, this warm weather," replied the conjurer, "across the Connecticut first, and then up through Vermont, and may be into Canada before the fall. But I must stop and see the breaking up of the camp meeting at Stamford."

I began to think that all the vagrants in New England were converging to the camp meeting, and had made this wagon their rendezvous by the way. The showman now proposed that, when the shower was over, they should pursue the road to Stamford together, it being sometimes the policy of these people to form a sort of league and confederacy.

"And the young lady too," observed the gallant bibliopolist, bowing to her profoundly, "and this foreign gentleman, as I understand, are on a jaunt of pleasure to the same spot. It would add incalculably to my own enjoyment, and I presume to that of my colleague and his friend, if they could be prevailed upon to join our party."

This arrangement met with approbation on all hands, nor were any of those concerned more sensible of its advantages than myself, who had no title to be included in it. Having already satisfied myself as to the several modes in which the four others attained felicity, I next set my mind at work to discover what enjoyments were peculiar to the old "Straggler", as the people of the country would have termed the wandering mendicant and prophet. As he pretended to familiarity with the Devil, so I fancied that he was fitted to pursue and take delight in his way of life, by possessing some of the mental and moral characteristics, the lighter and more comic ones, of the Devil in popular stories. Among them might be reckoned a love of deception for its own sake, a shrewd eye and keen relish for human weakness and ridiculous infirmity, and the talent of petty fraud. Thus to this old man there would be pleasure even in the consciousness, so insupportable to some minds, that his whole life was a cheat upon the world, and that, so far as he was concerned with the public, his little cunning had the upper hand of its united wisdom. Every day would furnish him with a succession of minute and pungent triumphs: as when, for instance, his importunity wrung a pittance out of the heart of a miser, or when my silly good nature transferred a part of my slender purse to his plump leather bag; or when some ostentatious gentleman should throw a coin to the ragged beggar who was richer than himself; or when, though he would not always be so decidedly diabolical, his pretended wants should make him a sharer in the scanty living of real indigence. And then what an inexhaustible field of enjoyment, both as enabling him to discern so much folly and achieve such quantities of minor mischief, was opened to his sneering spirit by his pretensions to prophetic knowledge.

All this was a sort of happiness which I could conceive of, though I had little sympathy with it. Perhaps, had I been then inclined to admit it, I might have found that the roving life was more proper to him than to either of his companions; for Satan, to whom I had compared the poor man, has delighted, ever since the time of Job, in "wandering up and down upon the earth";* and indeed a crafty disposition, which operates not in deep-laid plans, but in disconnected tricks, could not have an adequate scope, unless naturally impelled to a continual change of scene and society. My reflections were here interrupted.

"Another visitor!" exclaimed the old showman.

The door of the wagon had been closed against the tempest, which was roaring and blustering with prodigious fury and commotion, and beating violently against our shelter, as if it claimed all those homeless people for its lawful prey, while we, caring little for the displeasure of the elements, sat comfortably talking. There was now an attempt to open the door, succeeded by a voice, uttering some strange, unintelligible gibberish, which my companions mistook for Greek, and I suspected to be thieves' Latin. However, the showman stepped forward and gave admittance to a figure which made me imagine either that our wagon had rolled back two hundred years into past ages or that the forest and its old inhabitants had sprung up around us by enchantment.

It was a red Indian, armed with his bow and arrow. His dress was a sort of cap, adorned with a single feather of some wild bird, and a frock of blue cotton, girded tight about him; on his breast, like orders of knighthood, hung a crescent and a circle, and other ornaments of silver; while a small crucifix betokened that our Father the Pope had interposed between the Indian and the Great Spirit, whom he had worshipped in his simplicity. This son of the wilderness, and pilgrim of the storm, took his place silently in the midst of us. When the first surprise was over, I rightly conjectured him to be one of the Penobscot tribe, parties of which I had often seen in their summer excursions down our eastern rivers. There they paddle their birch canoes among the coasting schooners, and build their wigwam beside some roaring milldam, and drive a little trade in basketwork where their fathers hunted deer. Our new visitor was probably wandering through the country towards Boston, subsisting on the careless charity of the people, while he turned his archery to profitable account by shooting at cents, which were to be the prize of his successful aim.

The Indian had not long been seated, ere our merry damsel sought to draw him into conversation. She, indeed, seemed all made up of sunshine in the month of May, for there was nothing so dark and dismal that her pleasant mind could not cast a glow over it, and the wild man, like a fir tree in his native forest, soon began to brighten into a sort of sombre cheerfulness. At length, she enquired whether his journey had any particular end or purpose.

"I go shoot at the camp meeting at Stamford," replied the Indian.

"And here are five more," said the girl, "all aiming at the camp meeting too. You shall be one of us, for we travel with light hearts; and as for me, I sing merry songs, and tell merry tales, and am full of merry thoughts, and I dance merrily along the road, so that there is never any sadness among them that keep me company. But, oh, you would find it very dull indeed, to go all the way to Stamford alone!"

My ideas of the aboriginal character led me to fear that the Indian would prefer his own solitary musings to the gay society thus offered him; on the contrary, the girl's proposal met with immediate acceptance, and seemed to animate him with a misty expectation of enjoyment. I now gave myself up to a course of thought which, whether it flowed naturally from this combination of events, or was drawn forth by a wayward fancy, caused my mind to thrill as if I were listening to deep music. I saw mankind, in this weary old age of the world, either enduring a sluggish existence amid the smoke and dust of cities, or, if they breathed a purer air, still lying down at night with no hope but to wear out tomorrow, and all the tomorrows which make up life, among the same dull scenes and in the same wretched toil that had darkened the sunshine of today. But there were some, full of the primeval instinct, who preserved the freshness of youth to their latest years by the continual excitement of new objects, new pursuits and new associates; and cared little, though their birthplace might have been here in New England, if the grave should close over them in Central Asia. Fate was summoning a parliament of these free spirits; unconscious of the impulse which directed them to a common centre, they had come hither from far and near; and last of all appeared the representative of those mighty vagrants, who had chased the deer during thousands of years, and were chasing it now in the Spirit Land. Wandering down through the waste of ages, the woods had vanished around his path; his arm had lost somewhat of its strength, his foot of its fleetness, his mien of its wild regality, his heart and mind of their savage virtue and uncultured force; but here, untamable to the routine of artificial life, roving now along the dusty road, as of old over the forest leaves, here was the Indian still.

"Well," said the old showman, in the midst of my meditations, "here is an honest company of us – one, two, three, four, five, six – all going to the camp meeting at Stamford. Now, hoping no offence, I should like to know where this young gentleman may be going?"

I started. How came I among these wanderers? The free mind, that preferred its own folly to another's wisdom; the open spirit, that found companions everywhere; above all, the restless impulse, that had so often made me wretched in the midst of enjoyments: these were my claims to be of their society.

"My friends!" cried I, stepping into the centre of the wagon. "I am going with you to the camp meeting at Stamford."

"But in what capacity?" asked the old showman, after a moment's silence. "All of us here can get our bread in some creditable way. Every honest man should have his livelihood. You, sir, as I take it, are a mere strolling gentleman."

I proceeded to inform the company that, when Nature gave me a propensity to their way of life, she had not left me altogether destitute of qualifications for it, though I could not deny that my talent was less respectable, and might be less profitable, than the meanest of theirs. My design, in short, was to imitate the storytellers of whom oriental travellers have told us, and become an itinerant novelist, reciting my own extemporaneous fictions to such audiences as I could collect.

"Either this," said I, "is my vocation, or I have been born in vain."

The fortune-teller, with a sly wink to the company, proposed to take me as an apprentice to one or other of his professions, either of which, undoubtedly, would have given full scope to whatever inventive talent I might possess. The bibliopolist spoke a few words in opposition to my plan, influenced partly, I suspect, by the jealousy of authorship, and partly by an apprehension that the viva-voce practice would become general among novelists, to the infinite detriment of the book trade. Dreading a rejection, I solicited the interest of the merry damsel.

"Mirth," cried I, most aptly appropriating the words of 'L'Allegro',* "to thee I sue! Mirth, admit me of thy crew!"

"Let us indulge the poor youth," said Mirth, with a kindness which made me love her dearly, though I was no such coxcomb as to misinterpret her motives. "I have espied much promise in him. True, a shadow sometimes flits across his brow, but the sunshine is sure to follow in a moment. He is never guilty of a sad thought, but a merry one is twin-born with it. We will take him with us, and you shall see that he will set us all a-laughing before we reach the camp meeting at Stamford."

Her voice silenced the scruples of the rest, and gained me admittance into the league, according to the terms of which, without a community of goods or profits, we were to lend each other all the aid, and avert all the harm, that might be in our power. This affair settled, a marvellous jollity entered into the whole tribe of us, manifesting itself characteristically in each individual. The old showman, sitting down to his barrel organ, stirred up the souls of the pygmy people with one of the quickest tunes in the music book; tailors, blacksmiths, gentlemen and ladies, all seemed to share in the spirit of the occasion; and the Merry Andrew played his part more facetiously than ever, nodding and winking particularly at me. The young foreigner flourished his fiddle bow with a master's hand, and gave an inspiring echo to the showman's melody. The bookish man and the merry damsel started up simultaneously to dance; the former enacting the double shuffle in a style which everybody must have witnessed, ere election week was blotted out of time; while the girl, setting her arms akimbo with both hands at her slim waist, displayed such light rapidity of foot, and harmony of varying attitude and motion, that I could not conceive how she ever was to stop, imagining, at the moment, that Nature had made her, as the old showman had made his puppets, for no earthly purpose but to dance jigs. The Indian bellowed forth a succession of most hideous outcries, somewhat affrighting us, till we interpreted them as the war song with which, in imitation of his ancestors, he was prefacing the assault on Stamford. The conjurer, meanwhile, sat demurely in a corner, extracting a sly enjoyment from the whole scene and, like the facetious Merry Andrew, directing his queer glance particularly at me.

As for myself, with great exhilaration of fancy, I began to arrange and colour the incidents of a tale wherewith I proposed to amuse an audience that very evening, for I saw that my associates were a little ashamed of me, and that no time was to be lost in obtaining a public acknowledgement of my abilities.

"Come, fellow labourers," at last said the old showman, whom we had elected President. "The shower is over, and we must be doing our duty by these poor souls at Stamford."

"We'll come among them in procession, with music and dancing," cried the merry damsel.

Accordingly – for it must be understood that our pilgrimage was to be performed on foot – we sallied joyously out of the wagon, each of us, even the old gentleman in his white top boots, giving a great skip as we came down the ladder. Above our heads there was such a glory of sunshine and splendour of clouds, and such brightness of verdure below, that, as I modestly remarked at the time, Nature seemed to have washed her face and put on the best of her jewellery and a fresh green gown, in honour of our confederation. Casting our eyes northward, we beheld a horseman approaching leisurely and splashing through the little puddles on the Stamford road. Onward he came, sticking up in his saddle with rigid perpendicularity, a tall, thin figure in rusty black, whom the showman and the conjurer shortly recognized to be, what his aspect sufficiently indicated, a travelling preacher of great fame among the Methodists. What puzzled us was the fact that his face appeared turned from, instead of to the camp meeting at Stamford.

However, as this new votary of the wandering life drew near the little green space, where the guidepost and our wagon were situated, my six fellow vagabonds and myself rushed forward and surrounded him, crying out with united voices:

"What news, what news from the camp meeting at Stamford?"

The missionary looked down, in surprise, at as singular a knot of people as could have been selected from all his heterogeneous auditors. Indeed, considering that we might all be classified under the general head of Vagabond, there was great diversity of character among the grave old showman, the sly, prophetic beggar, the fiddling foreigner and his merry damsel, the smart bibliopolist, the sombre Indian and myself, the itinerant novelist, a slender youth of eighteen. I even fancied that a smile was endeavouring to disturb the iron gravity of the preacher's mouth.

"Good people," answered he, "the camp meeting is broke up."

So saying, the Methodist minister switched his steed, and rode westward. Our union being thus nullified by the removal of its object, we were sundered at once to the four winds of heaven. The fortune-teller, giving a nod to all, and a peculiar wink to me, departed on his northern tour, chuckling within himself as he took the Stamford road. The old showman and his literary coadjutor were already tackling their horses to the wagon, with a design to peregrinate south-west along the sea coast. The foreigner and the merry damsel took their laughing leave, and pursued the eastern road, which I had that day trodden; as they passed away, the young man played a lively strain, and the girl's happy spirit broke into a dance; and thus, dissolving, as it were, into sunbeams and gay music, that pleasant pair departed from my view. Finally, with a pensive shadow thrown across my mind, yet emulous of the light philosophy of my late companions, I joined myself to the Penobscot Indian, and set forth towards the distant city.

The Grey Champion

THERE WAS ONCE A TIME when New England groaned under the actual pressure of heavier wrongs than those threatened ones which brought on the Revolution. James II, the bigoted successor of Charles the Voluptuous, had annulled the charters of all the colonies, and sent a harsh and unprincipled soldier to take away our liberties and endanger our religion.* The administration of Sir Edmund Andros lacked scarcely a single characteristic of tyranny: a governor and council holding office from the King and wholly independent of the country; laws made and taxes levied without concurrence of the people, immediate or by their representatives; the rights of private citizens violated and the titles of all landed property declared void; the voice of complaint stifled by restrictions on the press; and, finally, disaffection overawed by the first band of mercenary troops that ever marched on our free soil. For two years our ancestors were kept in sullen submission by that filial love which had invariably secured their allegiance to the mother country, whether its head chanced to be a parliament, protector or Popish monarch. Till these evil times, however, such allegiance had been merely nominal, and the colonists had ruled themselves, enjoying far more freedom than is even yet the privilege of the native subjects of Great Britain.

At length a rumour reached our shores that the Prince of Orange had ventured on an enterprise, the success of which would be the triumph of civil and religious rights and the salvation of New England.* It was but a doubtful whisper; it might be false, or the attempt might fail; and, in either case, the man that stirred against King James would lose his head. Still, the intelligence produced a marked effect. The people smiled mysteriously in the streets, and threw bold glances at their oppressors, while, far and wide, there was a subdued and silent agitation, as if the slightest signal would rouse the whole land from its sluggish despondency. Aware of their danger, the rulers resolved to avert it by an imposing display of strength, and perhaps to confirm their despotism by yet harsher measures. One afternoon in April 1689, Sir Edmund Andros and his favourite councillors, being warm with wine, assembled the redcoats of the Governor's Guard, and made their appearance in the streets of Boston. The sun was near setting when the march commenced.

The roll of the drum, at that unquiet crisis, seemed to go through the streets, less as the martial music of the soldiers, than as a muster call to the inhabitants themselves. A multitude, by various avenues, assembled in King Street, which was destined to be the scene, nearly a century afterwards, of another encounter between the troops of Britain and a people struggling against her tyranny.* Though more than sixty years had elapsed since the Pilgrims came, this crowd of their descendants still showed the strong and sombre features of their character, perhaps more strikingly in such a stern emergency than on happier occasions. There were the sober garb, the general severity of mien, the gloomy but undismayed expression, the Scriptural forms of speech and the confidence in Heaven's blessing on a righteous cause, which would have marked a band of the original Puritans, when threatened by some peril of the wilderness. Indeed, it was not yet time for the old spirit to be extinct, since there were men in the street, that day, who had worshipped there beneath the trees, before a house was reared to the God for whom they had become exiles. Old soldiers of the Parliament were here too, smiling grimly at the thought that their aged arms might strike another blow against the house of Stuart. Here, also, were the veterans of King Philip's War,* who had burned villages and slaughtered young and old, with pious fierceness, while the godly souls throughout the land were helping them with prayer. Several ministers were scattered among the crowd, which, unlike all other mobs, regarded them with such reverence, as if there were sanctity in their very garments. These holy men exerted their influence to quiet the people, but not to disperse them. Meantime, the purpose of the Governor, in disturbing the peace of the town, at a period when the slightest commotion might throw the country into a ferment, was almost the universal subject of enquiry, and variously explained.

"Satan will strike his master stroke presently," cried some, "because he knoweth that his time is short. All our godly pastors are to be dragged to prison! We shall see them at a Smithfield fire* in King Street!"

Hereupon the people of each parish gathered closer round their minister, who looked calmly upwards and assumed a more apostolic dignity, as well befitted a candidate for the highest honour of his profession, the crown of martyrdom. It was actually fancied, at that period, that New England might have a John Rogers* of her own, to take the place of that worthy in the *Primer*.

"The Pope of Rome has given orders for a new St Bartholomew!"* cried others. "We are to be massacred, man and male child!"

"Neither was this rumour wholly discredited, although the wiser class believed the Governor's object somewhat less atrocious. His predecessor under the old charter, Bradstreet,* a venerable companion of the first settlers, was known to be in town. There were grounds for conjecturing that Sir Edmund Andros intended, at once, to strike terror, by a parade of military force, and to confound the opposite faction by possessing himself of their chief.

"Stand firm for the old charter Governor!" shouted the crowd, seizing upon the idea. "The good old Governor Bradstreet!"

While this cry was at the loudest, the people were surprised by the well-known figure of Governor Bradstreet himself, a patriarch of nearly ninety, who appeared on the elevated steps of a door and, with characteristic mildness, besought them to submit to the constituted authorities.

"My children," concluded this venerable person, "do nothing rashly. Cry not aloud, but pray for the welfare of New England, and expect patiently what the Lord will do in this matter!"

The event was soon to be decided. All this time, the roll of the drum had been approaching through Cornhill, louder and deeper, till with reverberations from house to house, and the regular tramp of martial footsteps, it burst into the street. A double rank of soldiers made their appearance, occupying the whole breadth of the passage, with shouldered matchlocks and matches burning, so as to present a row of fires in the dusk. Their steady march was like the progress of a machine that would roll irresistibly over everything in its way. Next, moving slowly, with a confused clatter of hoofs on the pavement, rode a party of mounted gentlemen, the central figure being Sir Edmund Andros, elderly, but erect and soldier-like. Those around him were his favourite councillors, and the bitterest foes of New England. At his right hand rode Edward Randolph, our arch-enemy, that "blasted wretch", as Cotton Mather calls him, who achieved the downfall of our ancient government, and was followed with a sensible curse, through life and to his grave.* On the other side was Bullivant,* scattering jests and mockery as he rode along. Dudley* came behind, with a downcast look, dreading, as well he might, to meet the indignant gaze of the people, who beheld him, their only countryman by birth, among the oppressors of his native land. The captain of a frigate in the harbour, and two or three civil officers under the

Crown, were also there. But the figure which most attracted the public eye, and stirred up the deepest feeling, was the Episcopal clergyman of King's Chapel, riding haughtily among the magistrates in his priestly vestments, the fitting representative of prelacy and persecution, the union of Church and State and all those abominations which had driven the Puritans to the wilderness. Another guard of soldiers, in double rank, brought up the rear.

The whole scene was a picture of the condition of New England, and its moral the deformity of any government that does not grow out of the nature of things and the character of the people. On one side the religious multitude, with their sad visages and dark attire, and on the other, the group of despotic rulers, with the High Churchman in the midst, and here and there a crucifix at their bosoms, all magnificently clad, flushed with wine, proud of unjust authority and scoffing at the universal groan. And the mercenary soldiers, waiting but the word to deluge the street with blood, showed the only means by which obedience could be secured.

"O Lord of Hosts," cried a voice among the crowd, "provide a Champion for thy people!"

This ejaculation was loudly uttered, and served as a herald's cry, to introduce a remarkable personage. The crowd had rolled back, and were now huddled together nearly at the extremity of the street, while the soldiers had advanced no more than a third of its length. The intervening space was empty – a paved solitude, between lofty edifices, which threw almost a twilight shadow over it. Suddenly, there was seen the figure of an ancient man, who seemed to have emerged from among the people and was walking by himself along the centre of the street to confront the armed band. He wore the old Puritan dress, a dark cloak and a steeple-crowned hat, in the fashion of at least fifty years before, with a heavy sword upon his thigh, but a staff in his hand to assist the tremulous gait of age.

When at some distance from the multitude, the old man turned slowly round, displaying a face of antique majesty, rendered doubly venerable by the hoary beard that descended on his breast. He made a gesture at once of encouragement and warning, then turned again and resumed his way.

"Who is this grey patriarch?" asked the young men of their sires.

"Who is this venerable brother?" asked the old men among themselves.

But none could make reply. The fathers of the people, those of fourscore years and upwards, were disturbed, deeming it strange that they should forget one of such evident authority, whom they must have known in their early days, the associate of Winthrop,* and all the old councillors, giving laws, and making prayers, and leading them against the savage. The elderly men ought to have remembered him too, with locks as grey in their youth as their own were now. And the young! How could he have passed so utterly from their memories – that hoary sire, the relic of long-departed times, whose awful benediction had surely been bestowed on their uncovered heads, in childhood?

"Whence did he come? What is his purpose? Who can this old man be?" whispered the wondering crowd.

Meanwhile, the venerable stranger, staff in hand, was pursuing his solitary walk along the centre of the street. As he drew near the advancing soldiers, and as the roll of their drums came full upon his ear, the old man raised himself to a loftier mien, while the decrepitude of age seemed to fall from his shoulders, leaving him in grey but unbroken dignity. Now, he marched onward with a warrior's step, keeping time to the military music. Thus the aged form advanced on one side, and the whole parade of soldiers and magistrates on the other, till, when scarcely twenty yards remained between, the old man grasped his staff by the middle and held it before him like a leader's truncheon.

"Stand!" cried he.

The eye, the face and attitude of command, the solemn, yet warlike peal of that voice, fit either to rule a host in the battlefield or be raised to God in prayer, were irresistible. At the old man's word and outstretched arm, the roll of the drum was hushed at once, and the advancing line stood still. A tremulous enthusiasm seized upon the multitude. That stately form, combining the leader and the saint, so grey, so dimly seen, in such an ancient garb, could only belong to some old champion of the righteous cause, whom the oppressor's drum had summoned from his grave. They raised a shout of awe and exultation, and looked for the deliverance of New England.

The Governor, and the gentlemen of his party, perceiving themselves brought to an unexpected stand, rode hastily forward, as if they would have pressed their snorting and affrighted horses right against the hoary apparition. He, however, blenched not a step, but, glancing his severe eye round the group, which half encompassed him, at last bent it sternly on Sir Edmund Andros. One would have thought that the dark old man was chief ruler there, and that the Governor and Council, with soldiers at their back, representing the whole power and authority of the Crown, had no alternative but obedience.

"What does this old fellow here?" cried Edward Randolph fiercely. "On, Sir Edmund! Bid the soldiers forward, and give the dotard the same choice that you give all his countrymen – to stand aside or be trampled on!"

"Nay, nay, let us show respect to the good grandsire," said Bullivant, laughing. "See you not he is some old round-headed dignitary, who hath lain asleep these thirty years, and knows nothing of the change of times? Doubtless, he thinks to put us down with a proclamation in Old Noll's name!"*

"Are you mad, old man?" demanded Sir Edmund Andros, in loud and harsh tones. "How dare you stay the march of King James's Governor?"

"I have stayed the march of a king himself, ere now," replied the grey figure, with stern composure. "I am here, Sir Governor, because the cry of an oppressed people hath disturbed me in my secret place, and beseeching this favour earnestly of the Lord, it was vouchsafed me to appear once again on earth, in the good old cause of the saints. And what speak ye of James? There is no longer a Popish tyrant on the throne of England, and by tomorrow noon his name shall be a byword in this very street, where ye would make it a word of terror. Back, thou that wast a governor, back! With this night thy power is ended – tomorrow, the prison! – back, lest I foretell the scaffold!"

The people had been drawing nearer and nearer, and drinking in the words of their champion, who spoke in accents long disused, like one unaccustomed to converse, except with the dead of many years ago. But his voice stirred their souls. They confronted the soldiers, not wholly without arms, and ready to convert the very stones of the street into deadly weapons. Sir Edmund Andros looked at the old man; then he cast his hard and cruel eye over the multitude, and beheld them burning with that lurid wrath, so difficult to kindle or to quench; and again he fixed his gaze on the aged form, which stood obscurely in an open space, where neither friend nor foe had thrust himself. What were his thoughts, he uttered no word which might discover. But whether the oppressor were overawed by the Grey Champion's look, or perceived his peril in the threatening attitude of the people, it is certain that he gave back, and ordered his soldiers to commence a slow and guarded retreat. Before another sunset, the Governor, and all that rode so proudly with him, were prisoners, and long ere it was known that James had abdicated, King William was proclaimed throughout New England.

But where was the Grey Champion? Some reported that when the troops had gone from King Street, and the people were thronging tumultuously in their rear, Bradstreet, the aged Governor, was seen to embrace a form more aged than his own. Others soberly affirmed that while they marvelled at the venerable grandeur of his aspect the old man had faded from their eyes, melting slowly into the hues of twilight, till, where he stood, there was an empty space. But all agreed that the hoary shape was gone. The men of that generation watched for his reappearance, in sunshine and in twilight, but never saw him more, nor knew when his funeral passed, nor where his gravestone was.

And who was the Grey Champion? Perhaps his name might be found in the records of that stern Court of Justice, which passed a sentence, too mighty for the age, but glorious in all after times, for its humbling lesson to the monarch and its high example to the subject. I have heard that whenever the descendants of the Puritans are to show the spirit of their sires the old man appears again. When eighty years had passed, he walked once more in King Street. Five years later, in the twilight of an April morning, he stood on the green, beside the meeting house, at Lexington, where now the obelisk of granite, with a slab of slate inlaid, commemorates the first fallen of the Revolution.* And when our fathers were toiling at the breastwork on Bunker's Hill,* all through that night the old warrior walked his rounds. Long, long may it be, ere he comes again! His hour is one of darkness, and adversity and peril. But should domestic tyranny oppress us, or the invader's step pollute our soil, still may the Grey Champion come, for he is the type of New England's hereditary spirit, and his shadowy march, on the eve of danger, must ever be the pledge that New England's sons will vindicate their ancestry.

Young Goodman Brown

YOUNG GOODMAN BROWN came forth at sunset into the street of Salem village, but put his head back, after crossing the threshold, to exchange a parting kiss with his young wife. And Faith, as the wife was aptly named, thrust her own pretty head into the street, letting the wind play with the pink ribbons of her cap while she called to Goodman Brown.

"Dearest heart," whispered she, softly and rather sadly, when her lips were close to his ear, "prithee put off your journey until sunrise and sleep in your own bed tonight. A lone woman is troubled with such dreams and such thoughts that she's afeared of herself sometimes. Pray tarry with me this night, dear husband, of all nights in the year."

"My love and my Faith," replied young Goodman Brown, "of all nights in the year, this one night must I tarry away from thee. My journey, as thou callest it, forth and back again, must needs be done 'twixt now and sunrise. What, my sweet, pretty wife, dost thou doubt me already, and we but three months married?"

"Then God bless you!" said Faith, with the pink ribbons. "And may you find all well when you come back."

"Amen!" cried Goodman Brown. "Say thy prayers, dear Faith, and go to bed at dusk, and no harm will come to thee." So they parted, and the young man pursued his way until, being about to turn the corner by the meeting house, he looked back and saw the head of Faith still peeping after him with a melancholy air, in spite of her pink ribbons.

"Poor little Faith!" thought he, for his heart smote him. "What a wretch am I to leave her on such an errand! She talks of dreams too. Methought as she spoke, there was trouble in her face, as if a dream had warned her what work is to be done tonight. But no, no: 'twould kill her to think it. Well, she's a blessed angel on earth, and after this one night I'll cling to her skirts and follow her to heaven."

With this excellent resolve for the future, Goodman Brown felt himself justified in making more haste on his present evil purpose. He had taken a dreary road, darkened by all the gloomiest trees of the forest, which barely stood aside to let the narrow path creep through, and closed immediately behind. It was all as lonely as could be, and there is this peculiarity in such a solitude that the traveller knows not who may be concealed by the innumerable trunks and the thick boughs overhead, so that with lonely footsteps he may yet be passing through an unseen multitude.

"There may be a devilish Indian behind every tree," said Goodman Brown to himself, and he glanced fearfully behind him as he added: "What if the Devil himself should be at my very elbow!"

His head being turned back, he passed a crook of the road and, looking forward again, beheld the figure of a man, in grave and decent attire, seated at the foot of an old tree. He arose at Goodman Brown's approach and walked onward side by side with him.

"You are late, Goodman Brown," said he. "The clock of the Old South was striking as I came through Boston, and that is full fifteen minutes agone."

"Faith kept me back awhile," replied the young man, with a tremor in his voice, caused by the sudden appearance of his companion, though not wholly unexpected.

It was now deep dusk in the forest, and deepest in that part of it where these two were journeying. As nearly as could be discerned, the second traveller was about fifty years old, apparently in the same rank of life as Goodman Brown and bearing a considerable resemblance to him, though perhaps more in expression than features. Still they might have been taken for father and son. And yet, though the elder person was as simply clad as the younger and as simple in manner too, he had an indescribable air of one who knew the world, and who would not have felt abashed at the governor's dinner table or in King William's court,* were it possible that his affairs should call him thither. But the only thing about him that could be fixed upon as remarkable was his staff, which bore the likeness of a great black snake, so curiously wrought that it might almost be seen to twist and wriggle itself like a living serpent. This, of course, must have been an ocular deception, assisted by the uncertain light.

"Come, Goodman Brown," cried his fellow traveller, "this is a dull pace for the beginning of a journey. Take my staff, if you are so soon weary."

"Friend," said the other, exchanging his slow pace for a full stop, "having kept covenant by meeting thee here, it is my purpose now to return whence I came. I have scruples touching the matter thou wot'st of."

"Sayest thou so?" replied he of the serpent, smiling apart. "Let us walk on, nevertheless, reasoning as we go, and if I convince thee not, thou shalt turn back. We are but a little way in the forest yet."

"Too far! Too far!" exclaimed the goodman, unconsciously resuming his walk. "My father never went into the woods on such an errand, nor his father before him. We have been a race of honest men and good Christians since the days of the martyrs, and shall I be the first by the name of Brown that ever took this path and kept..."

"Such company, thou wouldst say," observed the elder person, interpreting his pause. "Well said, Goodman Brown! I have been as well acquainted with your family as with ever a one among the Puritans, and that's no trifle to say. I helped your grandfather, the constable, when he lashed the Quaker woman so smartly through the streets of Salem; and it was I that brought your father a pitch-pine knot, kindled at my own hearth, to set fire to an Indian village, in King Philip's war. They were my good friends both, and many a pleasant walk have we had along this path, and returned merrily after midnight. I would fain be friends with you for their sake."

"If it be as thou sayest," replied Goodman Brown, "I marvel they never spoke of these matters – or, verily, I marvel not, seeing that the least rumour of the sort would have driven them from New England. We are a people of prayer, and good works to boot, and abide no such wickedness."

"Wickedness or not," said the traveller with the twisted staff, "I have a very general acquaintance here in New England. The deacons of many a church have drunk the communion wine with me; the selectmen of divers towns make me their chairman; and a majority of the Great and General Court are firm supporters of my interest. The governor and I too... But these are state secrets."

"Can this be so?" cried Goodman Brown, with a stare of amazement at his undisturbed companion. "Howbeit, I have nothing to do with the governor and council: they have their own ways, and are no rule for a simple husbandman like me. But, were I to go on with thee, how should I meet the eye of that good old man, our minister, at Salem village? Oh, his voice would make me tremble both Sabbath day and lecture day!"

Thus far the elder traveller had listened with due gravity, but now burst into a fit of irrepressible mirth, shaking himself so violently that his snake-like staff actually seemed to wriggle in sympathy.

"Ha! Ha! Ha!" shouted he again and again; then, composing himself: "Well, go on, Goodman Brown, go on – but, prithee, don't kill me with laughing."

"Well, then, to end the matter at once," said Goodman Brown, considerably nettled, "there is my wife, Faith. It would break her dear little heart – and I'd rather break my own."

"Nay, if that be the case," answered the other, "e'en go thy ways, Goodman Brown. I would not for twenty old women like the one hobbling before us that Faith should come to any harm."

As he spoke, he pointed his staff at a female figure on the path, in whom Goodman Brown recognized a very pious and exemplary dame, who had taught him his catechism in youth, and was still his moral and spiritual adviser, jointly with the minister and Deacon Gookin.

"A marvel, truly, that Goody Cloyse* should be so far in the wilderness at nightfall," said he. "But, with your leave, friend, I shall take a cut through the woods until we have left this Christian woman behind. Being a stranger to you, she might ask whom I was consorting with and whither I was going."

"Be it so," said his fellow traveller. "Betake you to the woods, and let me keep the path."

Accordingly the young man turned aside, but took care to watch his companion, who advanced softly along the road until he had come within a staff's length of the old dame. She, meanwhile, was making the best of her way, with singular speed for so aged a woman, and mumbling some indistinct words – a prayer, doubtless – as she went. The traveller put forth his staff and touched her withered neck with what seemed the serpent's tail.

"The Devil!" screamed the pious old lady.

"Then Goody Cloyse knows her old friend?" observed the traveller, confronting her and leaning on his writhing stick.

"Ah, forsooth, and is it Your Worship indeed?" cried the good dame. "Yea, truly is it, and in the very image of my old gossip,* Goodman Brown, the grandfather of the silly fellow that now is. But – would Your Worship believe it? – my broomstick hath strangely disappeared, stolen, as I suspect, by that unhanged witch, Goody Cory,* and that, too, when I was all anointed with the juice of smallage, and cinquefoil, and wolfsbane—"

"Mingled with fine wheat and the fat of a new-born babe," said the shape of old Goodman Brown.

"Ah, Your Worship knows the recipe," cried the old lady, cackling aloud. "So, as I was saying, being all ready for the meeting, and no horse to ride on, I made up my mind to foot it, for they tell me there is a nice young man to be taken into communion tonight. But now Your good Worship will lend me your arm, and we shall be there in a twinkling."

"That can hardly be," answered her friend. "I may not spare you my arm, Goody Cloyse; but here is my staff, if you will."

So saying, he threw it down at her feet, where, perhaps, it assumed life, being one of the rods which its owner had formerly lent to the Egyptian magi.* Of this fact, however, Goodman Brown could not take cognizance. He had cast up his eyes in astonishment and, looking down again, beheld neither Goody Cloyse nor the serpentine staff, but his fellow traveller alone, who waited for him as calmly as if nothing had happened.

"That old woman taught me my catechism," said the young man, and there was a world of meaning in this simple comment.

They continued to walk onward, while the elder traveller exhorted his companion to make good speed and persevere in the path, discoursing so aptly that his arguments seemed rather to spring up in the bosom of his auditor than to be suggested by himself. As they went, he plucked a branch of maple to serve for a walking stick, and began to strip it of the twigs and little boughs, which were wet with evening dew. The moment his fingers touched them they became strangely withered and dried up as with a week's sunshine. Thus the pair proceeded, at a good free pace, until suddenly, in a gloomy hollow of the road, Goodman Brown sat himself down on the stump of a tree and refused to go any farther.

"Friend," said he, stubbornly, "my mind is made up. Not another step will I budge on this errand. What if a wretched old woman do choose to go to the Devil when I thought she was going to heaven: is that any reason why I should quit my dear Faith and go after her?"

"You will think better of this by and by," said his acquaintance composedly. "Sit here and rest yourself awhile, and when you feel like moving again, there is my staff to help you along."

Without more words, he threw his companion the maple stick, and was as speedily out of sight as if he had vanished into the deepening gloom. The young man sat a few moments by the road-side, applauding himself greatly and thinking with how clear a conscience he should meet the minister in his morning walk, nor shrink from the eye of good old Deacon Gookin. And what calm sleep would be his that very night, which was to have been spent so wickedly, but so purely and sweetly now, in the arms of Faith! Amidst these pleasant and praiseworthy meditations, Goodman Brown heard the tramp of horses along the road, and deemed it advisable to conceal himself within the verge of the forest, conscious of the guilty purpose that had brought him thither, though now so happily turned from it.

On came the hoof tramps and the voices of the riders, two grave old voices, conversing soberly as they drew near. These mingled sounds appeared to pass along the road, within a few yards of the young man's hiding place; but, owing doubtless to the depth of the gloom at that particular spot, neither the travellers nor their steeds were visible. Though their figures brushed the small boughs by the wayside, it could not be seen that they intercepted, even for a moment, the faint gleam from the strip of bright sky athwart which they must have passed. Goodman Brown alternately crouched and stood on tiptoe, pulling aside the branches and thrusting forth his head as far as he durst, without discerning so much as a shadow. It vexed him the more, because he could have sworn, were such a thing possible, that he recognized the voices of the minister and Deacon Gookin, jogging along quietly, as they were wont to do, when bound to some ordination or ecclesiastical council. While yet within hearing, one of the riders stopped to pluck a switch.

"Of the two, reverend sir," said the voice like the deacon's, "I had rather miss an ordination dinner than tonight's meeting. They tell me that some of our community are to be here from Falmouth and beyond, and others from Connecticut and Rhode Island, besides several of the Indian pow-wows,* who, after their fashion, know almost as much deviltry as the best of us. Moreover, there is a goodly young woman to be taken into communion."

"Mighty well, Deacon Gookin!" replied the solemn old tones of the minister. "Spur up, or we shall be late. Nothing can be done, you know, until I get on the ground."

The hoofs clattered again, and the voices, talking so strangely in the empty air, passed on through the forest, where no church had ever been gathered or solitary Christian prayed. Whither, then, could these holy men be journeying so deep into the heathen wilderness? Young Goodman Brown caught hold of a tree for support, being ready to sink down on the ground, faint and overburdened with the heavy sickness of his heart. He looked up to the sky, doubting whether there really was a heaven above him. Yet there was the blue arch, and the stars brightening in it.

"With heaven above and Faith below, I will yet stand firm against the Devil!" cried Goodman Brown.

While he still gazed upward into the deep arch of the firmament and had lifted his hands to pray, a cloud, though no wind was stirring, hurried across the zenith and hid the brightening stars. The blue sky was still visible except directly overhead, where this black mass of cloud was sweeping swiftly northward. Aloft in the air, as if from the depths of the cloud, came a confused and doubtful sound of voices. Once the listener fancied that he could distinguish the accents of townspeople of his own, men and women, both pious and ungodly, many of whom he had met at the communion table, and had seen others rioting at the tavern. The next morning, so indistinct were the sounds, he doubted whether he had heard aught but the murmur of the old forest, whispering without a wind. Then came a stronger swell of those familiar tones, heard daily in the sunshine at Salem village, but never until now from a cloud of night. There was one voice, of a young woman, uttering lamentations, yet with an uncertain sorrow, and entreating for some favour, which, perhaps, it would grieve her to obtain; and all the unseen multitude, both saints and sinners, seemed to encourage her onward.

"Faith!" shouted Goodman Brown, in a voice of agony and desperation, and the echoes of the forest mocked him, crying, "Faith! Faith!" as if bewildered wretches were seeking her all through the wilderness.

The cry of grief, rage and terror was yet piercing the night, when the unhappy husband held his breath for a response. There was a scream, drowned immediately in a louder murmur of voices, fading into far-off laughter, as the dark cloud swept away, leaving the clear and silent sky above Goodman Brown. But something fluttered lightly down through the air and caught on the branch of a tree. The young man seized it, and beheld a pink ribbon.

"My Faith is gone!" cried he, after one stupefied moment. "There is no good on earth, and sin is but a name. Come, Devil – for to thee is this world given."

And, maddened with despair, so that he laughed loud and long, did Goodman Brown grasp his staff and set forth again, at such a rate that he seemed to fly along the forest path rather than to walk or run. The road grew wilder and drearier and more faintly traced, and vanished at length, leaving him in the heart of the dark wilderness, still rushing onward with the instinct that guides mortal man to evil. The whole forest was peopled with frightful sounds – the creaking of the trees, the howling of wild beasts and the yell of Indians – while sometimes the wind tolled like a distant church bell, and sometimes gave a broad roar around the traveller, as if all Nature were laughing him to scorn. But he was himself the chief horror of the scene, and shrank not from its other horrors.

"Ha! ha! ha!" roared Goodman Brown when the wind laughed at him. "Let us hear which will laugh loudest. Think not to frighten me with your deviltry. Come witch, come wizard, come Indian pow-wow, come Devil himself, and here comes Goodman Brown. You may as well fear him as he fear you."

In truth, all through the haunted forest there could be nothing more frightful than the figure of Goodman Brown. On he flew among the black pines, brandishing his staff with frenzied gestures, now giving vent to an inspiration of horrid blasphemy, and now shouting forth such laughter as set all the echoes of the forest laughing like demons around him. The fiend in his own shape is less hideous than when he rages in the breast of man. Thus sped the demoniac on his course, until, quivering among the trees, he saw a red light before him, as when the felled trunks and branches of a clearing have been set on fire and throw up their lurid blaze against the sky at the hour of midnight. He paused, in a lull of the tempest that had driven him onward, and heard the swell of what seemed a hymn rolling solemnly from a distance with the weight of many voices. He knew the tune: it was a familiar one in the choir of the village meeting house. The verse died heavily away, and was lengthened by a chorus, not of human voices, but of all the sounds of the benighted wilderness pealing in awful harmony together. Goodman Brown cried out – and his cry was lost to his own ear by its unison with the cry of the desert.

In the interval of silence he stole forward until the light glared full upon his eyes. At one extremity of an open space, hemmed in by the dark wall of the forest, arose a rock, bearing some rude, natural resemblance either to an altar or a pulpit, and surrounded by four blazing pines, their tops aflame, their stems untouched, like candles at an evening meeting. The mass of foliage that had overgrown the summit of the rock was all on fire, blazing high into the night and fitfully illuminating the whole field. Each pendent twig and leafy festoon was in a blaze. As the red light arose and fell, a numerous congregation alternately shone forth, then disappeared in shadow, and again grew, as it were, out of the darkness, peopling the heart of the solitary woods at once.

"A grave and dark-clad company," quoth Goodman Brown.

In truth they were such. Among them, quivering to and fro between gloom and splendour, appeared faces that would be seen next day at the council board of the province, and others which, Sabbath after Sabbath, looked devoutly heavenward, and benignantly over the crowded pews, from the holiest pulpits in the land. Some affirm that the lady of the governor was there. At least there were high dames well known to her, and wives of honoured husbands, and widows, a great multitude, and ancient maidens, all of excellent repute, and fair young girls who trembled lest their mothers should espy them. Either the sudden gleams of light flashing over the obscure field bedazzled Goodman Brown, or he recognized a score of the church members of Salem village famous for their especial sanctity, Good old Deacon Gookin had arrived, and waited at the skirts of that venerable saint, his revered pastor. But, irreverently consorting with these grave, reputable and pious people, these elders of the church, these chaste dames and dewy virgins, there were men of dissolute lives and women of spotted fame, wretches given over to all mean and filthy vice, and suspected even of horrid crimes. It was strange to see that the good shrank not from the wicked; nor were the sinners abashed by the saints. Scattered also among their pale-faced enemies were the Indian priests, or pow-wows, who had often scared their native forest with more hideous incantations than any known to English witchcraft.

"But where is Faith?" thought Goodman Brown, and, as hope came into his heart, he trembled.

Another verse of the hymn arose, a slow and mournful strain, such as the pious love, but joined to words which expressed all that our nature can conceive of sin, and darkly hinted at far more. Unfathomable to mere mortals is the lore of fiends. Verse after verse was sung; and still the chorus of the desert swelled between like the deepest tone of a mighty organ; and with the final peal of that dreadful anthem there came a sound, as if the roaring wind, the rushing streams and howling beasts, and every other voice of the unconverted wilderness were mingling and according with the voice of guilty man in homage to the prince of all. The four blazing pines threw up a loftier flame and obscurely discovered shapes and visages of horror on the smoke wreaths above the impious assembly. At the same moment the fire on the rock shot redly forth and formed a glowing arch above its base, where now appeared a figure. With reverence be it spoken, the figure bore no slight similitude, both in garb and manner, to some grave divine of the New England churches.

"Bring forth the converts!" cried a voice that echoed through the field and rolled into the forest.

At the word, Goodman Brown stepped forth from the shadow of the trees and approached the congregation, with whom he felt a loathful brotherhood by the sympathy of all that was wicked in his heart. He could have well-nigh sworn that the shape of his own dead father beckoned him to advance, looking downward from a smoke wreath, while a woman, with dim features of despair, threw out her hand to warn him back. Was it his mother? But he had no power to retreat one step, nor to resist, even in thought, when the minister and good old Deacon Gookin seized his arms and led him to the blazing rock. Thither came also the slender form of a veiled female, led between Goody Cloyse, that pious teacher of the catechism, and Martha Carrier, who had received the Devil's promise to be queen of hell. A rampant hag was she. And there stood the proselytes beneath the canopy of fire.

"Welcome, my children," said the dark figure, "to the communion of your race. Ye have found thus young your nature and your destiny. My children, look behind you!"

They turned, and flashing forth, as it were, in a sheet of flame, the fiend-worshippers were seen; the smile of welcome gleamed darkly on every visage.

"There," resumed the sable form, "are all whom ye have reverenced from youth. Ye deemed them holier than yourselves, and shrank from your own sin, contrasting it with their lives of righteousness and prayerful aspirations heavenward. Yet here are they all in my worshipping assembly. This night it shall be granted you to know their secret deeds; how hoary-bearded elders of the church have whispered wanton words to the young maids of their households; how many a woman, eager for widow's weeds, has given her husband a drink at bedtime and let him sleep his last sleep in her bosom; how beardless youths have made haste to inherit their father's wealth; and how fair damsels – blush not, sweet ones – have dug little graves in the garden, and bidden me, the sole guest, to an infant's funeral. By the sympathy of your human hearts for sin ye shall scent out all the places – whether in church, bedchamber, street, field or forest – where crime has been committed, and shall exult to behold the whole earth one stain of guilt, one mighty blood spot. Far more than this. It shall be yours to penetrate, in every bosom, the deep mystery of sin, the fountain of all wicked arts, and which inexhaustibly supplies more evil impulses than human power – than my power at its utmost – can make manifest in deeds. And now, my children, look upon each other."

They did so, and by the blaze of the hell-kindled torches the wretched man beheld his Faith, and the wife her husband, trembling before that unhallowed altar.

"Lo, there ye stand, my children," said the figure in a deep and solemn tone, almost sad with its despairing awfulness, as if his once angelic nature could yet mourn for our miserable race. "Depending upon one another's hearts, ye had still hoped that virtue were not all a dream. Now are ye undeceived. Evil is the nature of mankind. Evil must be your only happiness. Welcome again, my children, to the communion of your race."

"Welcome," repeated the fiend-worshippers, in one cry of despair and triumph.

And there they stood, the only pair, as it seemed, who were yet hesitating on the verge of wickedness in this dark world. A basin was hollowed, naturally, in the rock. Did it contain water, reddened by the lurid light? Or was it blood? Or, perchance, a liquid flame? Herein did the shape of evil dip his hand and prepare to lay the mark of baptism upon their foreheads, that they might be partakers of the mystery of sin, more conscious of the secret guilt of others, both in deed and thought, than they could now be of their own. The husband cast one look at his pale wife, and Faith at him. What polluted wretches would the next glance show them to each other, shuddering alike at what they disclosed and what they saw!

"Faith! Faith!" cried the husband. "Look up to Heaven, and resist the wicked one."

Whether Faith obeyed, he knew not. Hardly had he spoken, when he found himself amid calm night and solitude, listening to a roar of the wind which died heavily away through the forest. He staggered against the rock, and felt it chill and damp, while a hanging twig that had been all on fire besprinkled his cheek with the coldest dew.

The next morning young Goodman Brown came slowly into the street of Salem village, staring around him like a bewildered man. The good old minister was taking a walk along the graveyard to get an appetite for breakfast and meditate his sermon, and bestowed a blessing, as he passed, on Goodman Brown. He shrank from the venerable saint as if to avoid an anathema. Old Deacon Gookin was at domestic worship, and the holy words of his prayer were heard through the open window. "What God doth the wizard pray to?" quoth Goodman Brown. Goody Cloyse, that excellent old Christian, stood in the early sunshine at her own lattice, catechizing a little girl who had brought her a pint of morning's milk. Goodman Brown snatched away the child as from the grasp of the fiend himself. Turning the corner by the meeting house, he spied the head of Faith, with the pink ribbons, gazing anxiously forth, and bursting into such joy at sight of him that she skipped along the street and almost kissed her husband before the whole village. But Goodman Brown looked sternly and sadly into her face, and passed on without a greeting.

Had Goodman Brown fallen asleep in the forest, and only dreamt a wild dream of a witch meeting?

Be it so, if you will, but – alas! – it was a dream of evil omen for young Goodman Brown. A stern, a sad, a darkly meditative, a distrustful, if not a desperate man did he become from the night of that fearful dream. On the Sabbath day, when the congregation were singing a holy psalm, he could not listen, because an anthem of sin rushed loudly upon his ear and drowned all the blessed strain. When the minister spoke from the pulpit, with power and fervid eloquence, and with his hand on the open Bible, of the sacred truths of our religion, and of saint-like lives and triumphant deaths, and of future bliss or misery unutterable, then did Goodman Brown turn pale, dreading lest the roof should thunder down upon the grey blasphemer and his hearers. Often, awaking suddenly at midnight, he shrank from the bosom of Faith; and at morning or eventide, when the family knelt down to prayer, he scowled, and muttered to himself, and gazed sternly at his wife, and turned away. And when he had lived long, and was borne to his grave, a hoary corpse, followed by Faith, an aged woman, and children and grandchildren, a goodly procession, besides neighbours not a few, they carved no hopeful verse upon his tombstone, for his dying hour was gloom.

Wakefield

I N SOME OLD MAGAZINE OR NEWSPAPER,* I recollect a story, told as truth, of a man – let us call him Wakefield – who absented himself for a long time from his wife. The fact thus abstractedly stated is not very uncommon, nor – without a proper distinction of circumstances – to be condemned either as naughty or nonsensical. Howbeit, this, though far from the most aggravated, is perhaps the strangest instance on record of marital delinquency, and, moreover, as remarkable a freak as may be found in the whole list of human oddities. The wedded couple lived in London. The man, under pretence of going a journey, took lodgings in the next street to his own house, and there, unheard of by his wife or friends, and without the shadow of a reason for such self-banishment, dwelt upwards of twenty years. During that period, he beheld his home every day, and frequently the forlorn Mrs Wakefield. And after so great a gap in his matrimonial felicity – when his death was reckoned certain, his estate settled, his name dismissed from memory and his wife, long, long ago, resigned to her autumnal widowhood – he entered the door one evening, quietly, as from a day's absence, and became a loving spouse till death.

This outline is all that I remember. But the incident, though of the purest originality, unexampled, and probably never to be repeated, is one, I think, which appeals to the generous sympathies of mankind. We know, each for himself, that none of us would perpetrate such a folly, yet feel as if some other might. To my own contemplations, at least, it has often recurred, always exciting wonder, but with a sense that the story must be true, and a conception of its hero's character. Whenever any subject so forcibly affects the mind, time is well spent in thinking of it. If the reader choose, let him do his own meditation; or if he prefer to ramble with me through the twenty years of Wakefield's vagary, I bid him welcome, trusting that there will be a pervading spirit and a moral, even should we fail to find them, done up neatly, and condensed into the final sentence. Thought has always its efficacy, and every striking incident its moral.

What sort of a man was Wakefield? We are free to shape out our own idea and call it by his name. He was now in the meridian of life; his matrimonial affections, never violent, were sobered into a calm, habitual sentiment; of all husbands, he was likely to be the most constant, because a certain sluggishness would keep his heart at rest, wherever it might be placed. He was intellectual, but not actively so; his mind occupied itself in long and lazy musings that tended to no purpose, or had not vigour to attain it; his thoughts were seldom so energetic as to seize hold of words. Imagination, in the proper meaning of the term, made no part of Wakefield's gifts. With a cold but not depraved nor wandering heart, and a mind never feverish with riotous thoughts, nor perplexed with originality, who could have anticipated that our friend would entitle himself to a foremost place among the doers of eccentric deeds? Had his acquaintances been asked, who was the man in London, the surest to perform nothing today which should be remembered on the morrow, they would have thought of Wakefield. Only the wife of his bosom might have hesitated. She, without having analysed his character, was partly aware of a quiet selfishness that had rusted into his inactive mind; of a peculiar sort of vanity, the most uneasy attribute about him; of a disposition to craft, which had seldom produced more positive effects than the keeping of petty secrets, hardly worth revealing; and, lastly, of what she called a little strangeness, sometimes, in the good man. This latter quality is indefinable, and perhaps non-existent.

Let us now imagine Wakefield bidding adieu to his wife. It is the dusk of an October evening. His equipment is a drab greatcoat, a hat covered with an oilcloth, top boots, an umbrella in one hand and a small portmanteau in the other. He has informed Mrs Wakefield that he is to take the night coach into the country. She would fain enquire the length of his journey, its object and the probable time of his return, but, indulgent to his harmless love of mystery, interrogates him only by a look. He tells her not to expect him positively by the return coach, not to be alarmed should he tarry three or four days, but, at all events, to look for him at supper on Friday evening. Wakefield himself, be it considered, has no suspicion of what is before him. He holds out his hand; she gives her own, and meets his parting kiss, in the matter-of-course way of a ten years' matrimony; and forth goes the middle-aged Mr Wakefield, almost resolved to perplex his good lady by a whole week's absence. After the door has closed behind him, she perceives it thrust partly open, and a vision of her husband's face, through the aperture, smiling on her, and gone in a moment. For the time, this little incident is dismissed without a thought. But, long afterwards, when she has been more years a widow than a wife, that smile recurs, and flickers across all her reminiscences of Wakefield's visage. In her many musings, she surrounds the original smile with a multitude of fantasies, which make it strange and awful; as, for instance, if she imagines him in a coffin, that parting look is frozen on his pale features; or, if she dreams of him in heaven, still his blessed spirit wears a quiet and crafty smile. Yet, for its sake, when all others have given him up for dead, she sometimes doubts whether she is a widow.

But our business is with the husband. We must hurry after him, along the street, ere he lose his individuality and melt into the great mass of London life. It would be vain searching for him there. Let us follow close at his heels, therefore, until, after several superfluous turns and doublings, we find him comfortably established by the fireside of a small apartment previously bespoken. He is in the next street to his own, and at his journey's end. He can scarcely trust his good fortune in having got thither unperceived – recollecting that, at one time, he was delayed by the throng, in the very focus of a lighted lantern; and, again, there were footsteps, that seemed to tread behind his own, distinct from the multitudinous tramp around him; and, anon, he heard a voice shouting afar, and fancied that it called his name. Doubtless, a dozen busybodies had been watching him, and told his wife the whole affair. Poor Wakefield! Little knowest thou thine own insignificance in this great world! No mortal eye but mine has traced thee. Go quietly to thy bed, foolish man, and on the morrow, if thou wilt be wise, get thee home to good Mrs Wakefield and tell her the truth. Remove not thyself, even for a little week, from thy place in her chaste bosom. Were she, for a single moment, to deem thee dead, or lost, or lastingly divided from her, thou wouldst be woefully conscious of a change in thy true wife, for ever after. It is perilous to make a chasm in human affections – not that they gape so long and wide, but so quickly close again!

Almost repenting of his frolic, or whatever it may be termed, Wakefield lies down betimes and, starting from his first nap, spreads forth his arms into the wide and solitary waste of the unaccustomed bed. "No," thinks he, gathering the bedclothes about him, "I will not sleep alone another night."

In the morning, he rises earlier than usual, and sets himself to consider what he really means to do. Such are his loose and rambling modes of thought, that he has taken this very singular step, with the consciousness of a purpose, indeed, but without being able to define it sufficiently for his own contemplation. The vagueness of the project, and the convulsive effort with which he plunges into the execution of it, are equally characteristic of a feeble-minded man. Wakefield sifts his ideas, however, as minutely as he may, and finds himself curious to know the progress of matters at home – how his exemplary wife will endure her widowhood of a week, and, briefly, how the little sphere of creatures and circumstances, in which he was a central object, will be affected by his removal. A morbid vanity, therefore, lies nearest the bottom of the affair. But how is he to attain his ends? Not, certainly, by keeping close in this comfortable lodging, where, though he slept and awoke in the next street to his home, he is as effectually abroad, as if the stagecoach had been whirling him away all night. Yet, should he reappear, the whole project is knocked on the head. His poor brains being hopelessly puzzled with this dilemma, he at length ventures out, partly resolving to cross the head of the street and send one hasty glance towards his forsaken domicile. Habit – for he is a man of habits – takes him by the hand and guides him, wholly unaware, to his own door, where, just at the critical moment, he is aroused by the scraping of his foot upon the step. Wakefield! Whither are you going?

At that instant, his fate was turning on the pivot. Little dreaming of the doom to which his first backward step devotes him, he hurries away, breathless with agitation hitherto unfelt, and hardly dares turn his head, at the distant corner. Can it be that nobody caught sight of him? Will not the whole household – the decent Mrs Wakefield, the smart maidservant and the dirty little footboy – raise a hue and cry, through London streets, in pursuit of their fugitive lord and master? Wonderful escape! He gathers courage to pause and look homeward, but is perplexed with a sense of change about the familiar edifice, such as affects us all, when, after a separation of months or years, we again see some hill or lake, or work of art, with which we were friends of old. In ordinary cases, this indescribable impression is caused by the comparison and contrast between our imperfect reminiscences and the reality. In Wakefield, the magic of a single night has wrought a similar transformation, because, in that brief period, a great moral change has been effected. But this is a secret from himself. Before leaving the spot, he catches a far and momentary glimpse of his wife, passing athwart the front window, with her face turned towards the head of the street. The crafty nincompoop takes to his heels, scared with the idea that, among a thousand such atoms of mortality, her eye must have detected him. Right glad is his heart, though his brain be somewhat dizzy, when he finds himself by the coal fire of his lodgings.

So much for the commencement of this long whim-wham. After the initial conception and the stirring-up of the man's sluggish temperament to put it in practice, the whole matter evolves itself in a natural train. We may suppose him, as the result of deep deliberation, buying a new wig, of reddish hair, and selecting sundry garments, in a fashion unlike his customary suit of brown, from a Jew's old-clothes bag. It is accomplished. Wakefield is another man. The new system being now established, a retrograde movement to the old would be almost as difficult as the step that placed him in his unparalleled position. Furthermore, he is rendered obstinate by a sulkiness, occasionally incident to his temper, and brought on, at present, by the inadequate sensation which he conceives to have been produced in the bosom of Mrs Wakefield. He will not go back until she be frightened half to death. Well, twice or thrice has she passed before his sight, each time with a heavier step, a paler cheek and more anxious brow, and in the third week of his non-appearance he detects a portent of evil entering the house, in the guise of an apothecary. Next day, the knocker is muffled. Towards nightfall comes the chariot of a physician and deposits its big-wigged and solemn burden at Wakefield's door, whence, after a quarter of an hour's visit, he emerges, perchance the herald of a funeral. Dear woman! Will she die? By this time, Wakefield is excited to something like energy of feeling, but still lingers away from his wife's bedside, pleading with his conscience that she must not be disturbed at such a juncture. If aught else restrains him, he does not know it. In the course of a few weeks, she gradually recovers; the crisis is over; her heart is sad, perhaps, but quiet; and, let him return soon or late, it will never be feverish for him again. Such ideas glimmer through the mist of Wakefield's mind, and render him indistinctly conscious that an almost impassable gulf divides his hired apartment from his former home. "It is but in the next street!" he sometimes says. Fool! It is in another world. Hitherto, he has put off his return from one particular day to another; henceforward, he leaves the precise time undetermined. Not tomorrow – probably next week – pretty soon. Poor man! The dead have nearly as much chance of revisiting their earthly homes, as the self-banished Wakefield.

Would that I had a folio to write, instead of an article of a dozen pages! Then might I exemplify how an influence, beyond our control, lays its strong hand on every deed which we do and weaves its consequences into an iron tissue of necessity. Wakefield is spellbound. We must leave him, for ten years or so, to haunt around his house, without once crossing the threshold, and to be faithful to his wife, with all the affection of which his heart is capable, while he is slowly fading out of hers. Long since, it must be remarked, he has lost the perception of singularity in his conduct.

Now for a scene! Amid the throng of a London street, we distinguish a man, now waxing elderly, with few characteristics to attract careless observers, yet bearing, in his whole aspect, the handwriting of no common fate for such as have the skill to read it. He is meagre; his low and narrow forehead is deeply wrinkled, his eyes, small and lustreless, sometimes wander apprehensively about him, but oftener seem to look inward. He bends his head, and moves with an indescribable obliquity of gait, as if unwilling to display his full front to the world. Watch him, long enough to see what we have described, and you will allow that circumstances – which often produce remarkable men from nature's ordinary handiwork – have produced one such here. Next, leaving him to sidle along the footwalk, cast your eyes in the opposite direction, where a portly female, considerably in the wane of life, with a prayer book in her hand, is proceeding to yonder church. She has the placid mien of settled widowhood. Her regrets have either died away, or have become so essential to her heart that they would be poorly exchanged for joy. Just as the lean man and well-conditioned woman are passing, a slight obstruction occurs, and brings these two figures directly in contact. Their hands touch; the pressure of the crowd forces her bosom against his shoulder; they stand, face to face, staring into each other's eyes. After a ten years' separation, thus Wakefield meets his wife!

The throng eddies away, and carries them asunder. The sober widow, resuming her former pace, proceeds to church, but pauses in the portal, and throws a perplexed glance along the street. She passes in, however, opening her prayer book as she goes. And the man! With so wild a face, that busy and selfish London stands to gaze after him, he hurries to his lodgings, bolts the door and throws himself upon the bed. The latent feelings of years break out; his feeble mind acquires a brief energy from their strength; all the miserable strangeness of his life is revealed to him at a glance, and he cries out, passionately, "Wakefield! Wakefield! You are mad!"

Perhaps he was so. The singularity of his situation must have so moulded him to himself that, considered in regard to his fellow creatures and the business of life, he could not be said to possess his right mind. He had contrived, or rather he had happened to dissever himself from the world – to vanish – to give up his place and privileges with living men, without being admitted among the dead. The life of a hermit is nowise parallel to his. He was in the bustle of the city, as of old, but the crowd swept by and saw him not; he was, we may figuratively say, always beside his wife and at his hearth, yet must never feel the warmth of the one nor the affection of the other. It was Wakefield's unprecedented fate to retain his original share of human sympathies and to be still involved in human interests, while he had lost his reciprocal influence on them. It would be a most curious speculation to trace out the effect of such circumstances on his heart and intellect, separately and in unison. Yet, changed as he was, he would seldom be conscious of it, but deem himself the same man as ever; glimpses of the truth, indeed, would come, but only for the moment; and still he would keep saying, "I shall soon go back!" nor reflect that he had been saying so for twenty years.

I conceive, also, that these twenty years would appear, in the retrospect, scarcely longer than the week to which Wakefield had at first limited his absence. He would look on the affair as no more than an interlude in the main business of his life. When, after a little while more, he should deem it time to re-enter his parlour, his wife would clap her hands for joy on beholding the middle-aged Mr Wakefield. Alas, what a mistake! Would Time but await the close of our favourite follies, we should be young men, all of us, and till Doomsday.

One evening, in the twentieth year since he vanished, Wakefield is taking his customary walk towards the dwelling which he still calls his own. It is a gusty night of autumn, with frequent showers that patter down upon the pavement and are gone before a man can put up his umbrella. Pausing near the house, Wakefield discerns, through the parlour windows of the second floor, the red glow and the glimmer and fitful flash of a comfortable fire. On the ceiling appears a grotesque shadow of good Mrs Wakefield. The cap, the nose and chin and the broad waist form an admirable caricature, which dances, moreover, with the up-flickering and down-sinking blaze, almost too merrily for the shade of an elderly widow. At this instant, a shower chances to fall, and is driven, by the unmannerly gust, full into Wakefield's face and bosom. He is quite penetrated with its autumnal chill. Shall he stand, wet and shivering, here, when his own hearth has a good fire to warm him, and his own wife will run to fetch the grey coat and small clothes, which doubtless she has kept carefully in the closet of their bedchamber? No! Wakefield is no such fool. He ascends the steps – heavily! – for twenty years have stiffened his legs, since he came down – but he knows it not. Stay, Wakefield! Would you go to the sole home that is left you? Then step into your grave! The door opens. As he passes in, we have a parting glimpse of his visage and recognize the crafty smile, which was the precursor of the little joke that he has ever since been playing off at his wife's expense. How unmercifully has he quizzed the poor woman! Well, a good night's rest to Wakefield!

This happy event – supposing it to be such – could only have occurred at an unpremeditated moment. We will not follow our friend across the threshold. He has left us much food for thought, a portion of which shall lend its wisdom to a moral, and be shaped into a figure. Amid the seeming confusion of our mysterious world, individuals are so nicely adjusted to a system, and systems to one another, and to a whole, that, by stepping aside for a moment, a man exposes himself to a fearful risk of losing his place for ever. Like Wakefield, he may become, as it were, the Outcast of the Universe.

The White Old Maid

T HE MOONBEAMS CAME THROUGH two deep and narrow
windows and showed a spacious chamber, richly furnished in
an antique fashion. From one lattice, the shadow of the diamond
panes was thrown upon the floor; the ghostly light, through the
other, slept upon a bed, falling between the heavy silken curtains
and illuminating the face of a young man. But how quietly the
slumberer lay! How pale his features! And how like a shroud
the sheet was wound about his frame! Yes, it was a corpse, in its
burial clothes.

Suddenly the fixed features seemed to move, with dark emotion.
Strange fantasy! It was but the shadow of the fringed curtain,
waving betwixt the dead face and the moonlight, as the door of
the chamber opened and a girl stole softly to the bedside. Was
there delusion in the moonbeams, or did her gesture and her eye
betray a gleam of triumph, as she bent over the pale corpse – pale
as itself – and pressed her living lips to the cold ones of the dead?
As she drew back from that long kiss, her features writhed, as
if a proud heart were fighting with its anguish. Again it seemed
that the features of the corpse had moved responsive to her own.
Still an illusion! The silken curtain had waved, a second time,
betwixt the dead face and the moonlight, as another fair young
girl unclosed the door and glided, ghost-like, to the bedside. There
the two maidens stood, both beautiful, with the pale beauty of
the dead between them. But she who had first entered was proud
and stately, and the other a soft and fragile thing.

"Away!" cried the lofty one. "Thou hadst him living! The dead is mine!"

"Thine!" returned the other, shuddering. "Well hast thou spoken! The dead is thine!"

The proud girl started, and stared into her face, with a ghastly look. But a wild and mournful expression passed across the features of the gentle one; and, weak and helpless, she sank down on the bed, her head pillowed beside that of the corpse and her hair mingling with his dark locks. A creature of hope and joy, the first draught of sorrow had bewildered her.

"Edith!" cried her rival.

Edith groaned, as with a sudden compression of the heart; and, removing her cheek from the dead youth's pillow, she stood upright, fearfully encountering the eyes of the lofty girl.

"Wilt thou betray me?" said the latter calmly.

"Till the dead bid me speak, I will be silent," answered Edith. "Leave us alone together! Go, and live many years, and then return, and tell me of thy life. He too will be here! Then, if thou tellest of sufferings more than death, we will both forgive thee."

"And what shall be the token?" asked the proud girl, as if her heart acknowledged a meaning in these wild words.

"This lock of hair," said Edith, lifting one of the dark, clustering curls that lay heavily on the dead man's brow.

The two maidens joined their hands over the bosom of the corpse, and appointed a day and hour, far, far in time to come, for their next meeting in that chamber. The statelier girl gave one deep look at the motionless countenance and departed – yet turned again and trembled, ere she closed the door, almost believing that her dead lover frowned upon her. And Edith too! Was not her white form fading into the moonlight? Scorning her own weakness, she went forth, and perceived that a Negro slave was waiting in the passage with a wax light, which he held between her face and his own, and regarded her, as she thought, with an ugly expression of merriment. Lifting his torch on high, the slave lighted her down the staircase and undid the portal of the mansion. The young clergyman of the town had just ascended the steps, and, bowing to the lady, passed in without a word.

Years, many years rolled on; the world seemed new again, so much older was it grown since the night when those pale girls had clasped their hands across the bosom of the corpse. In the interval, a lonely woman had passed from youth to extreme age, and was known by all the town, as the "Old Maid in the Winding Sheet". A taint of insanity had affected her whole life, but so quiet, sad and gentle, so utterly free from violence, that she was suffered to pursue her harmless fantasies unmolested by the world, with whose business or pleasures she had naught to do. She dwelt alone, and never came into the daylight, except to follow funerals. Whenever a corpse was borne along the street, in sunshine, rain or snow, whether a pompous train of the rich and proud thronged after it or few and humble were the mourners, behind them came the lonely woman in a long, white garment, which the people called her shroud. She took no place among the kindred or the friends, but stood at the door to hear the funeral prayer and walked in the rear of the procession, as one whose earthly charge it was to haunt the house of mourning, and be the shadow of affliction, and see that the dead were duly buried. So long had this been her custom that the inhabitants of the town deemed her a part of every funeral, as much as the coffin pall or the very corpse itself, and augured ill of the sinner's destiny unless the "Old Maid in the Winding Sheet" came gliding, like a ghost, behind. Once, it is said, she affrighted a bridal party, with her pale presence, appearing suddenly in the illuminated hall, just as the priest was uniting a false maid to a wealthy man, before her lover had been dead a year. Evil was the omen to that marriage! Sometimes she stole forth by moonlight and visited the graves of venerable Integrity, and wedded Love, and virgin Innocence, and every spot where the ashes of a kind and faithful heart were mouldering. Over the hillocks of those favoured dead would she stretch out her arms, with a gesture as if she were scattering seeds, and many believed that she brought them from the garden of Paradise; for the graves which she had visited were green beneath the snow, and covered with sweet flowers from April to November. Her blessing was better than a holy verse upon the tombstone. Thus wore away her long, sad, peaceful and fantastic life, till few were so old as she, and the people of later generations wondered how the dead had ever been buried, or mourners had endured their grief, without the "Old Maid in the Winding Sheet".

Still, years went on, and still she followed funerals, and was not yet summoned to her own festival of death. One afternoon, the great street of the town was all alive with business and bustle, though the sun now gilded only the upper half of the church spire, having left the housetops and loftiest trees in shadow. The scene was cheerful and animated, in spite of the sombre shade between the high brick buildings. Here were pompous merchants in white wigs and laced velvet; the bronzed faces of sea captains; the foreign garb and air of Spanish creoles; and the disdainful port of natives of Old England; all contrasted with the rough aspect of one or two hack settlers, negotiating sales of timber from forests where axe had never sounded. Sometimes a lady passed, swelling roundly forth in an embroidered petticoat, balancing her steps in high-heeled shoes and curtsying, with lofty grace, to the punctilious obeisances of the gentlemen. The life of the town seemed to have its very centre not far from an old mansion that stood somewhat back from the pavement, surrounded by neglected grass, with a strange air of loneliness, rather deepened than dispelled by the throng so near it. Its site would have been suitably occupied by a magnificent Exchange, or a brick block, lettered all over with various signs; or the large house itself might have made a noble tavern, with the "King's Arms" swinging before it, and guests in every chamber, instead of the present solitude. But, owing to some dispute about the right of inheritance, the mansion had been long without a tenant, decaying from year to year and throwing the stately gloom of its shadow over the busiest part of the town. Such was the scene, and such the time, when a figure, unlike any that have been described, was observed at a distance down the street.

"I espy a strange sail, yonder," remarked a Liverpool captain, "that woman in the long, white garment!"

The sailor seemed much struck by the object, as were several others who, at the same moment, caught a glimpse of the figure that had attracted his notice. Almost immediately, the various topics of conversation gave place to speculations, in an undertone, on this unwonted occurrence.

"Can there be a funeral, so late this afternoon?" enquired some.

They looked for the signs of death at every door – the sexton, the hearse, the assemblage of black-clad relatives – all that makes up the woeful pomp of funerals. They raised their eyes, also, to the sun-gilt spire of the church, and wondered that no clang proceeded from its bell, which had always tolled till now, when this figure appeared in the light of day. But none had heard that a corpse was to be borne to its home that afternoon, nor was there any token of a funeral, except the apparition of the "Old Maid in the Winding Sheet".

"What may this portend?" asked each man of his neighbour.

All smiled as they put the question, yet with a certain trouble in their eyes, as if pestilence, or some other wide calamity, were prognosticated by the untimely intrusion among the living, of one whose presence had always been associated with death and woe. What a comet is to the earth was that sad woman to the town.

Still she moved on, while the hum of surprise was hushed at her approach, and the proud and the humble stood aside, that her white garment might not wave against them. It was a long, loose robe, of spotless purity. Its wearer appeared very old, pale, emaciated and feeble, yet glided onward, without the unsteady pace of extreme age. At one point of her course, a little rosy boy burst forth from a door and ran, with open arms, towards the ghostly woman, seeming to expect a kiss from her bloodless lips. She made a slight pause, fixing her eye upon him with an expression of no earthly sweetness, so that the child shivered and stood awestruck, rather than affrighted, while the Old Maid passed on. Perhaps her garment might have been polluted even by an infant's touch; perhaps her kiss would have been death to the sweet boy within a year.

"She is but a shadow," whispered the superstitious. "The child put forth his arms and could not grasp her robe!"

The wonder was increased when the Old Maid passed beneath the porch of the deserted mansion, ascended the moss-covered steps, lifted the iron knocker and gave three raps. The people could only conjecture that some old remembrance, troubling her bewildered brain, had impelled the poor woman hither to visit the friends of her youth; all gone from their home, long since and for ever, unless their ghosts still haunted it – fit company for the "Old Maid in the Winding Sheet". An elderly man approached the steps and, reverently uncovering his grey locks, essayed to explain the matter.

"None, madam," said he, "have dwelt in this house these fifteen years agone – no, not since the death of old Colonel Fenwicke, whose funeral you may remember to have followed. His heirs, being ill agreed among themselves, have let the mansion house go to ruin."

The Old Maid looked slowly round, with a slight gesture of one hand and a finger of the other upon her lip, appearing more shadow-like than ever, in the obscurity of the porch. But again she lifted the hammer, and gave, this time, a single rap. Could it be that a footstep was now heard, coming down the staircase of the old mansion, which all conceived to have been so long untenanted? Slowly, feebly yet heavily, like the pace of an aged and infirm person, the step approached, more distinct on every downward stair, till it reached the portal. The bar fell on the inside; the door was opened. One upward glance, towards the church spire, whence the sunshine had just faded, was the last that the people saw of the "Old Maid in the Winding Sheet".

"Who undid the door?" asked many.

This question, owing to the depth of shadow beneath the porch, no one could satisfactorily answer. Two or three aged men, while protesting against an inference, which might be drawn, affirmed that the person within was a Negro, and bore a singular resemblance to old Caesar, formerly a slave in the house, but freed by death some thirty years before.

"Her summons has waked up a servant of the old family," said one half-seriously.

"Let us wait here," replied another. "More guests will knock at the door, anon. But the gate of the graveyard should be thrown open!"

Twilight had overspread the town, before the crowd began to separate, or the comments on this incident were exhausted. One after another was wending his way homeward, when a coach – no common spectacle in those days – drove slowly into the street. It was an old-fashioned equipage, hanging close to the ground, with arms on the panels, a footman behind and a grave, corpulent coachman seated high in front – the whole giving an idea of solemn state and dignity. There was something awful in the heavy rumbling of the wheels. The coach rolled down the street till, coming to the gateway of the deserted mansion, it drew up, and the footman sprang to the ground.

"Whose grand coach is this?" asked a very inquisitive body.

The footman made no reply, but ascended the steps of the old house, gave three raps with the iron hammer and returned to open the coach door. An old man possessed of the heraldic lore so common in that day examined the shield of arms on the panel.

"Azure a lion's head erased between three flower-de-luces," said he, then whispered the name of the family to whom these bearings belonged. The last inheritor of its honours was recently dead, after a long residence amid the splendour of the British court, where his birth and wealth had given him no mean station. "He left no child," continued the herald, "and these arms, being in a lozenge, betoken that the coach appertains to his widow."

Further disclosures, perhaps, might have been made, had not the speaker suddenly been struck dumb by the stern eye of an ancient lady, who thrust forth her head from the coach, preparing to descend. As she emerged, the people saw that her dress was magnificent, and her figure dignified, in spite of age and infirmity – a stately ruin, but with a look, at once, of pride and wretchedness. Her strong and rigid features had an awe about them unlike that of the white Old Maid, but as of something evil. She passed up the steps, leaning on a gold-headed cane; the door swung open, as she ascended – and the light of a torch glittered on the embroidery of her dress and gleamed on the pillars of the porch. After a momentary pause – a glance backwards – and then a desperate effort – she went in. The decipherer of the coat of arms had ventured up the lowest step and, shrinking back immediately, pale and tremulous, affirmed that the torch was held by the very image of old Caesar.

"But, such a hideous grin," added he, "was never seen on the face of mortal man, black or white! It will haunt me till my dying day."

Meantime, the coach had wheeled round, with a prodigious clatter on the pavement, and rumbled up the street, disappearing in the twilight, while the ear still tracked its course. Scarcely was it gone, when the people began to question whether the coach and attendants, the ancient lady, the spectre of old Caesar and the Old Maid herself were not all a strangely combined delusion, with some dark purport in its mystery. The whole town was astir, so that, instead of dispersing, the crowd continually increased, and stood gazing up at the windows of the mansion, now silvered by the brightening moon. The elders, glad to indulge the narrative propensity of age, told of the long-faded splendour of the family, the entertainments they had given and the guests, the greatest of the land, and even titled and noble ones from abroad, who had passed beneath that portal. These graphic reminiscences seemed to call up the ghosts of those to whom they referred. So strong was the impression, on some of the more imaginative hearers, that two or three were seized with trembling fits, at one and the same moment, protesting that they had distinctly heard three other raps of the iron knocker.

"Impossible!" exclaimed others. "See! The moon shines beneath the porch, and shows every part of it, except in the narrow shade of that pillar. There is no one there!"

"Did not the door open?" whispered one of these fanciful persons.

"Didst thou see it too?" said his companion in a startled tone.

But the general sentiment was opposed to the idea that a third visitant had made application at the door of the deserted house. A few, however, adhered to this new marvel, and even declared that a red gleam, like that of a torch, had shone through the great front window, as if the Negro were lighting a guest up the staircase. This too was pronounced a mere fantasy. But at once the whole multitude started, and each man beheld his own terror painted in the faces of all the rest.

"What an awful thing is this!" cried they.

A shriek, too fearfully distinct for doubt, had been heard within the mansion, breaking forth suddenly and succeeded by a deep stillness, as if a heart had burst in giving it utterance. The people knew not whether to fly from the very sight of the house or to rush trembling in and search out the strange mystery. Amid their confusion and affright, they were somewhat reassured by the appearance of their clergyman, a venerable patriarch and equally a saint, who had taught them and their fathers the way to heaven, for more than the space of an ordinary lifetime. He was a reverend figure, with long, white hair upon his shoulders, a white beard upon his breast and a back so bent over his staff that he seemed to be looking downward, continually, as if to choose a proper grave for his weary frame. It was some time before the good old man, being deaf and of impaired intellect, could be made to comprehend such portions of the affair as were comprehensible at all. But, when possessed of the facts, his energies assumed unexpected vigour.

"Verily," said the old gentleman, "it will be fitting that I enter the mansion house of the worthy Colonel Fenwicke, lest any harm should have befallen that true Christian woman, whom ye call the 'Old Maid in the Winding Sheet'."

Behold, then, the venerable clergyman ascending the steps of the mansion, with a torchbearer behind him. It was the elderly man who had spoken to the Old Maid, and the same who had afterwards explained the shield of arms and recognized the features of the Negro. Like their predecessors, they gave three raps with the iron hammer.

"Old Caesar cometh not," observed the priest. "Well, I wot, he no longer doth service in this mansion."

"Assuredly, then, it was something worse, in old Caesar's likeness!" said the other adventurer.

"Be it as God wills," answered the clergyman. "See! My strength, though it be much decayed, hath sufficed to open this heavy door. Let us enter, and pass up the staircase."

Here occurred a singular exemplification of the dreamy state of a very old man's mind. As they ascended the wide flight of stairs, the aged clergyman appeared to move with caution, occasionally standing aside, and oftener bending his head, as it were in salutation, thus practising all the gestures of one who makes his way through a throng. Reaching the head of the staircase, he looked around, with sad and solemn benignity, laid aside his staff, bared his hoary locks and was evidently on the point of commencing a prayer.

"Reverend sir," said his attendant, who conceived this a very suitable prelude to their further search, "would it not be well that the people join with us in prayer?"

"Welladay!" cried the old clergyman, staring strangely around him. "Art thou here with me, and none other? Verily, past times were present to me, and I deemed that I was to make a funeral prayer, as many a time heretofore, from the head of this staircase. Of a truth, I saw the shades of many that are gone. Yea, I have prayed at their burials, one after another, and the 'Old Maid in the Winding Sheet' hath seen them to their graves!"

Being now more thoroughly awake to their present purpose, he took his staff and struck forcibly on the floor, till there came an echo from each deserted chamber, but no menial to answer their summons. They therefore walked along the passage, and again paused, opposite to the great front window, through which was seen the crowd, in the shadow and partial moonlight of the street beneath. On their right hand was the open door of a chamber, and a closed one on their left. The clergyman pointed his cane to the carved oak panel of the latter.

"Within that chamber," observed he, "a whole lifetime since, did I sit by the deathbed of a goodly young man who, being now at the last gasp—"

Apparently, there was some powerful excitement in the ideas which had now flashed across his mind. He snatched the torch from his companion's hand, and threw open the door with such sudden violence that the flame was extinguished, leaving them no other light than the moonbeams which fell through two windows into the spacious chamber. It was sufficient to discover all that could be known. In a high-backed oaken armchair, upright, with her hands clasped across her breast and her head thrown back, sat the "Old Maid in the Winding Sheet". The stately dame had fallen on her knees, with her forehead on the holy knees of the Old Maid, one hand upon the floor and the other pressed convulsively against her heart. It clutched a lock of hair, once sable, now discoloured with a greenish mould. As the priest and layman advanced into the chamber, the Old Maid's features assumed such a resemblance of shifting expression that they trusted to hear the whole mystery explained by a single word. But it was only the shadow of a tattered curtain, waving betwixt the dead face and the moonlight.

"Both dead!" said the venerable man. "Then who shall divulge the secret? Methinks it glimmers to and fro in my mind, like the light and shadow across the Old Maid's face. And now 'tis gone!"

The Ambitious Guest

ONE SEPTEMBER NIGHT a family had gathered round their hearth and piled it high with the driftwood of mountain streams, the dry cones of the pine and the splintered ruins of great trees that had come crashing down the precipice. Up the chimney roared the fire and brightened the room with its broad blaze. The faces of the father and mother had a sober gladness; the children laughed. The eldest daughter was the image of Happiness at seventeen, and the aged grandmother, who sat knitting in the warmest place, was the image of Happiness grown old. They had found the "herb heartsease" in the bleakest spot of all New England. This family were situated in the Notch of the White Hills, where the wind was sharp throughout the year and pitilessly cold in the winter, giving their cottage all its fresh inclemency before it descended on the valley of the Saco. They dwelt in a cold spot and a dangerous one, for a mountain towered above their heads so steep that the stones would often rumble down its sides and startle them at midnight.

The daughter had just uttered some simple jest that filled them all with mirth, when the wind came through the Notch and seemed to pause before their cottage, rattling the door with a sound of wailing and lamentation before it passed into the valley. For a moment it saddened them, though there was nothing unusual in the tones. But the family were glad again when they perceived that the latch was lifted by some traveller whose footsteps had been unheard amid the dreary blast which heralded his approach and wailed as he was entering and went moaning away from the door.

Though they dwelt in such a solitude, these people held daily converse with the world. The romantic pass of the Notch is a great artery through which the lifeblood of internal commerce is continually throbbing between Maine on one side and the Green Mountains and the shores of the St Lawrence on the other. The stagecoach always drew up before the door of the cottage. The wayfarer with no companion but his staff paused here to exchange a word, that the sense of loneliness might not utterly overcome him ere he could pass through the cleft of the mountain or reach the first house in the valley. And here the teamster on his way to Portland market would put up for the night and, if a bachelor, might sit an hour beyond the usual bedtime and steal a kiss from the mountain maid at parting. It was one of those primitive taverns where the traveller pays only for food and lodging, but meets with a homely kindness beyond all price. When the footsteps were heard, therefore, between the outer door and the inner one, the whole family rose up, grandmother, children and all, as if about to welcome someone who belonged to them, and whose fate was linked with theirs.

The door was opened by a young man. His face at first wore the melancholy expression, almost despondency, of one who travels a wild and bleak road at nightfall and alone, but soon brightened up when he saw the kindly warmth of his reception. He felt his heart spring forward to meet them all, from the old woman who wiped a chair with her apron to the little child that held out its arms to him. One glance and smile placed the stranger on a footing of innocent familiarity with the eldest daughter.

"Ah! This fire is the right thing," cried he, "especially when there is such a pleasant circle round it. I am quite benumbed, for the

Notch is just like the pipe of a great pair of bellows: it has blown a terrible blast in my face all the way from Bartlett."

"Then you are going towards Vermont?" said the master of the house as he helped to take a light knapsack off the young man's shoulders.

"Yes, to Burlington, and far enough beyond," replied he. "I meant to have been at Ethan Crawford's tonight, but a pedestrian lingers along such a road as this. It is no matter, for when I saw this good fire and all your cheerful faces, I felt as if you had kindled it on purpose for me and were waiting my arrival. So I shall sit down among you and make myself at home."

The frank-hearted stranger had just drawn his chair to the fire when something like a heavy footstep was heard without, rushing down the steep side of the mountain as with long and rapid strides, and taking such a leap in passing the cottage as to strike the opposite precipice. The family held their breath, because they knew the sound, and their guest held his by instinct.

"The old mountain has thrown a stone at us for fear we should forget him," said the landlord, recovering himself. "He sometimes nods his head and threatens to come down, but we are old neighbours, and agree together pretty well upon the whole. Besides, we have a sure place of refuge hard by if he should be coming in good earnest."

Let us now suppose the stranger to have finished his supper of bear's meat, and by his natural felicity of manner to have placed himself on a footing of kindness with the whole family, so that they talked as freely together as if he belonged to their mountain brood. He was of a proud yet gentle spirit, haughty and reserved among the rich and great, but ever ready to stoop his head to the lowly cottage door and be like a brother or a son at the poor man's fireside. In the household of the Notch he found warmth and simplicity of feeling, the pervading intelligence of New England

and a poetry of native growth which they had gathered when they little thought of it from the mountain peaks and chasms, and at the very threshold of their romantic and dangerous abode. He had travelled far and alone; his whole life, indeed, had been a solitary path, for, with the lofty caution of his nature, he had kept himself apart from those who might otherwise have been his companions. The family too, though so kind and hospitable, had that consciousness of unity among themselves and separation from the world at large which in every domestic circle should still keep a holy place where no stranger may intrude. But this evening a prophetic sympathy impelled the refined and educated youth to pour out his heart before the simple mountaineers, and constrained them to answer him with the same free confidence. And thus it should have been. Is not the kindred of a common fate a closer tie than that of birth?

The secret of the young man's character was a high and abstracted ambition. He could have borne to live an undistinguished life, but not to be forgotten in the grave. Yearning desire had been transformed to hope, and hope, long cherished, had become like certainty that, obscurely as he journeyed now, a glory was to beam on all his pathway, though not, perhaps, while he was treading it. But when posterity should gaze back into the gloom of what was now the present, they would trace the brightness of his footsteps, brightening as meaner glories faded, and confess that a gifted one had passed from his cradle to his tomb with none to recognize him.

"As yet," cried the stranger, his cheek glowing and his eye flashing with enthusiasm, "as yet I have done nothing. Were I to vanish from the earth tomorrow, none would know so much of me as you – that a nameless youth came up at nightfall from the valley of the Saco, and opened his heart to you in the evening, and passed through the Notch by sunrise, and was seen no more. Not a soul would ask, 'Who was he? Whither did the wanderer go?' But I cannot die till I have achieved my destiny. Then let Death come: I shall have built my monument."

There was a continual flow of natural emotion gushing forth amid abstracted reverie, which enabled the family to understand this young man's sentiments, though so foreign from their own. With quick sensibility of the ludicrous, he blushed at the ardour into which he had been betrayed.

"You laugh at me," said he, taking the eldest daughter's hand and laughing himself. "You think my ambition as nonsensical as if I were to freeze myself to death on the top of Mount Washington only that people might spy at me from the country roundabout. And truly that would be a noble pedestal for a man's statue."

"It is better to sit here by this fire," answered the girl, blushing, "and be comfortable and contented, though nobody thinks about us."

"I suppose," said her father, after a fit of musing, "there is something natural in what the young man says – and if my mind had been turned that way I might have felt just the same. It is strange, wife, how his talk has set my head running on things that are pretty certain never to come to pass."

"Perhaps they may," observed the wife. "Is the man thinking what he will do when he is a widower?"

"No, no!" cried he, repelling the idea with reproachful kindness. "When I think of your death, Esther, I think of mine too. But I was wishing we had a good farm in Bartlett or Bethlehem or Littleton, or some other township round the White Mountains, but not where they could tumble on our heads. I should want to stand well with my neighbours and be called squire and sent to General Court for a term or two; for a plain, honest man may do as much good there as a lawyer. And when I should be grown quite an old man, and you an old woman, so as not to be long apart, I might die happy enough in my bed and leave you all crying around me. A slate gravestone would suit me as well as a marble one, with just my name and age, and a verse of a hymn, and something to let people know that I lived an honest man and died a Christian."

"There, now!" exclaimed the stranger. "It is our nature to desire a monument, be it slate or marble, or a pillar of granite, or a glorious memory in the universal heart of man."

"We're in a strange way tonight," said the wife, with tears in her eyes. "They say it's a sign of something when folks' minds go a-wandering so. Hark to the children!"

They listened accordingly. The younger children had been put to bed in another room, but with an open door between, so that they could be heard talking busily among themselves. One and all seemed to have caught the infection from the fireside circle, and were outvying each other in wild wishes and childish projects of what they would do when they came to be men and women. At length a little boy, instead of addressing his brothers and sisters, called out to his mother.

"I'll tell you what I wish, mother," cried he. "I want you and father and grandma'm, and all of us, and the stranger too, to start right away and go and take a drink out of the basin of the Flume."

Nobody could help laughing at the child's notion of leaving a warm bed and dragging them from a cheerful fire to visit the basin of the Flume – a brook which tumbles over the precipice deep within the Notch.

The boy had hardly spoken, when a wagon rattled along the road and stopped a moment before the door. It appeared to contain two or three men who were cheering their hearts with the rough chorus of a song which resounded in broken notes between the cliffs, while the singers hesitated whether to continue their journey or put up here for the night.

"Father," said the girl, "they are calling you by name."

But the good man doubted whether they had really called him, and was unwilling to show himself too solicitous of gain by inviting people to patronize his house. He therefore did not hurry to the door, and, the lash being soon applied, the travellers plunged into the Notch, still singing and laughing, though their music and mirth came back drearily from the heart of the mountain.

"There, Mother!" cried the boy again. "They'd have given us a ride to the Flume."

Again they laughed at the child's pertinacious fancy for a night ramble. But it happened that a light cloud passed over the daughter's spirit; she looked gravely into the fire and drew a breath that was almost a sigh. It forced its way, in spite of a little struggle to repress it. Then, starting and blushing, she looked quickly around the circle, as if they had caught a glimpse into her bosom. The stranger asked what she had been thinking of.

"Nothing," answered she, with a downcast smile. "Only I felt lonesome just then."

"Oh, I have always had a gift of feeling what is in other people's hearts," said he half-seriously. "Shall I tell the secrets of yours? For I know what to think when a young girl shivers by a warm hearth and complains of lonesomeness at her mother's side. Shall I put these feelings into words?"

"They would not be a girl's feelings any longer if they could be put into words," replied the mountain nymph, laughing, but avoiding his eye.

All this was said apart. Perhaps a germ of love was springing in their hearts so pure that it might blossom in Paradise, since it could not be matured on earth; for women worship such gentle dignity as his, and the proud, contemplative yet kindly soul is oftenest captivated by simplicity like hers. But while they spoke softly, and he was watching the happy sadness, the lightsome shadows, the shy yearnings, of a maiden's nature, the wind through the

Notch took a deeper and drearier sound. It seemed as the fanciful stranger said, like the choral strain of the spirits of the blast who in old Indian times had their dwelling among these mountains and made their heights and recesses a sacred region. There was a wail along the road as if a funeral were passing. To chase away the gloom, the family threw pine branches on their fire till the dry leaves crackled and the flame arose, discovering once again a scene of peace and humble happiness. The light hovered about them fondly and caressed them all. There were the little faces of the children peeping from their bed apart, and here the father's frame of strength, the mother's subdued and careful mien, the high-browed youth, the budding girl and the good old grandam, still knitting in the warmest place.

The aged woman looked up from her task and, with fingers ever busy, was the next to speak.

"Old folks have their notions," said she, "as well as young ones. You've been wishing and planning and letting your heads run on one thing and another till you've set my mind a-wandering too. Now, what should an old woman wish for, when she can go but a step or two before she comes to her grave? Children, it will haunt me night and day till I tell you."

"What is it, mother?" cried the husband and wife at once.

Then the old woman, with an air of mystery which drew the circle closer round the fire, informed them that she had provided her grave clothes some years before – a nice linen shroud, a cap with a muslin ruff and everything of a finer sort than she had worn since her wedding day. But this evening an old superstition had strangely recurred to her. It used to be said in her younger days that if anything were amiss with a corpse – if only the ruff were not smooth or the cap did not set right – the corpse, in the coffin and beneath the clods, would strive to put up its cold hands and arrange it. The bare thought made her nervous.

"Don't talk so, Grandmother," said the girl, shuddering.

"Now," continued the old woman, with singular earnestness, yet smiling strangely at her own folly, "I want one of you, my children, when your mother is dressed and in the coffin – I want one of you to hold a looking glass over my face. Who knows but I may take a glimpse at myself and see whether all's right?"

"Old and young, we dream of graves and monuments," murmured the stranger youth. "I wonder how mariners feel when the ship is sinking and they, unknown and undistinguished, are to be buried together in the ocean, that wide and nameless sepulchre?"

For a moment the old woman's ghastly conception so engrossed the minds of her hearers that a sound abroad in the night, rising like the roar of a blast, had grown broad, deep and terrible before the fated group were conscious of it. The house and all within it trembled; the foundations of the earth seemed to be shaken, as if this awful sound were the peal of the last trump. Young and old exchanged one wild glance and remained an instant pale, affrighted, without utterance or power to move. Then the same shriek burst simultaneously from all their lips:

"The slide! The slide!"

The simplest words must intimate, but not portray, the unutterable horror of the catastrophe. The victims rushed from their cottage and sought refuge in what they deemed a safer spot, where, in contemplation of such an emergency, a sort of barrier had been reared. Alas! They had quitted their security and fled right into the pathway of destruction. Down came the whole side of the mountain in a cataract of ruin. Just before it reached the house the stream broke into two branches, shivered not a window there but overwhelmed the whole vicinity, blocked up the road and annihilated everything in its dreadful course. Long ere the thunder of that great slide had ceased to roar among the mountains, the mortal agony had been endured and the victims were at peace. Their bodies were never found.

The next morning the light smoke was seen stealing from the cottage chimney up the mountainside. Within, the fire was yet smouldering on the hearth, and the chairs in a circle round it, as if the inhabitants had but gone forth to view the devastation of the slide and would shortly return to thank Heaven for their miraculous escape. All had left separate tokens by which those who had known the family were made to shed a tear for each. Who has not heard their name? The story has been told far and wide, and will for ever be a legend of these mountains. Poets have sung their fate.

There were circumstances which led some to suppose that a stranger had been received into the cottage on this awful night, and had shared the catastrophe of all its inmates; others denied that there were sufficient grounds for such a conjecture. Woe for the high-souled youth with his dream of earthly immortality! His name and person utterly unknown, his history, his way of life, his plans, a mystery never to be solved, his death and his existence equally a doubt – whose was the agony of that death moment?

The Maypole of Merry Mount

There is an admirable foundation for a philosophic romance, in the curious history of the early settlement of Mount Wollaston, or Merry Mount. In the slight sketch here attempted, the facts recorded on the grave pages of our New England annalists have wrought themselves, almost spontaneously, into a sort of allegory. The masques, mummeries and festive customs described in the text are in accordance with the manners of the age. Authority on these points may be found in Strutt's *Book of English Sports and Pastimes*.*

B RIGHT WERE THE DAYS AT MERRY MOUNT, when the Maypole was the banner staff of that gay colony! They who reared it, should their banner be triumphant, were to pour sunshine over New England's rugged hills, and scatter flower seeds throughout the soil. Jollity and gloom were contending for an empire. Midsummer Eve had come, bringing deep verdure to the forest, and roses in her lap, of a more vivid hue than the tender buds of spring. But May, or her mirthful spirit, dwelt all the year round at Merry Mount, sporting with the summer months, and revelling with autumn, and basking in the glow of winter's fireside. Through a world of toil and care she flitted with dreamlike smile, and came hither to find a home among the lightsome hearts of Merry Mount.

Never had the Maypole been so gaily decked as at sunset on Midsummer Eve. This venerated emblem was a pine tree, which had preserved the slender grace of youth, while it equalled the loftiest height of the old wood monarchs. From its top streamed a silken banner, coloured like a rainbow. Down nearly to the ground, the pole was dressed with birchen boughs, and others of the liveliest green, and some silvery leaves, fastened by ribbons that fluttered in fantastic knots of twenty different colours, but no sad ones. Garden flowers and blossoms of the wilderness laughed gladly forth amid the verdure, so fresh and dewy that they must have grown by magic on that happy pine tree. Where this green and flowery splendour terminated, the shaft of the Maypole was stained with the seven brilliant hues of the banner at its top. On the lowest green bough hung an abundant wreath of roses – some that had been gathered in the sunniest spots of the forest, and others, of still richer blush, which the colonists had reared from English seed. Oh people of the Golden Age, the chief of your husbandry was to raise flowers!

But what was the wild throng that stood hand in hand about the Maypole? It could not be, that the fauns and nymphs, when driven from their classic groves and homes of ancient fable, had sought refuge, as all the persecuted did, in the fresh woods of the West. These were Gothic monsters, though perhaps of Grecian ancestry. On the shoulders of a comely youth uprose the head and branching antlers of a stag; a second, human in all other points, had the grim visage of a wolf; a third, still with the trunk and limbs of a mortal man, showed the beard and horns of a venerable he-goat. There was the likeness of a bear erect, brute in all but his hind legs, which were adorned with pink silk stockings. And here again, almost as wondrous, stood a real bear of the dark forest, lending each of his forepaws to the grasp of a human hand and as ready for the dance as any in that circle. His inferior nature rose halfway to meet his companions as they stooped. Other faces wore the similitude of man or woman, but distorted or extravagant, with red noses pendulous before their mouths, which seemed of awful depth and stretched from ear to ear in an eternal fit of laughter. Here might be seen the Salvage* Man, well known in heraldry, hairy as a baboon and girdled with green leaves. By his side, a nobler figure, but still a counterfeit, appeared an Indian hunter, with feathery crest and wampum belt. Many of this strange company wore foolscaps, and had little bells appended to their garments, tinkling with a silvery sound, responsive to the inaudible music of their gleesome spirits. Some youths and maidens were of soberer garb, yet well maintained their places in the irregular throng by the expression of wild revelry upon their features. Such were the colonists of Merry Mount, as they stood in the broad smile of sunset, round their venerated Maypole.

Had a wanderer, bewildered in the melancholy forest, heard their mirth, and stolen a half-affrighted glance, he might have fancied them the crew of Comus,* some already transformed to brutes, some midway between man and beast, and the others rioting in the flow of tipsy jollity that foreran the change. But a band of Puritans who watched the scene, invisible themselves, compared the masques to those devils and ruined souls with whom their superstition peopled the black wilderness.

Within the ring of monsters appeared the two airiest forms that had ever trodden on any more solid footing than a purple and golden cloud. One was a youth in glistening apparel, with a scarf of the rainbow pattern crosswise on his breast. His right hand held a gilded staff, the ensign of high dignity among the revellers, and his left grasped the slender fingers of a fair maiden, not less gaily decorated than himself. Bright roses glowed in contrast with the dark and glossy curls of each, and were scattered round their feet, or had sprung up spontaneously there. Behind this lightsome couple, so close to the Maypole that its boughs shaded his jovial face, stood the figure of an English priest, canonically dressed, yet decked with flowers, in heathen fashion, and wearing a chaplet of the native vine-leaves. By the riot of his rolling eye, and the pagan decorations of his holy garb, he seemed the wildest monster there, and the very Comus of the crew.

"Votaries of the Maypole," cried the flower-decked priest, "merrily, all day long, have the woods echoed to your mirth. But be this your merriest hour, my hearts! Lo, here stand the Lord and Lady of the May, whom I, a clerk of Oxford and high priest of Merry Mount, am presently to join in holy matrimony. Up with your nimble spirits, ye morris dancers, green men and glee maidens, bears and wolves and horned gentlemen! Come; a chorus now, rich with the old mirth of Merry England, and the wilder glee of this fresh forest; and then a dance, to show the youthful pair what life is made of, and how airily they should go through it! All ye that love the Maypole, lend your voices to the nuptial song of the Lord and Lady of the May!"

This wedlock was more serious than most affairs of Merry Mount, where jest and delusion, trick and fantasy kept up a continual carnival. The Lord and Lady of the May, though their titles must be laid down at sunset, were really and truly to be partners for the dance of life, beginning the measure that same bright eve. The wreath of roses that hung from the lowest green bough of the Maypole had been twined for them, and would be thrown over both their heads in symbol of their flowery union. When the priest had spoken, therefore, a riotous uproar burst from the rout of monstrous figures.

"Begin you the stave, reverend sir," cried they all. "And never did the woods ring to such a merry peal, as we of the Maypole shall send up!"

Immediately a prelude of pipe, cithern and viol, touched with practised minstrelsy, began to play from a neighbouring thicket, in such a mirthful cadence that the boughs of the Maypole quivered to the sound. But the May Lord, he of the gilded staff, chancing to look into his Lady's eyes, was wonderstruck at the almost pensive glance that met his own.

"Edith, sweet Lady of the May," whispered he reproachfully, "is yon wreath of roses a garland to hang above our graves, that you look so sad? O Edith, this is our golden time! Tarnish it not by any pensive shadow of the mind, for it may be that nothing of futurity will be brighter than the mere remembrance of what is now passing."

"That was the very thought that saddened me! How came it in your mind too?" said Edith in a still lower tone than he, for it was high treason to be sad at Merry Mount. "Therefore do I sigh amid this festive music. And besides, dear Edgar, I struggle as with a dream, and fancy that these shapes of our jovial friends are visionary, and their mirth unreal, and that we are no true Lord and Lady of the May. What is the mystery in my heart?"

Just then, as if a spell had loosened them, down came a little shower of withering rose leaves from the Maypole. Alas, for the young lovers! No sooner had their hearts glowed with real passion than they were sensible of something vague and unsubstantial in their former pleasures and felt a dreary presentiment of inevitable change. From the moment that they truly loved, they had subjected themselves to earth's doom of care and sorrow, and troubled joy, and had no more a home at Merry Mount. That was Edith's mystery. Now leave we the priest to marry them, and the masquers to sport round the Maypole, till the last sunbeam be withdrawn from its summit, and the shadows of the forest mingle gloomily in the dance. Meanwhile, we may discover who these gay people were.

Two hundred years ago, and more, the Old World and its inhabitants became mutually weary of each other. Men voyaged by thousands to the West: some to barter glass beads, and suchlike jewels, for the furs of the Indian hunter; some to conquer virgin empires; and one stern band to pray. But none of these motives had much weight with the colonists of Merry Mount. Their leaders were men who had sported so long with life that, when Thought and Wisdom came, even these unwelcome guests were led astray by the crowd of vanities which they should have put to flight. Erring Thought and perverted Wisdom were made to put on masques, and play the fool. The men of whom we speak, after losing the heart's fresh gaiety, imagined a wild philosophy of pleasure, and came hither to act out their latest daydream. They gathered followers from all that giddy tribe, whose whole life is like the festal days of soberer men. In their train were minstrels, not unknown in London streets; wandering players, whose theatres had been the halls of noblemen; mummers, rope-dancers and mountebanks, who would long be missed at wakes, church ales and fairs – in a word, mirth-makers of every sort, such as abounded in that age, but now began to be discountenanced by the rapid growth of Puritanism. Light had their footsteps been on land, and as lightly they came across the sea. Many had been maddened by their previous troubles into a gay despair; others were as madly gay in the flush of youth, like the May Lord and his Lady; but whatever might be the quality of their mirth, old and young were gay at Merry Mount. The young deemed themselves happy. The elder spirits, if they knew that mirth was but the counterfeit of happiness, yet followed the false shadow wilfully, because at least her garments glittered brightest. Sworn triflers of a lifetime, they would not venture among the sober truths of life, not even to be truly blest.

All the hereditary pastimes of Old England were transplanted hither. The King of Christmas was duly crowned, and the Lord of Misrule bore potent sway. On the eve of St John,* they felled whole acres of the forest to make bonfires, and danced by the blaze all night, crowned with garlands and throwing flowers into the flame. At harvest time, though their crop was of the smallest, they made an image with the sheaves of Indian corn, and wreathed it with autumnal garlands, and bore it home triumphantly. But what chiefly characterized the colonists of Merry Mount was their veneration for the Maypole. It has made their true history a poet's tale. Spring decked the hallowed emblem with young blossoms and fresh green boughs; summer brought roses of the deepest blush, and the perfected foliage of the forest; autumn enriched it with that red and yellow gorgeousness which converts each wildwood leaf into a painted flower; and winter silvered it with sleet, and hung it round with icicles, till it flashed in the cold sunshine, itself a frozen sunbeam. Thus each alternate season did homage to the Maypole, and paid it a tribute of its own richest splendour. Its votaries danced round it, once, at least, in every month; sometimes they called it their religion, or their altar; but always, it was the banner staff of Merry Mount.

Unfortunately, there were men in the New World of a sterner faith than these Maypole worshippers. Not far from Merry Mount was a settlement of Puritans, most dismal wretches, who said their prayers before daylight, and then wrought in the forest or the cornfield till evening made it prayer time again. Their weapons were always at hand, to shoot down the straggling savage. When they met in conclave, it was never to keep up the old English mirth, but to hear sermons three hours long, or to proclaim bounties on the heads of wolves and the scalps of Indians. Their festivals were fast days, and their chief pastime the singing of psalms. Woe to the youth or maiden who did but dream of a dance! The selectman nodded to the constable; and there sat the light-heeled reprobate in the stocks; or if he danced, it was round the whipping post, which might be termed the Puritan Maypole.

A party of these grim Puritans, toiling through the difficult woods, each with a horse-load of iron armour to burden his footsteps, would sometimes draw near the sunny precincts of Merry Mount. There were the silken colonists, sporting round their Maypole; perhaps teaching a bear to dance, or striving to communicate their mirth to the grave Indian; or masquerading in the skins of deer and wolves, which they had hunted for that especial purpose. Often the whole colony were playing at blindman's buff, magistrates and all with their eyes bandaged, except a single scapegoat, whom the blinded sinners pursued by the tinkling of the bells at his garments. Once, it is said, they were seen following a flower-decked corpse, with merriment and festive music, to his grave. But did the dead man laugh? In their quietest times, they sang ballads and told tales for the edification of their pious visitors; or perplexed them with juggling tricks; or grinned at them through horse collars; and when sport itself grew wearisome, they made game of their own stupidity and began a yawning match. At the very least of these enormities, the men of iron shook their heads and frowned so darkly that the revellers looked up, imagining that a momentary cloud had overcast the sunshine, which was to be perpetual there. On the other hand, the Puritans affirmed that, when a psalm was pealing from their place of worship, the echo which the forest sent them back seemed often like the chorus of a jolly catch, closing with a roar of laughter. Who but the fiend, and his bond slaves, the crew of Merry Mount, had thus disturbed them? In due time, a feud arose, stern and bitter on one side and as serious on the other as anything could be among such light spirits as had sworn allegiance to the Maypole. The future complexion of New England was involved in this important quarrel. Should the grizzly saints establish their jurisdiction over the gay sinners, then would their spirits darken all the clime, and make it a land of clouded visages, of hard toil, of sermon and psalm for ever. But should the banner staff of Merry Mount be fortunate, sunshine would break upon the hills, and flowers would beautify the forest, and late posterity do homage to the Maypole.

After these authentic passages from history, we return to the nuptials of the Lord and Lady of the May. Alas! We have delayed too long, and must darken our tale too suddenly. As we glance again at the Maypole, a solitary sunbeam is fading from the summit, and leaves only a faint, golden tinge, blended with the hues of the rainbow banner. Even that dim light is now withdrawn, relinquishing the whole domain of Merry Mount to the evening gloom, which has rushed so instantaneously from the black surrounding woods. But some of these black shadows have rushed forth in human shape.

Yes, with the setting sun, the last day of mirth had passed from Merry Mount. The ring of gay masquers was disordered and broken; the stag lowered his antlers in dismay; the wolf grew weaker than a lamb; the bells of the morris dancers tinkled with tremulous affright. The Puritans had played a characteristic part in the Maypole mummeries. Their darksome figures were intermixed with the wild shapes of their foes, and made the scene a picture of the moment, when waking thoughts start up amid the scattered fantasies of a dream. The leader of the hostile party stood in the centre of the circle, while the rout of monsters cowered around him, like evil spirits in the presence of a dread magician. No fantastic foolery could look him in the face. So stern was the energy of his aspect, that the whole man, visage, frame and soul, seemed wrought of iron, gifted with life and thought, yet all of one substance with his headpiece and breastplate. It was the Puritan of Puritans; it was Endicott himself!

"Stand off, priest of Baal!" said he, with a grim frown, and laying no reverent hand upon the surplice. "I know thee, Blackstone!* Thou art the man who couldst not abide the rule even of thine own corrupted church, and hast come hither to preach iniquity, and to give example of it in thy life. But now shall it be seen that the Lord hath sanctified this wilderness for his peculiar people. Woe unto them that would defile it! And first, for this flower-decked abomination, the altar of thy worship!"

And with his keen sword Endicott assaulted the hallowed Maypole. Nor long did it resist his arm. It groaned with a dismal sound; it showered leaves and rosebuds upon the remorseless enthusiast; and finally, with all its green boughs, and ribbons, and flowers, symbolic of departed pleasures, down fell the banner staff of Merry Mount. As it sank, tradition says, the evening sky drew darker, and the woods threw forth a more sombre shadow.

"There," cried Endicott, looking triumphantly on his work, "there lies the only Maypole in New England! The thought is strong within me that, by its fall, is shadowed forth the fate of light and idle mirth-makers, amongst us and our posterity. Amen, saith John Endicott."

"Amen!" echoed his followers.

But the votaries of the Maypole gave one groan for their idol. At the sound, the Puritan leader glanced at the crew of Comus, each a figure of broad mirth, yet, at this moment, strangely expressive of sorrow and dismay.

"Valiant captain," quoth Peter Palfrey, the Ancient* of the band, "what order shall be taken with the prisoners?"

"I thought not to repent me of cutting down a Maypole," replied Endicott, "yet now I could find in my heart to plant it again, and give each of these bestial pagans one other dance round their idol. It would have served rarely for a whipping post!"

"But there are pine trees enow," suggested the lieutenant.

"True, good Ancient," said the leader. "Wherefore, bind the heathen crew, and bestow on them a small matter of stripes apiece, as earnest of our future justice. Set some of the rogues in the stocks to rest themselves, so soon as Providence shall bring us to one of our own well-ordered settlements, where such accommodations may be found. Further penalties, such as branding and cropping of ears, shall be thought of hereafter."

"How many stripes for the priest?" enquired Ancient Palfrey.

"None as yet," answered Endicott, bending his iron frown upon the culprit. "It must be for the Great and General Court to determine whether stripes and long imprisonment, and other grievous penalty, may atone for his transgressions. Let him look to himself! For such as violate our civil order, it may be permitted us to show mercy. But woe to the wretch that troubleth our religion!"

"And this dancing bear," resumed the officer. "Must he share the stripes of his fellows?"

"Shoot him through the head!" said the energetic Puritan. "I suspect witchcraft in the beast."

"Here be a couple of shining ones," continued Peter Palfrey, pointing his weapon at the Lord and Lady of the May. "They seem to be of high station among these misdoers. Methinks their dignity will not be fitted with less than a double share of stripes."

Endicott rested on his sword, and closely surveyed the dress and aspect of the hapless pair. There they stood, pale, downcast and apprehensive. Yet there was an air of mutual support, and of pure affection, seeking aid and giving it, that showed them to be man and wife, with the sanction of a priest upon their love. The youth, in the peril of the moment, had dropped his gilded staff, and thrown his arm about the Lady of the May, who leant against his breast, too lightly to burden him, but with weight enough to express that their destinies were linked together, for good or evil. They looked first at each other, and then into the grim captain's face. There they stood, in the first hour of wedlock, while the idle pleasures, of which their companions were the emblems, had given place to the sternest cares of life, personified by the dark Puritans.

But never had their youthful beauty seemed so pure and high as when its glow was chastened by adversity.

"Youth," said Endicott, "ye stand in an evil case, thou and thy maiden wife. Make ready presently, for I am minded that ye shall both have a token to remember your wedding day!"

"Stern man," cried the May Lord, "how can I move thee? Were the means at hand, I would resist to the death. Being powerless, I entreat! Do with me as thou wilt, but let Edith go untouched!"

"Not so," replied the immitigable zealot. "We are not wont to show an idle courtesy to that sex which requireth the stricter discipline. What sayest thou, maid? Shall thy silken bridegroom suffer thy share of the penalty, besides his own?"

"Be it death," said Edith, "and lay it all on me!"

Truly, as Endicott had said, the poor lovers stood in a woeful case. Their foes were triumphant, their friends captive and abased, their home desolate, the benighted wilderness around them, and rigorous destiny, in the shape of the Puritan leader, their only guide. Yet the deepening twilight could not altogether conceal that the iron man was softened; he smiled at the fair spectacle of early love; he almost sighed for the inevitable blight of early hopes.

"The troubles of life have come hastily on this young couple," observed Endicott. "We will see how they comport themselves under their present trials, ere we burden them with greater. If, among the spoil, there be any garments of a more decent fashion, let them be put upon this May Lord and his Lady, instead of their glistening vanities. Look to it, some of you."

"And shall not the youth's hair be cut?" asked Peter Palfrey, looking with abhorrence at the lovelock and long glossy curls of the young man.

"Crop it forthwith, and that in the true pumpkin-shell fashion," answered the captain. "Then bring them along with us, but more gently than their fellows. There be qualities in the youth which may make him valiant to fight, and sober to toil, and pious to pray; and in the maiden that may fit her to become a mother in our Israel, bringing up babes in better nurture than her own hath been. Nor think ye, young ones, that they are the happiest, even in our lifetime of a moment, who misspend it in dancing round a Maypole!"

And Endicott, the severest Puritan of all who laid the rock foundation of New England, lifted the wreath of roses from the ruin of the Maypole and threw it, with his own gauntleted hand, over the heads of the Lord and Lady of the May. It was a deed of prophecy. As the moral gloom of the world overpowers all systematic gaiety, even so was their home of wild mirth made desolate amid the sad forest. They returned to it no more. But, as their flowery garland was wreathed of the brightest roses that had grown there, so, in the tie that united them, were intertwined all the purest and best of their early joys. They went heavenward, supporting each other along the difficult path which it was their lot to tread, and never wasted one regretful thought on the vanities of Merry Mount.

The Minister's Black Veil

A *Parable**

T HE SEXTON STOOD IN THE PORCH of Milford meeting house, pulling busily at the bell rope. The old people of the village came stooping along the street. Children with bright faces tripped merrily beside their parents or mimicked a graver gait, in the conscious dignity of their Sunday clothes. Spruce bachelors looked sidelong at the pretty maidens, and fancied that the Sabbath sunshine made them prettier than on weekdays. When the throng had mostly streamed into the porch, the sexton began to toll the bell, keeping his eye on the Reverend Mr Hooper's door. The first glimpse of the clergyman's figure was the signal for the bell to cease its summons.

"But what has good Parson Hooper got upon his face?" cried the sexton in astonishment.

All within hearing immediately turned about and beheld the semblance of Mr Hooper, pacing slowly his meditative way towards the meeting house. With one accord they started, expressing more wonder than if some stranger minister were coming to dust the cushions of Mr Hooper's pulpit.

"Are you sure it is our parson?" enquired Goodman Gray of the sexton.

"Of a certainty it is good Mr Hooper," replied the sexton. "He was to have exchanged pulpits with Parson Shute, of Westbury; but Parson Shute sent to excuse himself yesterday, being to preach a funeral sermon."

The cause of so much amazement may appear sufficiently slight. Mr Hooper, a gentlemanly person of about thirty, though still a bachelor, was dressed with due clerical neatness, as if a careful wife had starched his band and brushed the weekly dust from his Sunday's garb. There was but one thing remarkable in his appearance. Swathed about his forehead, and hanging down over his face, so low as to be shaken by his breath, Mr Hooper had on a black veil. On a nearer view, it seemed to consist of two folds of crape, which entirely concealed his features, except the mouth and chin, but probably did not intercept his sight further than to give a darkened aspect to all living and inanimate things. With this gloomy shade before him, good Mr Hooper walked onward, at a slow and quiet pace, stooping somewhat and looking on the ground, as is customary with abstracted men, yet nodding kindly to those of his parishioners who still waited on the meeting-house steps. But so wonderstruck were they that his greeting hardly met with a return.

"I can't really feel as if good Mr Hooper's face was behind that piece of crape," said the sexton.

"I don't like it," muttered an old woman, as she hobbled into the meeting house. "He has changed himself into something awful, only by hiding his face."

"Our parson has gone mad!" cried Goodman Gray, following him across the threshold.

A rumour of some unaccountable phenomenon had preceded Mr Hooper into the meeting house, and set all the congregation astir. Few could refrain from twisting their heads towards the door; many stood upright, and turned directly about; while several little boys clambered upon the seats and came down again with a terrible racket. There was a general bustle, a rustling of the women's gowns and shuffling of the men's feet, greatly at variance with that hushed repose which should attend the entrance of the minister. But Mr Hooper appeared not to notice the perturbation of his people. He entered with an almost noiseless step, bent his head mildly to the pews on each side and bowed as he passed his oldest parishioner, a white-haired great-grandsire who occupied an armchair in the centre of the aisle. It was strange to observe how slowly this venerable man became conscious of something singular in the appearance of his pastor. He seemed not fully to partake of the prevailing wonder, till Mr Hooper had ascended the stairs and showed himself in the pulpit, face to face with his congregation, except for the black veil. The mysterious emblem was never once withdrawn. It shook with his measured breath as he gave out the psalm; it threw its obscurity between him and the holy page, as he read the Scriptures; and while he prayed, the veil lay heavily on his uplifted countenance. Did he seek to hide it from the dread Being whom he was addressing?

Such was the effect of this simple piece of crape that more than one woman of delicate nerves was forced to leave the meeting house. Yet perhaps the pale-faced congregation was almost as fearful a sight to the minister as his black veil to them.

Mr Hooper had the reputation of a good preacher, but not an energetic one: he strove to win his people heavenward by mild, persuasive influences rather than to drive them thither by the thunders of the Word. The sermon which he now delivered was marked by the same characteristics of style and manner as the general series of his pulpit oratory. But there was something, either in the sentiment of the discourse itself, or in the imagination of the auditors, which made it greatly the most powerful effort that they had ever heard from their pastor's lips. It was tinged, rather more darkly than usual, with the gentle gloom of Mr Hooper's temperament. The subject had reference to secret sin, and those sad mysteries which we hide from our nearest and dearest, and would fain conceal from our own consciousness, even forgetting that the Omniscient can detect them. A subtle power was breathed into his words. Each member of the congregation, the most innocent girl and the man of hardened breast, felt as if the preacher had crept upon them, behind his awful veil, and discovered their hoarded iniquity of deed or thought. Many spread their clasped hands on their bosoms. There was nothing terrible in what Mr Hooper said – at least, no violence – and yet, with every tremor of his melancholy voice, the hearers quaked. An unsought pathos came hand in hand with awe. So sensible were the audience of some unwonted attribute in their minister that they longed for a breath of wind to blow aside the veil, almost believing that a stranger's visage would be discovered, though the form, gesture and voice were those of Mr Hooper.

At the close of the service, the people hurried out with indecorous confusion, eager to communicate their pent-up amazement, and conscious of lighter spirits, the moment they lost sight of the black veil. Some gathered in little circles, huddled closely together, with their mouths all whispering in the centre; some went homeward alone, wrapt in silent meditation; some talked loudly, and profaned the Sabbath day with ostentatious laughter. A few shook their sagacious heads, intimating that they could penetrate the mystery; while one or two affirmed that there was no mystery at all, but only that Mr Hooper's eyes were so weakened by the midnight lamp, as to require a shade. After a brief interval, forth came good Mr Hooper also, in the rear of his flock. Turning his veiled face from one group to another, he paid due reverence to the hoary heads, saluted the middle-aged with kind dignity, as their friend and spiritual guide, greeted the young with mingled authority and love and laid his hands on the little children's heads to bless them. Such was always his custom on the Sabbath day. Strange and bewildered looks repaid him for his courtesy. None, as on former occasions, aspired to the honour of walking by their pastor's side. Old Squire Saunders, doubtless by an accidental lapse of memory, neglected to invite Mr Hooper to his table, where the good clergyman had been wont to bless the food almost every Sunday since his settlement. He returned, therefore, to the parsonage and, at the moment of closing the door, was observed to look back upon the people, all of whom had their eyes fixed upon the minister. A sad smile gleamed faintly from beneath the black veil, and flickered about his mouth, glimmering as he disappeared.

"How strange," said a lady, "that a simple black veil, such as any woman might wear on her bonnet, should become such a terrible thing on Mr Hooper's face!"

"Something must surely be amiss with Mr Hooper's intellects," observed her husband, the physician of the village. "But the strangest part of the affair is the effect of this vagary, even on a sober-minded man like myself. The black veil, though it covers only our pastor's face, throws its influence over his whole person, and makes him ghost-like from head to foot. Do you not feel it so?"

"Truly do I," replied the lady, "and I would not be alone with him for the world. I wonder he is not afraid to be alone with himself!"

"Men sometimes are so," said her husband.

The afternoon service was attended with similar circumstances. At its conclusion, the bell tolled for the funeral of a young lady. The relatives and friends were assembled in the house, and the more distant acquaintances stood about the door, speaking of the good qualities of the deceased, when their talk was interrupted by the appearance of Mr Hooper, still covered with his black veil. It was now an appropriate emblem. The clergyman stepped into the room where the corpse was laid and bent over the coffin, to take a last farewell of his deceased parishioner. As he stooped, the veil hung straight down from his forehead, so that, if her eyelids had not been closed for ever, the dead maiden might have seen his face. Could Mr Hooper be fearful of her glance, that he so hastily caught back the black veil? A person who watched the interview between the dead and living scrupled not to affirm that, at the instant when the clergyman's features were disclosed, the corpse had slightly shuddered, rustling the shroud and muslin cap, though the countenance retained the composure of death. A superstitious old woman was the only witness of this prodigy. From the coffin Mr Hooper passed into the chamber of the mourners, and thence to the head of the staircase, to make the funeral prayer. It was a tender and heart-dissolving prayer, full of sorrow, yet so imbued with celestial hopes that the music of a heavenly harp, swept by the fingers of the dead, seemed faintly to be heard among the saddest accents of the minister. The people trembled, though they but darkly understood him when he prayed that they, and himself, and all of mortal race, might be ready, as he trusted this young maiden had been, for the dreadful hour that should snatch the veil from their faces. The bearers went heavily forth, and the mourners followed, saddening all the street, with the dead before them, and Mr Hooper in his black veil behind.

"Why do you look back?" said one in the procession to his partner.

"I had a fancy," replied she, "that the minister and the maiden's spirit were walking hand in hand."

"And so had I, at the same moment," said the other.

That night, the handsomest couple in Milford village were to be joined in wedlock. Though reckoned a melancholy man, Mr Hooper had a placid cheerfulness for such occasions, which often excited a sympathetic smile, where livelier merriment would have been thrown away. There was no quality of his disposition which made him more beloved than this. The company at the wedding awaited his arrival with impatience, trusting that the strange awe which had gathered over him throughout the day would now be dispelled. But such was not the result. When Mr Hooper came, the first thing that their eyes rested on was the same horrible black veil which had added deeper gloom to the funeral and could portend nothing but evil to the wedding. Such was its immediate effect on the guests, that a cloud seemed to have rolled duskily from beneath the black crape and dimmed the light of the candles. The bridal pair stood up before the minister. But the bride's cold fingers quivered in the tremulous hand of the bridegroom, and her deathlike paleness caused a whisper that the maiden who had been buried a few hours before was come from her grave to be married. If ever another wedding were so dismal, it was that famous one where they tolled the wedding knell.* After performing the ceremony, Mr Hooper raised a glass of wine to his lips, wishing happiness to the new-married couple, in a strain of mild pleasantry that ought to have brightened the features of the guests, like a cheerful gleam from the hearth. At that instant, catching a glimpse of his figure in the looking glass, the black veil involved his own spirit in the horror with which it overwhelmed all others. His frame shuddered – his lips grew white – he spilt the untasted wine upon the carpet – and rushed forth into the darkness. For the Earth, too, had on her Black Veil.

The next day, the whole village of Milford talked of little else than Parson Hooper's black veil. That, and the mystery concealed behind it, supplied a topic for discussion between acquaintances meeting in the street and good women gossiping at their open windows. It was the first item of news that the tavern-keeper told to his guests. The children babbled of it on their way to school. One imitative little imp covered his face with an old black handkerchief, thereby so affrighting his playmates that the panic seized himself, and he well-nigh lost his wits by his own waggery.

It was remarkable that, of all the busybodies and impertinent people in the parish, not one ventured to put the plain question to Mr Hooper wherefore he did this thing. Hitherto, whenever there appeared the slightest call for such interference, he had never lacked advisers, nor shown himself averse to be guided by their judgement. If he erred at all, it was by so painful a degree of self-distrust that even the mildest censure would lead him to consider an indifferent action as a crime. Yet, though so well acquainted with this amiable weakness, no individual among his parishioners chose to make the black veil a subject of friendly remonstrance. There was a feeling of dread, neither plainly confessed nor carefully concealed, which caused each to shift the responsibility upon another, till at length it was found expedient to send a deputation of the church in order to deal with Mr Hooper about the mystery before it should grow into a scandal. Never did an embassy so ill discharge its duties. The minister received them with friendly courtesy, but became silent, after they were seated, leaving to his visitors the whole burden of introducing their important business. The topic, it might be supposed, was obvious enough. There was the black veil swathed round Mr Hooper's forehead and concealing every feature above his placid mouth, on which, at times, they could perceive the glimmering of a melancholy smile. But that piece of crape, to their imagination, seemed to hang down before his heart, the symbol of a fearful secret between him and them. Were the veil but cast aside, they might speak freely of it, but not till then. Thus they sat a considerable time, speechless, confused and shrinking uneasily from Mr Hooper's eye, which they felt to be fixed upon them with an invisible glance. Finally, the deputies returned abashed to their constituents, pronouncing the matter too weighty to be handled, except by a council of the churches, if, indeed, it might not require a general synod.

But there was one person in the village unappalled by the awe with which the black veil had impressed all beside herself. When the deputies returned without an explanation, or even venturing to demand one, she, with the calm energy of her character, determined to chase away the strange cloud that appeared to be settling round Mr Hooper every moment more darkly than before. As his plighted wife, it should be her privilege to know what the black veil concealed. At the minister's first visit, therefore, she entered upon the subject, with a direct simplicity which made the task easier both for him and her. After he had seated himself, she fixed her eyes steadfastly upon the veil, but could discern nothing of the dreadful gloom that had so overawed the multitude; it was but a double fold of crape, hanging down from his forehead to his mouth, and slightly stirring with his breath.

"No," said she aloud, and smiling, "there is nothing terrible in this piece of crape, except that it hides a face which I am always glad to look upon. Come, good sir, let the sun shine from behind the cloud. First lay aside your black veil: then tell me why you put it on."

Mr Hooper's smile glimmered faintly.

"There is an hour to come," said he, "when all of us shall cast aside our veils. Take it not amiss, beloved friend, if I wear this piece of crape till then."

"Your words are a mystery too," returned the young lady. "Take away the veil from them, at least."

"Elizabeth, I will," said he, "so far as my vow may suffer me. Know, then, this veil is a type and a symbol, and I am bound to wear it ever, both in light and darkness, in solitude and before the gaze of multitudes, and as with strangers, so with my familiar friends. No mortal eye will see it withdrawn. This dismal shade must separate me from the world: even you, Elizabeth, can never come behind it!"

"What grievous affliction hath befallen you," she earnestly enquired, "that you should thus darken your eyes for ever?"

"If it be a sign of mourning," replied Mr Hooper, "I, perhaps, like most other mortals, have sorrows dark enough to be typified by a black veil."

"But what if the world will not believe that it is the type of an innocent sorrow?" urged Elizabeth. "Beloved and respected as you are, there may be whispers that you hide your face under the consciousness of secret sin. For the sake of your holy office, do away this scandal!"

The colour rose into her cheeks as she intimated the nature of the rumours that were already abroad in the village. But Mr Hooper's mildness did not forsake him. He even smiled again – that same sad smile, which always appeared like a faint glimmering of light, proceeding from the obscurity beneath the veil.

"If I hide my face for sorrow, there is cause enough," he merely replied, "and if I cover it for secret sin, what mortal might not do the same?"

And with this gentle but unconquerable obstinacy did he resist all her entreaties. At length Elizabeth sat silent. For a few moments she appeared lost in thought, considering, probably, what new methods might be tried to withdraw her lover from so dark a fantasy, which, if it had no other meaning, was perhaps a symptom of mental disease. Though of a firmer character than his own, the tears rolled down her cheeks. But, in an instant, as it were, a new feeling took the place of sorrow; her eyes were fixed insensibly on the black veil, when, like a sudden twilight in the air, its terrors fell around her. She arose, and stood trembling before him.

"And do you feel it then at last?" said he mournfully.

She made no reply, but covered her eyes with her hand and turned to leave the room. He rushed forward and caught her arm.

"Have patience with me, Elizabeth!" cried he passionately.

"Do not desert me, though this veil must be between us here on earth. Be mine, and hereafter there shall be no veil over my face, no darkness between our souls! It is but a mortal veil – it is not for eternity! Oh, you know not how lonely I am, and how frightened, to be alone behind my black veil! Do not leave me in this miserable obscurity for ever!"

"Lift the veil but once, and look me in the face," said she.

"Never! It cannot be!" replied Mr Hooper.

"Then, farewell!" said Elizabeth.

She withdrew her arm from his grasp, and slowly departed, pausing at the door, to give one long, shuddering gaze that seemed almost to penetrate the mystery of the black veil. But, even amid his grief, Mr Hooper smiled to think that only a material emblem had separated him from happiness, though the horrors which it shadowed forth must be drawn darkly between the fondest of lovers.

From that time no attempts were made to remove Mr Hooper's black veil or, by a direct appeal, to discover the secret which it was supposed to hide. By persons who claimed a superiority to popular prejudice it was reckoned merely an eccentric whim, such as often mingles with the sober actions of men otherwise rational, and tinges them all with its own semblance of insanity. But with the multitude, good Mr Hooper was irreparably a bugbear. He could not walk the street with any peace of mind, so conscious was he that the gentle and timid would turn aside to avoid him, and that others would make it a point of hardihood to throw themselves in his way. The impertinence of the latter class compelled him to give up his customary walk, at sunset, to the burial ground; for when he leant pensively over the gate there would always be faces behind the gravestones, peeping at his black veil. A fable went the rounds that the stare of the dead people drove him thence. It grieved him, to the very depth of his kind heart, to observe how the children fled from his approach, breaking up their merriest sports, while his melancholy figure was yet afar off. Their instinctive dread caused him to feel, more strongly than aught else, that a preternatural horror was interwoven with the threads of the black crape. In truth, his own antipathy to the veil was known to be so great that he never willingly passed before a mirror, nor stooped to drink at a still fountain, lest, in its peaceful bosom, he should be affrighted by himself. This was what gave plausibility to the whispers that Mr Hooper's conscience tortured him for some great crime too horrible to be entirely concealed, or otherwise than so obscurely intimated. Thus, from beneath the black veil there rolled a cloud into the sunshine, an ambiguity of sin or sorrow, which enveloped the poor minister, so that love or sympathy could never reach him. It was said that ghost and fiend consorted with him there. With self-shudderings and outward terrors, he walked continually in its shadow, groping darkly within his own soul, or gazing through a medium that saddened the whole world. Even the lawless wind, it was believed, respected his dreadful secret, and never blew aside the veil. But still good Mr Hooper sadly smiled at the pale visages of the worldly throng as he passed by.

Among all its bad influences, the black veil had the one desirable effect of making its wearer a very efficient clergyman. By the aid of his mysterious emblem – for there was no other apparent cause – he became a man of awful power, over souls that were in agony for sin. His converts always regarded him with a dread peculiar to themselves, affirming, though but figuratively, that, before he brought them to celestial light, they had been with him behind the black veil. Its gloom, indeed, enabled him to sympathize with all dark affections. Dying sinners cried aloud for Mr Hooper, and would not yield their breath till he appeared; though ever, as he stooped to whisper consolation, they shuddered at the veiled face so near their own. Such were the terrors of the black veil, even when Death had bared his visage! Strangers came long distances to attend service at his church, with the mere idle purpose of gazing at his figure, because it was forbidden them to behold his face. But many were made to quake ere they departed! Once, during Governor Belcher's* administration, Mr Hooper was appointed to preach the election sermon. Covered with his black veil, he stood before the chief magistrate, the council and the representatives, and wrought so deep an impression that the legislative measures of that year were characterized by all the gloom and piety of our earliest ancestral sway.

In this manner Mr Hooper spent a long life, irreproachable in outward act, yet shrouded in dismal suspicions; kind and loving, though unloved, and dimly feared; a man apart from men, shunned in their health and joy, but ever summoned to their aid in mortal anguish. As years wore on, shedding their snows above his sable veil, he acquired a name throughout the New England churches, and they called him Father Hooper. Nearly all his parishioners, who were of mature age when he was settled, had been borne away by many a funeral: he had one congregation in the church, and a more crowded one in the churchyard; and having wrought so late into the evening, and done his work so well, it was now good Father Hooper's turn to rest.

Several persons were visible by the shaded candlelight in the death chamber of the old clergyman. Natural connections he had none. But there was the decorously grave, though unmoved physician, seeking only to mitigate the last pangs of the patient whom he could not save. There were the deacons, and other eminently pious members of his church. There, also, was the Reverend Mr Clark, of Westbury, a young and zealous divine, who had ridden in haste to pray by the bedside of the expiring minister. There was the nurse, no hired handmaiden of death, but one whose calm affection had endured thus long in secrecy, in solitude, amid the chill of age, and would not perish, even at the dying hour. Who, but Elizabeth! And there lay the hoary head of good Father Hooper upon the death pillow, with the black veil still swathed about his brow, and reaching down over his face, so that each more difficult gasp of his faint breath caused it to stir. All through life that piece of crape had hung between him and the world; it had separated him from cheerful brotherhood and woman's love, and kept him in that saddest of all prisons, his own heart; and still it lay upon his face, as if to deepen the gloom of his darksome chamber, and shade him from the sunshine of eternity.

For some time previous, his mind had been confused, wavering doubtfully between the past and the present, and hovering forward, as it were, at intervals, into the indistinctness of the world to come. There had been feverish turns, which tossed him from side to side, and wore away what little strength he had. But in his most convulsive struggles, and in the wildest vagaries of his intellect, when no other thought retained its sober influence, he still showed an awful solicitude lest the black veil should slip aside. Even if his bewildered soul could have forgotten, there was a faithful woman at his pillow, who, with averted eyes, would have covered that aged face, which she had last beheld in the comeliness of manhood. At length the death-stricken old man lay quietly in the torpor of mental and bodily exhaustion, with an imperceptible pulse, and breath that grew fainter and fainter, except when a long, deep and irregular inspiration seemed to prelude the flight of his spirit.

The minister of Westbury approached the bedside.

"Venerable Father Hooper," said he, "the moment of your release is at hand. Are you ready for the lifting of the veil that shuts in time from eternity?"

Father Hooper at first replied merely by a feeble motion of his head; then, apprehensive, perhaps, that his meaning might be doubtful, he exerted himself to speak.

"Yea," said he, in faint accents, "my soul hath a patient weariness until that veil be lifted."

"And is it fitting," resumed the Reverend Mr Clark, "that a man so given to prayer, of such a blameless example, holy in deed and thought, so far as mortal judgement may pronounce – is it fitting that a father in the church should leave a shadow on his memory that may seem to blacken a life so pure? I pray you, my venerable brother, let not this thing be! Suffer us to be gladdened by your triumphant aspect, as you go to your reward. Before the veil of eternity be lifted, let me cast aside this black veil from your face!"

And thus speaking, the Reverend Mr Clark bent forward to reveal the mystery of so many years. But, exerting a sudden energy that made all the beholders stand aghast, Father Hooper snatched both his hands from beneath the bedclothes, and pressed them strongly on the black veil, resolute to struggle if the minister of Westbury would contend with a dying man.

"Never!" cried the veiled clergyman. "On earth, never!"

"Dark old man!" exclaimed the affrighted minister. "With what horrible crime upon your soul are you now passing to the judgement?"

Father Hooper's breath heaved; it rattled in his throat; but, with a mighty effort, grasping forward with his hands, he caught hold of life, and held it back till he should speak. He even raised himself in bed; and there he sat, shivering with the arms of death around him, while the black veil hung down, awful, at that last moment, in the gathered terrors of a lifetime. And yet the faint, sad smile, so often there, now seemed to glimmer from its obscurity, and linger on Father Hooper's lips.

"Why do you tremble at me alone?" cried he, turning his veiled face round the circle of pale spectators. "Tremble also at each other! Have men avoided me, and women shown no pity, and children screamed and fled, only for my black veil? What, but the mystery which it obscurely typifies, has made this piece of crape so awful? When the friend shows his inmost heart to his friend; the lover to his best beloved; when man does not vainly shrink from the eye of his Creator, loathsomely treasuring up the secret of his sin; then deem me a monster, for the symbol beneath which I have lived, and die! I look around me, and – lo! – on every visage a Black Veil!"

While his auditors shrank from one another, in mutual affright, Father Hooper fell back upon his pillow, a veiled corpse, with a faint smile lingering on the lips. Still veiled, they laid him in his coffin and a veiled corpse they bore him to the grave. The grass of many years has sprung up and withered on that grave, the burial stone is moss-grown, and good Mr Hooper's face is dust – but awful is still the thought that it mouldered beneath the Black Veil!

Dr Heidegger's Experiment

T HAT VERY SINGULAR MAN, old Dr Heidegger, once invited four venerable friends to meet him in his study. There were three white-bearded gentlemen, Mr Medbourne, Colonel Killigrew and Mr Gascoigne, and a withered gentlewoman, whose name was the Widow Wycherly. They were all melancholy old creatures, who had been unfortunate in life, and whose greatest misfortune it was that they were not long ago in their graves. Mr Medbourne, in the vigour of his age, had been a prosperous merchant, but had lost his all by a frantic speculation, and was now little better than a mendicant. Colonel Killigrew had wasted his best years, and his health and substance, in the pursuit of sinful pleasures, which had given birth to a brood of pains, such as the gout, and divers other torments of soul and body. Mr Gascoigne was a ruined politician, a man of evil fame, or at least had been so till time had buried him from the knowledge of the present generation and made him obscure instead of infamous. As for the Widow Wycherly, tradition tells us that she was a great beauty in her day; but, for a long while past, she had lived in deep seclusion, on account of certain scandalous stories which had prejudiced the gentry of the town against her. It is a circumstance worth mentioning that each of these three old gentlemen, Mr Medbourne, Colonel Killigrew and Mr Gascoigne, were early lovers of the Widow Wycherly, and had once been on the point of cutting each other's throats for her sake. And, before proceeding farther, I will merely hint that Dr Heidegger and all his four guests were sometimes thought to be a little beside themselves – as is not unfrequently the case with old people, when worried either by present troubles or woeful recollections.

"My dear old friends," said Dr Heidegger, motioning them to be seated, "I am desirous of your assistance in one of those little experiments with which I amuse myself here in my study."

If all stories were true, Dr Heidegger's study must have been a very curious place. It was a dim, old-fashioned chamber, festooned with cobwebs and besprinkled with antique dust. Around the walls stood several oaken bookcases, the lower shelves of which were filled with rows of gigantic folios and black-letter quartos, and the upper with little parchment-covered duodecimos. Over the central bookcase was a bronze bust of Hippocrates,* with which, according to some authorities, Dr Heidegger was accustomed to hold consultations, in all difficult cases of his practice. In the obscurest corner of the room stood a tall and narrow oaken closet, with its door ajar, within which doubtfully appeared a skeleton. Between two of the bookcases hung a looking glass, presenting its high and dusty plate within a tarnished gilt frame. Among many wonderful stories related of this mirror, it was fabled that the spirits of all the doctor's deceased patients dwelt within its verge, and would stare him in the face whenever he looked thitherward. The opposite side of the chamber was ornamented with the full-length portrait of a young lady, arrayed in the faded magnificence of silk, satin and brocade, and with a visage as faded as her dress. Above half a century ago, Dr Heidegger had been on the point of marriage with his young lady, but, being affected with some slight disorder, she had swallowed one of her lover's prescriptions and died on the bridal evening. The greatest curiosity of the study remains to be mentioned: it was a ponderous folio volume, bound in black leather, with massive silver clasps. There were no letters on the back, and nobody could tell the title of the book. But it was well known to be a book of magic, and once, when a chambermaid had lifted it, merely to brush away the dust, the skeleton had rattled in its closet, the picture of the young lady had stepped one foot upon the floor and several ghastly faces had peeped forth from the mirror, while the brazen head of Hippocrates frowned, and said, "Forbear!"

Such was Dr Heidegger's study. On the summer afternoon of our tale, a small round table, as black as ebony, stood in the centre of the room, sustaining a cut-glass vase, of beautiful form and elaborate workmanship. The sunshine came through the window, between the heavy festoons of two faded damask curtains, and fell directly across this vase, so that a mild splendour was reflected from it on the ashen visages of the five old people who sat around. Four champagne glasses were also on the table.

"My dear old friends," repeated Dr Heidegger, "may I reckon on your aid in performing an exceedingly curious experiment?"

Now Dr Heidegger was a very strange old gentleman, whose eccentricity had become the nucleus for a thousand fantastic stories. Some of these fables, to my shame be it spoken, might possibly be traced back to mine own veracious self, and if any passages of the present tale should startle the reader's faith, I must be content to bear the stigma of a fiction-monger.

When the doctor's four guests heard him talk of his proposed experiment, they anticipated nothing more wonderful than the murder of a mouse in an air pump, or the examination of a cobweb by the microscope, or some similar nonsense with which he was constantly in the habit of pestering his intimates. But without waiting for a reply, Dr Heidegger hobbled across the chamber and returned with the same ponderous folio, bound in black leather, which common report affirmed to be a book of magic. Undoing the silver clasps, he opened the volume and took from among its black-letter pages a rose, or what was once a rose, though now the green leaves and crimson petals had assumed one brownish hue, and the ancient flower seemed ready to crumble to dust in the doctor's hands.

"This rose," said Dr Heidegger with a sigh, "this same withered and crumbling flower, blossomed five-and-fifty years ago. It was given me by Sylvia Ward, whose portrait hangs yonder, and I meant to wear it in my bosom at our wedding. Five-and-fifty years it has been treasured between the leaves of this old volume. Now, would you deem it possible that this rose of half a century could ever bloom again?"

"Nonsense!" said the Widow Wycherly, with a peevish toss of her head. "You might as well ask whether an old woman's wrinkled face could ever bloom again."

"See!" answered Dr Heidegger.

He uncovered the vase, and threw the faded rose into the water which it contained. At first, it lay lightly on the surface of the fluid, appearing to imbibe none of its moisture. Soon, however, a singular change began to be visible. The crushed and dried petals stirred, and assumed a deepening tinge of crimson, as if the flower were reviving from a deathlike slumber; the slender stalk and twigs of foliage became green; and there was the rose of half a century, looking as fresh as when Sylvia Ward had first given it to her lover. It was scarcely full blown, for some of its delicate red leaves curled modestly around its moist bosom, within which two or three dewdrops were sparkling.

"That is certainly a very pretty deception," said the doctor's friends – carelessly, however, for they had witnessed greater miracles at a conjurer's show. "Pray how was it effected?"

"Did you never hear of the 'Fountain of Youth'," asked Dr Heidegger, "which Ponce de León,* the Spanish adventurer, went in search of, two or three centuries ago?"

"But did Ponce de León ever find it?" said the Widow Wycherly.

"No," answered Dr Heidegger, "for he never sought it in the right place. The famous Fountain of Youth, if I am rightly informed, is situated in the southern part of the Floridan peninsula, not far from Lake Macaco. Its source is overshadowed by several gigantic magnolias, which, though numberless centuries old, have been kept as fresh as violets by the virtues of this wonderful water. An acquaintance of mine, knowing my curiosity in such matters, has sent me what you see in the vase."

"Ahem!" said Colonel Killigrew, who believed not a word of the doctor's story. "And what may be the effect of this fluid on the human frame?"

"You shall judge for yourself, my dear Colonel," replied Dr Heidegger. "And all of you, my respected friends, are welcome to so much of this admirable fluid as may restore to you the bloom of youth. For my own part, having had much trouble in growing old, I am in no hurry to grow young again. With your permission, therefore, I will merely watch the progress of the experiment."

While he spoke, Dr Heidegger had been filling the four champagne glasses with the water of the Fountain of Youth. It was apparently impregnated with an effervescent gas, for little bubbles were continually ascending from the depths of the glasses and bursting in silvery spray at the surface. As the liquor diffused a pleasant perfume, the old people doubted not that it possessed cordial and comfortable properties; and, though utter sceptics as to its rejuvenescent power, they were inclined to swallow it at once. But Dr Heidegger besought them to stay a moment.

"Before you drink, my respectable old friends," said he, "it would be well that, with the experience of a lifetime to direct you, you should draw up a few general rules for your guidance, in passing a second time through the perils of youth. Think what a sin and shame it would be if, with your peculiar advantages, you should not become patterns of virtue and wisdom to all the young people of the age."

The doctor's four venerable friends made him no answer, except by a feeble and tremulous laugh; so very ridiculous was the idea that, knowing how closely repentance treads behind the steps of error, they should ever go astray again.

"Drink, then," said the doctor, bowing. "I rejoice that I have so well selected the subjects of my experiment."

With palsied hands, they raised the glasses to their lips. The liquor, if it really possessed such virtues as Dr Heidegger imputed to it, could not have been bestowed on four human beings who needed it more woefully. They looked as if they had never known what youth or pleasure was, but had been the offspring of Nature's dotage, and always the grey, decrepit, sapless, miserable creatures who now sat stooping round the doctor's table, without life enough in their souls or bodies to be animated even by the prospect of growing young again. They drank off the water, and replaced their glasses on the table.

Assuredly there was an almost immediate improvement in the aspect of the party, now unlike what might have been produced by a glass of generous wine, together with a sudden glow of cheerful sunshine, brightening over all their visages at once. There was a healthful suffusion on their cheeks, instead of the ashen hue that had made them look so corpselike. They gazed at one another, and fancied that some magic power had really begun to smooth away the deep and sad inscription which Father Time had been so long engraving on their brows. The Widow Wycherly adjusted her cap, for she felt almost like a woman again.

"Give us more of this wondrous water!" cried they eagerly. "We are younger – but we are still too old! Quick – give us more!"

"Patience, patience!" quoth Dr Heidegger, who sat watching the experiment, with philosophic coolness. "You have been a long time growing old. Surely, you might be content to grow young in half an hour! But the watch is at your service."

Again he filled their glasses with the liquor of youth, enough of which still remained in the vase to turn half the old people in the city to the age of their own grandchildren. While the bubbles were yet sparkling on the brim, the doctor's four guests snatched their glasses from the table and swallowed the contents at a single gulp. Was it delusion? Even while the draught was passing down their throats, it seemed to have wrought a change on their whole systems. Their eyes grew clear and bright; a dark shade deepened among their silvery locks; they sat around the table, three gentlemen of middle age and a woman hardly beyond her buxom prime.

"My dear widow, you are charming!" cried Colonel Killigrew, whose eyes had been fixed upon her face, while the shadows of age were flitting from it like darkness from the crimson daybreak.

The fair widow knew, of old, that Colonel Killigrew's compliments were not always measured by sober truth, so she started up and ran to the mirror, still dreading that the ugly visage of an old woman would meet her gaze. Meanwhile, the three gentlemen behaved in such a manner as proved that the water of the Fountain of Youth possessed some intoxicating qualities – unless, indeed, their exhilaration of spirits were merely a lightsome dizziness caused by the sudden removal of the weight of years. Mr Gascoigne's mind seemed to run on political topics, but whether relating to the past, present or future, could not easily be determined, since the same ideas and phrases have been in vogue these fifty years. Now he rattled forth full-throated sentences about patriotism, national glory and the people's right; now he muttered some perilous stuff or other, in a sly and doubtful whisper, so cautiously that even his own conscience could scarcely catch the secret; and now, again, he spoke in measured accents, and a deeply deferential tone, as if a royal ear were listening to his well-turned periods. Colonel Killigrew all this time had been trolling forth a jolly bottle song, and ringing his glass in symphony with the chorus, while his eyes wandered towards the buxom figure of the Widow Wycherly. On the other side of the table, Mr Medbourne was involved in a calculation of dollars and cents, with which was strangely intermingled a project for supplying the East Indies with ice by harnessing a team of whales to the polar icebergs.

As for the Widow Wycherly, she stood before the mirror curtsying and simpering to her own image, and greeting it as the friend whom she loved better than all the world beside. She thrust her face close to the glass to see whether some long-remembered wrinkle or crow's foot had indeed vanished. She examined whether the snow had so entirely melted from her hair that the venerable cap could be safely thrown aside. At last, turning briskly away, she came with a sort of dancing step to the table.

"My dear old doctor," cried she, "pray favour me with another glass!"

"Certainly, my dear madam, certainly!" replied the complaisant doctor. "See! I have already filled the glasses."

There, in fact, stood the four glasses, brimful of this wonderful water, the delicate spray of which, as it effervesced from the surface, resembled the tremulous glitter of diamonds. It was now so nearly sunset that the chamber had grown duskier than ever, but a mild and moonlike splendour gleamed from within the vase and rested alike on the four guests, and on the doctor's venerable figure. He sat in a high-backed, elaborately carved oaken armchair, with a grey dignity of aspect that might have well befitted that very Father Time whose power had never been disputed, save by this fortunate company. Even while quaffing the third draught of the Fountain of Youth, they were almost awed by the expression of his mysterious visage.

But, the next moment, the exhilarating gush of young life shot through their veins. They were now in the happy prime of youth. Age, with its miserable train of cares, and sorrows, and diseases, was remembered only as the trouble of a dream from which they had joyously awoke. The fresh gloss of the soul, so early lost, and without which the world's successive scenes had been but a gallery of faded pictures, again threw its enchantment over all their prospects. They felt like new-created beings, in a new-created universe.

"We are young! We are young!" they cried exultingly.

Youth, like the extremity of age, had effaced the strongly marked characteristics of middle life, and mutually assimilated them all. They were a group of merry youngsters, almost maddened with the exuberant frolicsomeness of their years. The most singular effect of their gaiety was an impulse to mock the infirmity and decrepitude of which they had so lately been the victims. They laughed loudly at their old-fashioned attire, the wide-skirted coats and flapped waistcoats of the young men and the ancient cap and gown of the blooming girl. One limped across the floor, like a gouty grandfather; one set a pair of spectacles astride of his nose and pretended to pore over the black-letter pages of the book of magic; a third seated himself in an armchair and strove to imitate the venerable dignity of Dr Heidegger. Then all shouted mirthfully and leaped about the room. The Widow Wycherly – if so fresh a damsel could be called a widow – tripped up to the doctor's chair, with a mischievous merriment in her rosy face.

"Doctor, you dear old soul," cried she, "get up and dance with me!" And then the four young people laughed louder than ever, to think what a queer figure the poor old doctor would cut.

"Pray excuse me," answered the doctor quietly. "I am old and rheumatic, and my dancing days were over long ago. But either of these gay young gentlemen will be glad of so pretty a partner."

"Dance with me, Clara!" cried Colonel Killigrew.

"No, no, I will be her partner!" shouted Mr Gascoigne.

"She promised me her hand fifty years ago!" exclaimed Mr Medbourne.

They all gathered round her. One caught both her hands in his passionate grasp – another threw his arm about her waist – the third buried his hand among the glossy curls that clustered beneath the widow's cap. Blushing, panting, struggling, chiding, laughing, her warm breath fanning each of their faces by turns, she strove to disengage herself, yet still remained in their triple embrace. Never was there a livelier picture of youthful rivalship, with bewitching beauty for the prize. Yet, by a strange deception, owing to the duskiness of the chamber and the antique dresses which they still wore, the tall mirror is said to have reflected the figures of three old, grey, withered grandsires, ridiculously contending for the skinny ugliness of a shrivelled grandam.

But they were young: their burning passions proved them so. Inflamed to madness by the coquetry of the girl-widow, who neither granted nor quite withheld her favours, the three rivals began to interchange threatening glances. Still keeping hold of the fair prize, they grappled fiercely at one another's throats. As they struggled to and fro, the table was overturned and the vase dashed into a thousand fragments. The precious Water of Youth flowed in a bright stream across the floor, moistening the wings of a butterfly, which, grown old in the decline of summer, had alighted there to die. The insect fluttered lightly through the chamber, and settled on the snowy head of Dr Heidegger.

"Come, come, gentlemen! Come, Madam Wycherly," exclaimed the doctor, "I really must protest against this riot."

They stood still and shivered, for it seemed as if grey Time were calling them back from their sunny youth, far down into the chill and darksome vale of years. They looked at old Dr Heidegger, who sat in his carved armchair, holding the rose of half a century, which he had rescued from among the fragments of the shattered vase. At the motion of his hand, the four rioters resumed their seats, the more readily because their violent exertions had wearied them, youthful though they were.

"My poor Sylvia's rose!" ejaculated Dr Heidegger, holding it in the light of the sunset clouds. "It appears to be fading again."

And so it was. Even while the party were looking at it, the flower continued to shrivel up, till it became as dry and fragile as when the doctor had first thrown it into the vase. He shook off the few drops of moisture which clung to its petals.

"I love it as well thus, as in its dewy freshness," observed he, pressing the withered rose to his withered lips. While he spoke, the butterfly fluttered down from the doctor's snowy head, and fell upon the floor.

His guests shivered again. A strange chilliness, whether of the body or spirit they could not tell, was creeping gradually over them all. They gazed at one another, and fancied that each fleeting moment snatched away a charm, and left a deepening furrow where none had been before. Was it an illusion? Had the changes of a lifetime been crowded into so brief a space, and were they now four aged people, sitting with their old friend, Dr Heidegger?

"Are we grown old again, so soon?" cried they dolefully.

In truth, they had. The Water of Youth possessed merely a virtue more transient than that of wine. The delirium which it created had effervesced away. Yes! They were old again. With a shuddering impulse that showed her a woman still, the widow clasped her skinny hands before her face and wished that the coffin lid were over it, since it could be no longer beautiful.

"Yes, friends, ye are old again," said Dr Heidegger. "And lo! – the Water of Youth is all lavished on the ground. Well, I bemoan it not, for if the fountain gushed at my very doorstep, I would not stoop to bathe my lips in it – no, though its delirium were for years instead of moments. Such is the lesson ye have taught me!"

But the doctor's four friends had taught no such lesson to themselves. They resolved forthwith to make a pilgrimage to Florida, and quaff at morning, noon and night from the Fountain of Youth.

Note. In an English review, not long since, I have been accused of plagiarizing the idea of this story from a chapter in one of the novels of Alexandre Dumas.* There has undoubtedly been a plagiarism on one side or the other, but as my story was written a good deal more than twenty years ago, and as the novel is of considerably more recent date, I take pleasure in thinking that M. Dumas has done me the honour to appropriate one of the fanciful conceptions of my earlier days. He is heartily welcome to it; nor is it the only instance, by many, in which the great French romancer has exercised the privilege of commanding genius by confiscating the intellectual property of less famous people to his own use and behoof.

September 1860

The Man of Adamant

I N THE OLD TIMES OF RELIGIOUS GLOOM and intolerance lived Richard Digby, the gloomiest and most intolerant of a stern brotherhood. His plan of salvation was so narrow that, like a plank in a tempestuous sea, it could avail no sinner but himself, who bestrode it triumphantly, and hurled anathemas against the wretches whom he saw struggling with the billows of eternal death. In his view of the matter, it was a most abominable crime – as, indeed, it is a great folly – for men to trust to their own strength, or even to grapple to any other fragment of the wreck, save this narrow plank, which, moreover, he took special care to keep out of their reach. In other words, as his creed was like no man's else, and being well pleased that Providence had entrusted him alone, of mortals, with the treasure of a true faith, Richard Digby determined to seclude himself to the sole and constant enjoyment of his happy fortune.

"And verily," thought he, "I deem it a chief condition of Heaven's mercy to myself that I hold no communion with those abominable myriads which it hath cast off to perish. Peradventure, were I to tarry longer in the tents of Kedar, the gracious boon would be revoked, and I also be swallowed up in the deluge of wrath, or consumed in the storm of fire and brimstone, or involved in whatever new kind of ruin is ordained for the horrible perversity of this generation."

So Richard Digby took an axe, to hew space enough for a tabernacle in the wilderness, and some few other necessaries, especially a sword and gun, to smite and slay any intruder upon his hallowed seclusion – and plunged into the dreariest depths of the forest. On its verge, however, he paused a moment to shake off the dust of his feet against the village where he had dwelt, and to invoke a curse on the meeting house, which he regarded as a temple of heathen idolatry. He felt a curiosity, also, to see whether the fire and brimstone would not rush down from heaven at once, now that the one righteous man had provided for his own safety. But, as the sunshine continued to fall peacefully on the cottages and fields, and the husbandmen laboured and children played, and as there were many tokens of present happiness, and nothing ominous of a speedy judgement, he turned away, somewhat disappointed. The farther he went, however, and the lonelier he felt himself, and the thicker the trees stood along his path, and the darker the shadow overhead, so much the more did Richard Digby exult. He talked to himself, as he strode onward; he read his Bible to himself, as he sat beneath the trees; and, as the gloom of the forest hid the blessed sky, I had almost added, that, at morning, noon and eventide, he prayed to himself. So congenial was this mode of life to his disposition that he often laughed to himself, but was displeased when an echo tossed him back the long loud roar.

In this manner, he journeyed onward three days and two nights, and came, on the third evening, to the mouth of a cave, which, at first sight, reminded him of Elijah's cave at Horeb, though perhaps it more resembled Abraham's sepulchral cave at Machpelah.* It entered into the heart of a rocky hill. There was so dense a veil of tangled foliage about it that none but a sworn lover of gloomy recesses would have discovered the low arch of its entrance, or have dared to step within its vaulted chamber, where the burning eyes of a panther might encounter him. If Nature meant this remote and dismal cavern for the use of man, it could only be to bury in its gloom the victims of a pestilence, and then to block up its mouth with stones, and avoid the spot for ever after. There was nothing bright nor cheerful near it, except a bubbling fountain, some twenty paces off, at which Richard Digby hardly threw away a glance. But he thrust his head into the cave, shivered and congratulated himself.

"The finger of Providence hath pointed my way!" cried he, aloud, while the tomb-like den returned a strange echo, as if some-one within were mocking him. "Here my soul will be at peace, for the wicked will not find me. Here I can read the Scriptures, and be no more provoked with lying interpretations. Here I can offer up acceptable prayers, because my voice will not be mingled with the sinful supplications of the multitude. Of a truth, the only way to heaven leadeth through the narrow entrance of this cave – and I alone have found it!"

In regard to this cave it was observable that the roof, so far as the imperfect light permitted it to be seen, was hung with substances resembling opaque icicles; for the damps of unknown centuries, dripping down continually, had become as hard as adamant; and wherever that moisture fell, it seemed to possess the power of converting what it bathed to stone. The fallen leaves and sprigs of foliage, which the wind had swept into the cave, and the little feathery shrubs, rooted near the threshold, were not wet with a natural dew but had been embalmed by this wondrous process. And here I am put in mind that Richard Digby, before he withdrew himself from the world, was supposed by skilful physicians to have contracted a disease for which no remedy was written in their medical books. It was a deposition of calculous particles within his heart, caused by an obstructed circulation of the blood; and, unless a miracle should be wrought for him, there was danger that the malady might act on the entire substance of the organ and change his fleshy heart to stone. Many, indeed, affirmed that the process was already near its consummation. Richard Digby, however, could never be convinced that any such direful work was going on within him; nor when he saw the sprigs of marble foliage did his heart even throb the quicker at the similitude suggested by these once tender herbs. It may be that this same insensibility was a symptom of the disease.

Be that as it might, Richard Digby was well contented with his sepulchral cave. So dearly did he love this congenial spot that, instead of going a few paces to the bubbling spring for water, he allayed his thirst with now and then a drop of moisture from the roof, which, had it fallen anywhere but on his tongue, would have been congealed into a pebble. For a man predisposed to stoniness of the heart, this surely was unwholesome liquor. But there he dwelt, for three days more, eating herbs and roots, drinking his own destruction, sleeping, as it were, in a tomb and awaking to the solitude of death, yet esteeming this horrible mode of life as hardly inferior to celestial bliss. Perhaps superior – for, above the sky, there would be angels to disturb him. At the close of the third day, he sat in the portal of his mansion, reading the Bible aloud, because no other ear could profit by it, and reading it amiss, because the rays of the setting sun did not penetrate the dismal depth of shadow round about him, nor fall upon the sacred page. Suddenly, however, a faint gleam of light was thrown over the volume, and, raising his eyes, Richard Digby saw that a young woman stood before the mouth of the cave, and that the sunbeams bathed her white garment, which thus seemed to possess a radiance of its own.

"Good evening, Richard," said the girl. "I have come from afar to find thee."

The slender grace and gentle loveliness of this young woman were at once recognized by Richard Digby. Her name was Mary Goffe. She had been a convert to his preaching of the word in England, before he yielded himself to that exclusive bigotry which now enfolded him with such an iron grasp that no other sentiment could reach his bosom. When he came a pilgrim to America, she had remained in her father's hall, but now, as it appeared, had crossed the ocean after him, impelled by the same faith that led other exiles hither, and perhaps by love almost as holy. What else but faith and love united could have sustained so delicate a creature, wandering thus far into the forest, with her golden hair dishevelled by the boughs and her feet wounded by the thorns? Yet, weary and faint though she must have been, and affrighted at the dreariness of the cave, she looked on the lonely man with a mild and pitying expression, such as might beam from an angel's eyes, towards an afflicted mortal. But the recluse, frowning sternly upon her and keeping his finger between the leaves of his half-closed Bible, motioned her away with his hand.

"Off!" cried he. "I am sanctified, and thou art sinful. Away!"

"O Richard," said she earnestly, "I have come this weary way because I heard that a grievous distemper had seized upon thy heart, and a great physician hath given me the skill to cure it. There is no other remedy than this which I have brought thee. Turn me not away, therefore, nor refuse my medicine, for then must this dismal cave be thy sepulchre."

"Away!" replied Richard Digby, still with a dark frown. "My heart is in better condition than thine own. Leave me, earthly one, for the sun is almost set, and when no light reaches the door of the cave, then is my prayer time."

Now, great as was her need, Mary Goffe did not plead with this stony-hearted man for shelter and protection, nor ask anything whatever for her own sake. All her zeal was for his welfare.

"Come back with me!" she exclaimed, clasping her hands. "Come back to thy fellow men, for they need thee, Richard, and thou hast tenfold need of them. Stay not in this evil den, for the air is chill, and the damps are fatal; nor will any that perish within it ever find the path to heaven. Hasten hence, I entreat thee, for thine own soul's sake; for either the roof will fall upon thy head, or some other speedy destruction is at hand."

"Perverse woman!" answered Richard Digby, laughing aloud – for he was moved to bitter mirth by her foolish vehemence. "I tell thee that the path to heaven leadeth straight through this narrow portal where I sit. And, moreover, the destruction thou speakest of is ordained, not for this blessed cave, but for all other habitations of mankind, throughout the earth. Get thee hence speedily, that thou mayst have thy share!"

So saving, he opened his Bible again, and fixed his eyes intently on the page, being resolved to withdraw his thoughts from this child of sin and wrath, and to waste no more of his holy breath upon her. The shadow had now grown so deep, where he was sitting, that he made continual mistakes in what he read, converting all that was gracious and merciful to denunciations of vengeance and unutterable woe on every created being but himself. Mary Goffe, meanwhile, was leaning against a tree, beside the sepulchral cave, very sad, yet with something heavenly and ethereal in her unselfish sorrow. The light from the setting sun still glorified her form, and was reflected a little way within the darksome den, discovering so terrible a gloom that the maiden shuddered for its self-doomed inhabitant. Espying the bright fountain near at hand, she hastened thither, and scooped up a portion of its water, in a cup of birchen bark. A few tears mingled with the draught, and perhaps gave it all its efficacy. She then returned to the mouth of the cave, and knelt down at Richard Digby's feet.

"Richard," she said, with passionate fervour, yet a gentleness in all her passion, "I pray thee, by thy hope of heaven, and as thou wouldst not dwell in this tomb for ever, drink of this hallowed water, be it but a single drop! Then, make room for me by thy side, and let us read together one page of that blessed volume – and, lastly, kneel down with me and pray! Do this, and thy stony heart shall become softer than a babe's, and all be well."

But Richard Digby, in utter abhorrence of the proposal, cast the Bible at his feet, and eyed her with such a fixed and evil frown that he looked less like a living man than a marble statue, wrought by some dark-imagined sculptor to express the most repulsive mood that human features could assume. And, as his look grew even devilish, so with an equal change did Mary Goffe become more sad, more mild, more pitiful, more like a sorrowing angel. But the more heavenly she was, the more hateful did she seem to Richard Digby, who at length raised his hand, and smote down the cup of hallowed water upon the threshold of the cave, thus rejecting the only medicine that could have cured his stony heart. A sweet perfume lingered in the air for a moment, and then was gone.

"Tempt me no more, accursed woman," exclaimed he, still with his marble frown, "lest I smite thee down also! What hast thou to do with my Bible? What with my prayers? What with my heaven?"

No sooner had he spoken these dreadful words, than Richard Digby's heart ceased to beat; while – so the legend says – the form of Mary Goffe melted into the last sunbeams, and returned from the sepulchral cave to heaven. For Mary Golfe had been buried in an English churchyard, months before, and either it was her ghost that haunted the wild forest, or else a dream-like spirit, typifying pure Religion.

Above a century afterwards, when the trackless forest of Richard Digby's day had long been interspersed with settlements, the children of a neighbouring farmer were playing at the foot of a hill. The trees, on account of the rude and broken surface of this acclivity, had never been felled, and were crowded so densely together as to hide all but a few rocky prominences, wherever their roots could grapple with the soil. A little boy and girl, to conceal themselves from their playmates, had crept into the deepest shade, where not only the darksome pines, but a thick veil of creeping plants suspended from an overhanging rock, combined to make a twilight at noonday, and almost a midnight at all other seasons. There the children hid themselves, and shouted, repeating the cry at intervals, till the whole party of pursuers were drawn thither and, pulling aside the matted foliage, let in a doubtful glimpse of daylight. But scarcely was this accomplished when the little group uttered a simultaneous shriek and tumbled headlong down the hill, making the best of their way homeward, without a second glance into the gloomy recess. Their father, unable to comprehend what had so startled them, took his axe and, by felling one or two trees, and tearing away the creeping plants, laid the mystery open to the day. He had discovered the entrance of a cave, closely resembling the mouth of a sepulchre, within which sat the figure of a man, whose gesture and attitude warned the father and children to stand back, while his visage wore a most forbidding frown. This repulsive personage seemed to have been carved in the same grey stone that formed the walls and portal of the cave. On minuter inspection, indeed, such blemishes were observed as made it doubtful whether the figure were really a statue, chiselled by human art and somewhat worn and defaced by the lapse of ages, or a freak of Nature, who might have chosen to imitate, in stone, her usual handiwork of flesh. Perhaps it was the least unreasonable idea, suggested by this strange spectacle, that the moisture of the cave possessed a petrifying quality, which had thus awfully embalmed a human corpse.

There was something so frightful in the aspect of this Man of Adamant that the farmer, the moment that he recovered from the fascination of his first gaze, began to heap stones into the mouth of the cavern. His wife, who had followed him to the hill, assisted her husband's efforts. The children also approached as near as they durst, with their little hands full of pebbles, and cast them on the pile. Earth was then thrown into the crevices, and the whole fabric overlaid with sods. Thus all traces of the discovery were obliterated, leaving only a marvellous legend, which grew wilder from one generation to another, as the children told it to their grandchildren, and they to their posterity, till few believed that there had ever been a cavern or a statue, where now they saw but a grassy patch on the shadowy hillside. Yet grown people avoid the spot, nor do children play there. Friendship, and Love, and Piety, all human and celestial sympathies, should keep aloof from that hidden cave; for there still sits and, unless an earthquake crumble down the roof upon his head, shall sit for ever the shape of Richard Digby, in the attitude of repelling the whole race of mortals – not from heaven – but from the horrible loneliness of his dark, cold sepulchre!

The Great Carbuncle

A Mystery of the White Mountains

A T NIGHTFALL ONCE IN THE OLDEN TIME, on the rugged side of one of the Crystal Hills, a party of adventurers were refreshing themselves after a toilsome and fruitless quest for the Great Carbuncle. They had come thither, not as friends nor partners in the enterprise, but each, save one youthful pair, impelled by his own selfish and solitary longing for this wondrous gem. Their feeling of brotherhood, however, was strong enough to induce them to contribute a mutual aid in building a rude hut of branches and kindling a great fire of shattered pines that had drifted down the headlong current of the Ammonoosuc, on the lower bank of which they were to pass the night. There was but one of their number, perhaps, who had become so estranged from natural sympathies by the absorbing spell of the pursuit as to acknowledge no satisfaction at the sight of human faces in the remote and solitary region whither they had ascended. A vast extent of wilderness lay between them and the nearest settlement, while scant a mile above their heads was that bleak verge where the hills throw off their shaggy mantle of forest trees and either robe themselves in clouds or tower naked into the sky. The roar of the Ammonoosuc would have been too awful for endurance if only a solitary man had listened while the mountain stream talked with the wind.

The adventurers, therefore, exchanged hospitable greetings and welcomed one another to the hut where each man was the host and all were the guests of the whole company. They spread their individual supplies of food on the flat surface of a rock and partook of a general repast – at the close of which a sentiment of good-fellowship was perceptible among the party, though repressed by the idea that the renewed search for the Great Carbuncle must make them strangers again in the morning. Seven men and one young woman, they warmed themselves together at the fire, which extended its bright wall along the whole front of their wigwam. As they observed the various and contrasted figures that made up the assemblage, each man looking like a caricature of himself in the unsteady light that flickered over him, they came mutually to the conclusion that an odder society had never met in city or wilderness, on mountain or plain.

The eldest of the group – a tall, lean, weather-beaten man some sixty years of age – was clad in the skins of wild animals whose fashion of dress he did well to imitate, since the deer, the wolf and the bear had long been his most intimate companions. He was one of those ill-fated mortals, such as the Indians told of, whom in their early youth the Great Carbuncle smote with a peculiar madness and became the passionate dream of their existence. All who visited that region knew him as "the Seeker", and by no other name. As none could remember when he first took up the search, there went a fable in the valley of the Saco that for his inordinate lust after the Great Carbuncle he had been condemned to wander among the mountains till the end of time, still with the same feverish hopes at sunrise, the same despair at eve. Near this miserable Seeker sat a little elderly personage wearing a high-crowned hat shaped somewhat like a crucible. He was from beyond the sea – a Doctor Cacaphodel, who had wilted and dried himself into a mummy by continually stooping over charcoal furnaces and inhaling unwholesome fumes during his researches in chemistry and alchemy. It was told of him – whether truly or not – that at the commencement of his studies he had drained his body of all its richest blood and wasted it, with other inestimable ingredients, in an unsuccessful experiment, and had never been a well man since. Another of the adventurers was Master Ichabod Pigsnort, a weighty merchant and selectman of Boston, and an elder of the famous Mr Norton's church. His enemies had a ridiculous story that Master Pigsnort was accustomed to spend a whole hour after prayer time every morning and evening in wallowing naked among an immense quantity of pine-tree shillings, which were the earliest silver coinage of Massachusetts. The fourth whom we shall notice had no name that his companions knew of, and was chiefly distinguished by a sneer that always contorted his thin visage, and by a prodigious pair of spectacles which were supposed to deform and discolour the whole face of nature to this gentleman's perception. The fifth adventurer likewise lacked a name, which was the greater pity, as he appeared to be a poet. He was a bright-eyed man, but woefully pined away, which was no more than natural if, as some people affirmed, his ordinary diet was fog, morning mist and a slice of the densest cloud within his reach, sauced with moonshine whenever he could get it. Certain it is that the poetry which flowed from him had a smack of all these dainties. The sixth of the party was a young man of haughty mien and sat somewhat apart from the rest, wearing his plumed hat loftily among his elders, while the fire glittered on the rich embroidery of his dress and gleamed intensely on the jewelled pommel of his sword. This was the Lord De Vere, who when at home was said to spend much of his time in the burial vault of his dead progenitors rummaging their mouldy coffins in search of all the earthly pride and vainglory that was hidden among bones and dust; so that, besides his own share, he had the collected haughtiness of his whole line of ancestry. Lastly, there was a handsome youth in rustic garb, and by his side a blooming little person in whom a delicate shade of maiden reserve was just melting into the rich glow of a young wife's affection. Her name was Hannah, and her husband's Matthew – two homely names, yet well enough adapted to the simple pair who seemed strangely out of place among the whimsical fraternity whose wits had been set agog by the Great Carbuncle.

Beneath the shelter of one hut, in the bright blaze of the same fire, sat this varied group of adventurers, all so intent upon a single object that of whatever else they began to speak their closing words were sure to be illuminated with the Great Carbuncle. Several related the circumstances that brought them thither. One had listened to a traveller's tale of this marvellous stone in his own distant country, and had immediately been seized with such a thirst for beholding it as could only be quenched in its intensest lustre. Another, so long ago as when the famous Captain Smith visited these coasts,* had seen it blazing far at sea, and had felt no rest in all the intervening years till now that he took up the search. A third, being encamped on a hunting expedition full forty miles south of the White Mountains, awoke at midnight and beheld the Great Carbuncle gleaming like a meteor, so that the shadows of the trees fell backward from it. They spoke of the innumerable attempts which had been made to reach the spot, and of the singular fatality which had hitherto withheld success from all adventurers, though it might seem so easy to follow to its source a light that overpowered the moon and almost matched the sun. It was observable that each smiled scornfully at the madness of every other in anticipating better fortune than the past, yet nourished a scarcely hidden conviction that he would himself be the favoured one. As if to allay their too sanguine hopes, they recurred to the Indian traditions that a spirit kept watch about the gem and bewildered those who sought it either by removing it from peak to peak of the higher hills or by calling up a mist from the enchanted lake over which it hung. But these tales were deemed unworthy of credit, all professing to believe that the search had been baffled by want of sagacity or perseverance in the adventurers, or such other causes as might naturally obstruct the passage to any given point among the intricacies of forest, valley and mountain.

In a pause of the conversation, the wearer of the prodigious spectacles looked round upon the party, making each individual in turn the object of the sneer which invariably dwelt upon his countenance.

"So, fellow pilgrims," said he, "here we are, seven wise men and one fair damsel, who doubtless is as wise as any greybeard of the company. Here we are, I say, all bound on the same goodly enterprise. Methinks, now, it were not amiss that each of us declare what he proposes to do with the Great Carbuncle, provided he have the good hap to clutch it. What says our friend in the bear-skin? How mean you, good sir, to enjoy the prize which you have been seeking the Lord knows how long among the Crystal Hills?"

"How enjoy it!" exclaimed the aged Seeker bitterly. "I hope for no enjoyment from it – that folly has passed long ago! I keep up the search for this accursed stone, because the vain ambition of my youth has become a fate upon me, in old age. The pursuit alone is my strength – the energy of my soul – the warmth of my blood and the pith and marrow of my bones! Were I to turn my back upon it, I should fall down dead, on the hither side of the Notch, which is the gateway of this mountain region. Yet, not to have my wasted lifetime back again, would I give up my hopes of the Great Carbuncle! Having found it, I shall bear it to a certain cavern that I wot of, and there, grasping it in my arms, lie down and die, and keep it buried with me for ever."

"Oh, wretch, regardless of the interests of science!" cried Doctor Cacaphodel, with philosophic indignation. "Thou art not worthy to behold, even from afar off, the lustre of this most precious gem that ever was concocted in the laboratory of Nature. Mine is the sole purpose for which a wise man may desire the possession of the Great Carbuncle. Immediately on obtaining it – for I have a presentiment, good people, that the prize is reserved to crown my scientific reputation – I shall return to Europe, and employ my remaining years in reducing it to its first elements. A portion of the stone will I grind to impalpable powder; other parts shall be dissolved in acids, or whatever solvents will act upon so admirable a composition; and the remainder I design to melt in the crucible, or set on fire with the blowpipe. By these various methods I shall gain an accurate analysis, and finally bestow the result of my labours upon the world, in a folio volume."

"Excellent!" quoth the man with the spectacles. "Nor need you hesitate, learned sir, on account of the necessary destruction of the gem, since the perusal of your folio may teach every mother's son of us to concoct a Great Carbuncle of his own."

"But, verily," said Master Ichabod Pigsnort, "for mine own part, I object to the making of these counterfeits, as being calculated to reduce the marketable value of the true gem. I tell ye frankly, sirs, I have an interest in keeping up the price. Here have I quitted my regular traffic, leaving my warehouse in the care of my clerks and putting my credit to great hazard, and, furthermore, have put myself to peril of death or captivity by the accursed heathen savages – and all this without daring to ask the prayers of the congregation, because the quest for the Great Carbuncle is deemed little better than a traffic with the evil one. Now think ye that I would have done this grievous wrong to my soul, body, reputation and estate, without a reasonable chance of profit?"

"Not I, pious Master Pigsnort," said the man with the spectacles. "I never laid such a great folly to thy charge."

"Truly, I hope not," said the merchant. "Now, as touching this Great Carbuncle, I am free to own that I have never had a glimpse of it, but, be it only the hundredth part so bright as people tell, it will surely outvalue the Great Mogul's best diamond, which he holds at an incalculable sum; wherefore I am minded to put the Great Carbuncle on shipboard and voyage with it to England, France, Spain, Italy or into heathendom if Providence should send me thither, and, in a word, dispose of the gem to the best bidder among the potentates of the earth, that he may place it among his crown jewels. If any of ye have a wiser plan, let him expound it."

"That have I, thou sordid man!" exclaimed the poet. "Dost thou desire nothing brighter than gold, that thou wouldst transmute all this ethereal lustre into such dross as thou wallowest in already? For myself, hiding the jewel under my cloak, I shall hie me back to my attic chamber in one of the darksome alleys of London. There night and day will I gaze upon it. My soul shall drink its radiance; it shall be diffused throughout my intellectual powers and gleam brightly in every line of poesy that I indite. Thus long ages after I am gone the splendour of the Great Carbuncle will blaze around my name."

"Well said, Master Poet!" cried he of the spectacles. "Hide it under thy cloak, sayest thou? Why, it will gleam through the holes and make thee look like a jack-o'-lantern!"

"To think," ejaculated the Lord De Vere, rather to himself than his companions, the best of whom he held utterly unworthy of his intercourse – "to think that a fellow in a tattered cloak should talk of conveying the Great Carbuncle to a garret in Grubb Street! Have not I resolved within myself that the whole earth contains no fitter ornament for the great hall of my ancestral castle? There shall it flame for ages, making a noonday of midnight, glittering on the suits of armour, the banners and escutcheons that hang around the wall, and keeping bright the memory of heroes.

Wherefore have all other adventurers sought the prize in vain but that I might win it and make it a symbol of the glories of our lofty line? And never on the diadem of the White Mountains did the Great Carbuncle hold a place half so honoured as is reserved for it in the hall of the De Veres."

"It is a noble thought," said the cynic, with an obsequious sneer. "Yet, might I presume to say so, the gem would make a rare sepulchral lamp, and would display the glories of Your Lordship's progenitors more truly in the ancestral vault than in the castle hall."

"Nay, forsooth," observed Matthew, the young rustic, who sat hand in hand with his bride, "the gentleman has bethought himself of a profitable use for this bright stone. Hannah here and I are seeking it for a like purpose."

"How, fellow?" exclaimed His Lordship, in surprise. "What castle hall hast thou to hang it in?"

"No castle," replied Matthew, "but as neat a cottage as any within sight of the Crystal Hills. Ye must know, friends, that Hannah and I, being wedded the last week, have taken up the search of the Great Carbuncle because we shall need its light in the long winter evenings and it will be such a pretty thing to show the neighbours when they visit us! It will shine through the house, so that we may pick up a pin in any corner, and will set all the windows a-glowing as if there were a great fire of pine knots in the chimney. And then how pleasant, when we awake in the night, to be able to see one another's faces!"

There was a general smile among the adventurers at the simplicity of the young couple's project in regard to this wondrous and invaluable stone, with which the greatest monarch on earth might have been proud to adorn his palace. Especially the man with spectacles, who had sneered at all the company in turn, now twisted his visage into such an expression of ill-natured mirth that Matthew asked him rather peevishly what he himself meant to do with the Great Carbuncle.

"The Great Carbuncle!" answered the cynic, with ineffable scorn. "Why, you blockhead, there is no such thing *in rerum natura*.* I have come three thousand miles, and am resolved to set my foot on every peak of these mountains and poke my head into every chasm for the sole purpose of demonstrating to the satisfaction of any man one whit less an ass than thyself that the Great Carbuncle is all a humbug."

Vain and foolish were the motives that had brought most of the adventurers to the Crystal Hills, but none so vain, so foolish and so impious too, as that of the scoffer with the prodigious spectacles. He was one of those wretched and evil men whose yearnings are downward to the darkness instead of heavenward, and who, could they but extinguish the lights which God hath kindled for us, would count the midnight gloom their chiefest glory.

As the cynic spoke several of the party were startled by a gleam of red splendour that showed the huge shapes of the surrounding mountains and the rock-bestrewn bed of the turbulent river, with an illumination unlike that of their fire, on the trunks and black boughs of the forest trees. They listened for the roll of thunder, but heard nothing, and were glad that the tempest came not near them. The stars – those dial points of heaven – now warned the adventurers to close their eyes on the blazing logs and open them in dreams to the glow of the Great Carbuncle.

The young married couple had taken their lodgings in the farthest corner of the wigwam, and were separated from the rest of the party by a curtain of curiously woven twigs such as might have hung in deep festoons around the bridal bower of Eve. The modest little wife had wrought this piece of tapestry while the other guests were talking. She and her husband fell asleep with hands tenderly clasped, and awoke from visions of unearthly radiance to meet the more blessed light of one another's eyes. They awoke at the same instant and with one happy smile beaming over their two faces, which grew brighter with their consciousness of the reality of life and love. But no sooner did she recollect where they were than the bride peeped through the interstices of the leafy curtain and saw that the outer room of the hut was deserted.

"Up, dear Matthew!" cried she, in haste. "The strange folk are all gone. Up this very minute, or we shall lose the Great Carbuncle!"

In truth, so little did these poor young people deserve the mighty prize which had lured them thither that they had slept peacefully all night and till the summits of the hills were glittering with sunshine, while the other adventurers had tossed their limbs in feverish wakefulness or dreamt of climbing precipices, and set off to realize their dreams with the curliest peep of dawn. But Matthew and Hannah after their calm rest were as light as two young deer, and merely stopped to say their prayers and wash themselves in a cold pool of the Ammonoosuc, and then to taste a morsel of food ere they turned their faces to the mountainside. It was a sweet emblem of conjugal affection as they toiled up the difficult ascent gathering strength from the mutual aid which they afforded.

After several little accidents, such as a torn robe, a lost shoe and the entanglement of Hannah's hair in a bough, they reached the upper verge of the forest and were now to pursue a more adventurous course. The innumerable trunks and heavy foliage of the trees had hitherto shut in their thoughts, which now shrank affrighted from the region of wind and cloud and naked rocks and desolate sunshine that rose immeasurably above them. They gazed back at the obscure wilderness which they had traversed, and longed to be buried again in its depths rather than trust themselves to so vast and visible a solitude.

"Shall we go on?" said Matthew, throwing his arm round Hannah's waist both to protect her and to comfort his heart by drawing her close to it.

But the little bride, simple as she was, had a woman's love of jewels, and could not forgo the hope of possessing the very brightest in the world, in spite of the perils with which it must be won.

"Let us climb a little higher," whispered she, yet tremulously, as she turned her face upward to the lonely sky.

"Come, then," said Matthew, mustering his manly courage and drawing her along with him, for she became timid again the moment that he grew bold.

And upward, accordingly, went the pilgrims of the Great Carbuncle, now treading upon the tops and thickly interwoven branches of dwarf pines which by the growth of centuries, though mossy with age, had barely reached three feet in altitude. Next they came to masses and fragments of naked rock heaped confusedly together like a cairn reared by giants in memory of a giant chief. In this bleak realm of upper air nothing breathed, nothing grew; there was no life but what was concentred in their two hearts; they had climbed so high that Nature herself seemed no longer to keep them company. She lingered beneath them within the verge of the forest trees, and sent a farewell glance after her children as they strayed where her own green footprints had never been. But soon they were to be hidden from her eye. Densely and dark the mists began to gather below, casting black spots of shadow on the vast landscape and sailing heavily to one centre, as if the loftiest mountain peak had summoned a council of its kindred clouds. Finally the vapours welded themselves, as it were, into a mass, presenting the appearance of a pavement over which the wanderers might have trodden, but where they would vainly have sought an avenue to the blessed earth which they had lost. And the lovers yearned to behold that green earth again, more intensely – alas!

– than beneath a clouded sky they had ever desired a glimpse of heaven. They even felt it a relief to their desolation when the mists, creeping gradually up the mountain, concealed its lonely peak, and thus annihilated – at least, for them – the whole region of visible space. But they drew closer together with a fond and melancholy gaze, dreading lest the universal cloud should snatch them from each other's sight. Still, perhaps, they would have been resolute to climb as far and as high between earth and heaven as they could find foothold if Hannah's strength had not begun to fail, and with that her courage also. Her breath grew short. She refused to burden her husband with her weight, but often tottered against his side, and recovered herself each time by a feebler effort. At last she sank down on one of the rocky steps of the acclivity.

"We are lost, dear Matthew," said she mournfully. "We shall never find our way to the earth again. And oh how happy we might have been in our cottage!"

"Dear heart, we will yet be happy there," answered Matthew. "Look! In this direction the sunshine penetrates the dismal mist; by its aid I can direct our course to the passage of the Notch. Let us go back, love, and dream no more of the Great Carbuncle."

"The sun cannot be yonder," said Hannah, with despondence. "By this time it must be noon; if there could ever be any sunshine here, it would come from above our heads."

"But look!" repeated Matthew, in a somewhat altered tone. "It is brightening every moment. If not sunshine, what can it be?"

Nor could the young bride any longer deny that a radiance was breaking through the mist and changing its dim hue to a dusky red, which continually grew more vivid, as if brilliant particles were interfused with the gloom. Now, also, the cloud began to roll away from the mountain, while, as it heavily withdrew, one object after another started out of its impenetrable obscurity into sight with precisely the effect of a new creation before the indistinctness of the old chaos had been completely swallowed up. As the process went on they saw the gleaming of water close at their feet, and found themselves on the very border of a mountain lake, deep, bright, clear and calmly beautiful, spreading from brim to brim of a basin that had been scooped out of the solid rock. A ray of glory flashed across its surface. The pilgrims looked whence it should proceed, but closed their eyes, with a thrill of awful admiration, to exclude the fervid splendour that glowed from the brow of a cliff impending over the enchanted lake.

For the simple pair had reached that lake of mystery and found the long-sought shrine of the Great Carbuncle. They threw their arms around each other and trembled at their own success, for as the legends of this wondrous gem rushed thick upon their memory they felt themselves marked out by fate, and the consciousness was fearful. Often from childhood upward they had seen it shining like a distant star, and now that star was throwing its intensest lustre on their hearts. They seemed changed to one another's eyes in the red brilliancy that flamed upon their cheeks, while it lent the same fire to the lake, the rocks and sky, and to the mists which had rolled back before its power. But with their next glance they beheld an object that drew their attention even from the mighty stone. At the base of the cliff, directly beneath the Great Carbuncle, appeared the figure of a man with his arms extended in the act of climbing and his face turned upward as if to drink the full gush of splendour. But he stirred not, no more than if changed to marble.

"It is the Seeker," whispered Hannah, convulsively grasping her husband's arm. "Matthew, he is dead."

"The joy of success has killed him," replied Matthew, trembling violently. "Or perhaps the very light of the Great Carbuncle was death."

"'The Great Carbuncle'!" cried a peevish voice behind them. "The great humbug! If you have found it, prithee point it out to me."

They turned their heads, and there was the cynic with his pro-digious spectacles set carefully on his nose, staring now at the lake, now at the rocks, now at the distant masses of vapour, now right at the Great Carbuncle itself, yet seemingly as unconscious of its light as if all the scattered clouds were condensed about his person. Though its radiance actually threw the shadow of the unbeliever at his own feet as he turned his back upon the glorious jewel, he would not be convinced that there was the least glimmer there.

"Where is your great humbug?" he repeated. "I challenge you to make me see it."

"There!" said Matthew, incensed at such perverse blindness, and turning the cynic round toward the illuminated cliff. "Take off those abominable spectacles, and you cannot help seeing it."

Now, these coloured spectacles probably darkened the cynic's sight in at least as great a degree as the smoked glasses through which people gaze at an eclipse. With resolute bravado, however, he snatched them from his nose and fixed a bold stare full upon the ruddy blaze of the Great Carbuncle. But scarcely had he encoun-tered it when, with a deep, shuddering groan, he dropped his head and pressed both hands across his miserable eyes. Thenceforth there was in very truth no light of the Great Carbuncle, nor any other light on earth, nor light of heaven itself, for the poor cynic. So long accustomed to view all objects through a medium that deprived them of every glimpse of brightness, a single flash of so glorious a phenomenon, striking upon his naked vision, had blinded him for ever.

"Matthew," said Hannah, clinging to him, "let us go hence."

Matthew saw that she was faint and, kneeling down, supported her in his arms while he threw some of the thrillingly cold water of the enchanted lake upon her face and bosom. It revived her, but could not renovate her courage.

"Yes, dearest," cried Matthew, pressing her tremulous form to his breast, "we will go hence and return to our humble cottage. The blessed sunshine and the quiet moonlight shall come through our window. We will kindle the cheerful glow of our hearth at eventide and be happy in its light. But never again will we desire more light than all the world may share with us."

"No," said his bride, "for how could we live by day or sleep by night in this awful blaze of the Great Carbuncle?"

Out of the hollow of their hands they drank each a draught from the lake, which presented them its waters uncontaminated by an earthly lip. Then, lending their guidance to the blinded cynic, who uttered not a word, and even stifled his groans in his own most wretched heart, they began to descend the mountain. Yet as they left the shore, till then untrodden, of the spirit's lake, they threw a farewell glance toward the cliff and beheld the vapours gathering in dense volumes, through which the gem burned duskily.

As touching the other pilgrims of the Great Carbuncle, the legend goes on to tell that the worshipful Master Ichabod Pigsnort soon gave up the quest as a desperate speculation, and wisely resolved to betake himself again to his warehouse, near the town dock, in Boston. But as he passed through the Notch of the mountains a war party of Indians captured our unlucky merchant and carried him to Montreal, there holding him in bondage till by the payment of a heavy ransom he had woefully subtracted from his hoard of pine-tree shillings. By his long absence, moreover, his affairs had become so disordered that for the rest of his life, instead of wallowing in silver, he had seldom a sixpence-worth of copper. Doctor Cacaphodel, the alchemist, returned to his laboratory with a prodigious fragment of granite, which he ground to powder, dissolved in acids, melted in the crucible and burned with the blowpipe, and published the result of his experiments in one of the heaviest folios of the day. And for all these purposes the gem itself could not have answered better than the granite. The poet, by a somewhat similar mistake, made prize of a great piece of ice which he found in a sunless chasm of the mountains, and swore that it corresponded in all points with his idea of the Great Carbuncle. The critics say that, if his poetry lacked the splendour of the gem, it retained all the coldness of the ice. The Lord De Vere went back to his ancestral hall, where he contented himself with a wax-lighted chandelier, and filled in due course of time another coffin in the ancestral vault. As the funeral torches gleamed within that dark receptacle, there was no need of the Great Carbuncle to show the vanity of earthly pomp.

The cynic, having cast aside his spectacles, wandered about the world a miserable object, and was punished with an agonizing desire of light for the wilful blindness of his former life. The whole night long he would lift his splendour-blasted orbs to the moon and stars; he turned his face eastward at sunrise as duly as a Persian idolater; he made a pilgrimage to Rome to witness the magnificent illumination of St Peter's church and finally perished in the Great Fire of London, into the midst of which he had thrust himself with the desperate idea of catching one feeble ray from the blaze that was kindling earth and heaven.

Matthew and his bride spent many peaceful years and were fond of telling the legend of the Great Carbuncle. The tale, however, towards the close of their lengthened lives, did not meet with the full credence that had been accorded to it by those who remembered the ancient lustre of the gem. For it is affirmed that from the hour when two mortals had shown themselves so simply wise as to reject a jewel which would have dimmed all earthly things its splendour waned. When our pilgrims reached the cliff, they found only an opaque stone with particles of mica glittering on its surface. There is also a tradition that as the youthful pair departed the gem was loosened from the forehead of the cliff and fell into the enchanted lake, and that at noontide the Seeker's form may still be seen to bend over its quenchless gleam.

Some few believe that this inestimable stone is blazing as of old, and say that they have caught its radiance, like a flash of summer lightning, far down the valley of the Saco. And be it owned that many a mile from the Crystal Hills I saw a wondrous light around their summits, and was lured by the faith of poesy to be the latest pilgrim of the Great Carbuncle.

Note on the Text

The stories in this collection have been selected from *Twice-Told Tales* (1837), *Mosses from an Old Manse* (1846) and *The Snow-Image, and Other Twice-Told Tales* (1852). In some instances, variant readings from previously published versions have been adopted. Spelling and punctuation have been Anglicized, standardized, modernized and made consistent throughout.

Notes

p. 4, *in the year 1659… the crown of martyrdom*: A reference to the public hanging of the Quakers Marmaduke Stephenson and William Robinson on 27th October 1659.

p. 5, *the person then at the head of the government*: John Endecott (*c.*1588–1665) was governor of the Massachusetts Bay Colony.

p. 5, *The historian of the sect*: A reference to the Dutch historian Willem Sewel (1653–1720) and his book *The History of the Rise, Increase, and Progress of the Christian People Called Quakers* (1717, English translation 1722).

p. 15, *Cobler of Aggawam*: A reference to the fictional narrator of the satirical pamphlet *The Simple Cobler of Aggawam* (1647) by the Puritan clergyman Nathaniel Ward (1578–1652).

p. 17, *Archbishop Laud*: William Laud (1573–1645) became Archbishop of Canterbury in 1633 and staunchly opposed Puritanism.

p. 32, *his interference was not prompt*: A reference to the fact that Charles II only responded to the persecution of the Quakers in New England, by signing an order for imprisoned Quakers to be sent to England, in September 1661.

p. 42, *the kings of Great Britain... the colonial governors*: Charles II suspended the right of the Massachusetts Bay Colony to elect its own governors in 1684, and in 1691 James II officialized their direct appointment by the crown.

p. 42, *six governors... peaceful sway*: A reference to Edmund Andros (1637–1714, in office 1686–89), Joseph Dudley (1647–1720, in office 1702–15), Samuel Shute (1662–1742, in office 1716–28), William Burnet (1688–1729, in office 1728–29), William Phipps (1651–95, in office 1692–94) and Richard Coote, 1st Earl of Bellomont (1636–1700, in office 1699–1700) respectively. Thomas Hutchinson (1711–80), himself governor from 1769 to 1774, wrote *The History of the Province of Massachusetts Bay* (1764–1828).

p. 44, *Ramillies wig*: A fashionable wig, named after a town in Belgium, featuring a long plait tied with bows at the top and bottom.

p. 51, *the Moonshine of Pyramus and Thisbe*: A reference to the character of *A Midsummer Night's Dream*'s play within a play.

p. 65, *Lovell's Fight*: A famous battle in Pequawket, Maine, between the British forces led by Richard Lovewell (also known as Lovell, 1691–1725) and the Abenaki tribe.

p. 93, *Castalia*: According to Greek myth, a fountain on Mount Parnassus that provided inspiration to those who drank from it.

p. 96, *the Oregon expedition*: A reference to a failed expedition from Massachusetts to Oregon, led in 1832 by Nathaniel Jarvis Wyeth (1802–56) to set up a trading post.

p. 100, *Gulliver's portable mansion among the Brobdingnags*: In the second part of the satirical novel *Gulliver's Travels* (1726) by the Irish writer Jonathan Swift (1667–1745), Gulliver travels to the land of Brobdingnag, where everything, including the inhabitants, is of huge size. The queen of Brobdingnag constructs for Gulliver a small house, a "travelling box" in which he can be carried around.

p. 102, *Don Quixote*: The eponymous hero of the satirical novel by the Spanish writer Miguel de Cervantes (1547–1616), published between 1605 and 1615. Don Quixote is a confused old man who, fixated with stories of romance, comes to believe he is a knight on a heroic quest.

p. 103, *the Scottish Chiefs and Thomas Thumb*: A reference to the novels of Sir Walter Scott (1771–1832) and the classic folk tale of Tom Thumb, first published in 1621 as *The History of Tom Thumb*.

p. 103, *New England Primer*: A book of learning aids based on religious content, first published in 1690.

p. 103, *Life of Franklin*: *The Life of Benjamin Franklin, Written by Himself* (1793) by the American statesman and scientist Benjamin Franklin (1706–90).

p. 104, *Webster's spelling book*: *A Grammatical Institute of the English Language* (1783–85) by Noah Webster (1758–1843).

p. 108, *Where are you going... an old song*: 'Where Are You Going My Pretty Maid?' is a traditional song, the earliest known printed record of which dates from 1790.

p. 112, *wandering up and down upon the earth*: Job 1:7.

p. 116, *'L'Allegro'*: A poem by John Milton (1608–74) first published in 1645.

p. 119, *James II... endanger our religion*: Soon after he had ascended to the throne of England in 1685, the Catholic James II (1633–1701) merged all the north-western American colonies into the Dominion of New England, and sent the much resented Sir Edmund Andros (1637–1714) to govern it.

p. 119, *the Prince of Orange... salvation of New England*: A reference to the bloodless Glorious Revolution of 1688, which brought to the British throne the Protestant William of Orange (1650–1702) as King William III, who ruled from 1689 until his death.

p. 120, *A multitude... a people struggling against her tyranny*: A reference to the Boston Massacre of 5th March 1770, in which British troops killed five rioters.

p. 121, *King Philip's War*: A 1675–78 conflict which opposed the New England colonists and the Native American forces led by Metacomet (1638–76), also known as King Philip. Although it resulted in a colonial victory, it decimated the settlers' population.

p. 121, *Smithfield fire*: Smithfield Market in London was the scene of many executions, particularly of Protestants.

p. 121, *John Rogers*: John Rogers (*c.*1505–55) was an English clergyman who converted to Protestantism and was executed for heresy.

p. 121, *St Bartholomew*: A reference to the St Bartholomew's Day Massacre of 23rd–24th August 1572, in which thousands of Protestants were killed across France.

p. 121, *Bradstreet*: Simon Bradstreet (1603–97) was the governor of the Massachusetts Bay Colony from 1679 to 1686 and 1689 to 1692.

p. 122, *Edward Randolph... through life and to his grave*: Edward Randolph (1632–1703) was envoy sent by Britain to the North American colonies. His reports led to the suspension of elected governors in 1684 (see note to p. 42), and he later served in the administration of the Dominion of New England (see first note to p. 119). Cotton Mather (1663–1728) was a Puritan minister who was very influential in New England politics and involved in the Salem witch trials of 1692–93.

p. 122, *Bullivant*: Benjamin Bullivant was the first Attorney General of the Dominion of New England (in office 1686–87).

p. 122, *Dudley*: Joseph Dudley (see second note to p. 42).

p. 124, *Winthrop*: John Winthrop (1588–1649) was the governor of the Massachusetts Bay Colony (in office 1629–34, 1637–40, 1642–44 and 1646–49).

p. 125, *Old Noll's name*: Old Noll was one of the nicknames of Oliver Cromwell (1599–1658).

p. 127, *at Lexington... the first fallen of the Revolution*: The Battle of Lexington of 9th April 1775 marked the beginning of the American Revolutionary War.

p. 127, *Bunker's Hill*: The Battle of Bunker's Hill of 17th June 1775, although technically a British victory, was celebrated as a turning point for the American forces.

p. 130, *King William's court*: A reference to William III (see second note to p. 119).

p. 132, *Goody Cloyse*: Sarah Cloyce (1648–1703) was the name of a woman accused of witchcraft during the Salem witch trials of 1692–93.

p. 133, *gossip*: Used here in the original sense of "spiritual relation".

p. 133, *Goody Cory*: Martha Corey (1619–92) was another woman accused and convicted of witchcraft during the Salem witch trials.

p. 133, *one of the rods... lent to the Egyptian magi*: A reference to Exodus 7:11–13, in which Pharaoh instructs his sorcerers to turn their rods into serpents.

p. 135, *pow-wows*: Native American medicine men.

p. 144, *some old magazine or newspaper*: The source has been identified as *Political and Literary Anecdotes of His Own Times* (1818) by William King (1786–1865).

p. 176, *Strutt's Book of English Sports and Pastimes*: The English antiquary Joseph Strutt (1749–1802) was, among other things, an authority on the costumes of the past. *Sports and Pastimes of the People of England* was published in 1801.

p. 178, *Salvage*: An archaic form of "savage".

p. 178, *the crew of Comus*: A reference to the masque *Comus* (1634) by the English poet John Milton (1608–74), in which the evil sorcerer Comus offers unsuspecting travellers a magical potion that transforms "their human countenance... / Into some brutish form of wolf, or bear, / Or ounce, or tiger, hog, or bearded goat, / All other parts remaining as they were".

p. 181, *the eve of St John*: Midsummer's Eve, 23rd June.

p. 184, *I know thee, Blackstone*: Did Governor Endicott speak less positively, we should suspect a mistake here. The Rev. Mr Blackstone, though an eccentric, is not known to have been an immoral man. We rather doubt his identity with the priest of Merry Mount. (HAWTHORNE'S NOTE)

p. 185, *Ancient*: I.e. standard-bearer.

p. 189, *A Parable*: Another clergyman in New England, Mr Joseph Moody, of York, Maine, who died about eighty years since, made himself remarkable by the same eccentricity that is here related of the Reverend Mr Hooper. In his case, however, the symbol had a different import. In early life he had accidentally killed a beloved friend; and from that day till the hour of his own death, he hid his face from men. (HAWTHORNE'S NOTE)

p. 195, *that famous one where they tolled the wedding knell*: A reference to Hawthorne's tale 'The Wedding Knell' (1836).

p. 201, *Governor Belcher's administration*: Jonathan Belcher (1682–1757) was governor of Massachusetts Bay from 1730 to 1741.

p. 206, *Hippocrates*: The Greek philosopher Hippocrates (460–370 BC), known as the father of medicine.

p. 208, *Ponce de León*: Juan Ponce de León (1460–1521) was a Spanish explorer who travelled to Florida in 1513 and 1521, although the notion that he was on a quest to find the Fountain of Youth is a popular myth.

p. 216, *an English review... one of the novels of Alexandre Dumas*: An 1860 article in the *Universal Review* claimed that Hawthorne had taken the idea for this story from *Mémoires d'un médecin: Joseph Balsamo* (1846–48) by the French writer Alexandre Dumas *père* (1802–70), about the Italian occultist Giuseppe Balsamo (1743–95), also known as Alessandro Cagliostro.

p. 218, *Elijah's cave at Horeb... Abraham's sepulchral cave at Machpelah*: Respectively, a cave in which the prophet Elijah took shelter during his journey into the wilderness (1 Kings 19:8) and the Cave of Machpelah, or the Cave of the Patriarchs, in the Palestinian city of Hebron, where Abraham, Isaac and Jacob, along with their wives Sarah, Rebecca and Leah, are said to be buried. It is the second holiest site in Judaism.

p. 229, *when the famous Captain Smith visited these coasts*: The English explorer John Smith (1580–1631) was one of the founders of the Jamestown Colony, the first permanent English settlement in North America, and is famous for exploring and mapping the coast of New England.

p. 234, *in rerum natura*: "In the nature of things" (Latin).

Extra Material

on

Nathaniel Hawthorne's

*Young Goodman Brown
and Other Stories*

Nathaniel Hawthorne's Life

Nathaniel Hathorne (the *w* would be added in the 1830s) was *Birth and Family* born on 4th July 1804 in Salem, Massachusetts, to Nathaniel *Background* Hathorne and Elizabeth Clarke Manning Hathorne, with an older and a younger sister, Elizabeth and Louisa, both of whom would retain a strong influence upon Hawthorne well into maturity. Hathorne had hitherto been a name of some illustriousness, and not a little notoriety, in the history of New England: Hawthorne's predecessors – including the judge that condemned the supposed witches of the Salem witch trials – are the progenitors of the many ghastly puritans that stalk Hawthorne's fiction. Major William Hathorne (*c.*1606/7–1681) left England for the colonies in the 1630s, where, amongst other achievements, he was famed for his prosecutions of the Quakers, a propensity memorialized in short stories 'The Gentle Boy' and 'The Maypole of Merry Mount'. His son Justice John Hathorne (1641–1717) continued the family tradition of intolerance, sitting as an associate magistrate at the notorious Salem witch trials. He never publicly repented his verdict. By the turn of the nineteenth century, the Hathornes were primarily a seafaring family, with Hawthorne's father and other close family members captaining merchant ships out of Salem (at this point still a bustling competitor to Boston and New Bedford – in contrast to the moribund days of 'The Custom House' section of *The Scarlet Letter*). Salem would attain a central and ambivalent presence in Hawthorne's work and life; it was at once the locale of the author's originating myths and represented, like his Hathorne antecedents, a repressive burden to be dislodged. Hawthorne tried to leave Salem geographically and spiritually throughout his whole life: he achieved the first of these goals, though it might be argued that he never truly managed the second.

Early Life   In 1808 Captain Nathaniel Hathorne (b. 1775) died in Surinam of yellow fever, occasioning his and his sisters' removal to his mother's Manning family home, under the roof of Robert Manning at 10 ½ Herbert Street, Salem. Hawthorne's original "Castle Dismal", this large home was crowded with Mannings and Hathornes – young Nathaniel reportedly sharing a bed with his uncle. The bereaved Hathornes were thrown upon the charity of the Mannings, a dependency Nathaniel would resent throughout his youth, railing against uncle Robert's frugality in the letters of his university years. Hawthorne apparently never felt himself fully integrated into the Manning family: although the Mannings, heirs of the Salem and Boston Stagecoach Line, were also a venerable New England family, it is notable that it is always the Hathornes that the author returns to in his work. Despite his early death, it is clearly his father's side of the family that Hawthorne identifies himself with.

In 1813 the nine-year-old Hawthorne injured his foot playing ball. Though no external injury could be detected, one leg soon showed signs of stunted growth, and the child became lame and was confined to his home. He was thus prevented from regular school attendance for two years and four months. At this time the lexicographer Joseph Emerson Worcester, who would later become Noah Webster's main competitor in the race to provide America with a standard dictionary, was hired by the Mannings to tutor Hawthorne at home. The incident that seems to have had a not inconsiderable influence on Hawthorne's character and literary career: it is, for instance, reflected in the lengthy confinement and traumatic re-emergence of Ilbrahim in the author's first notable success, 'The Gentle Boy' (1832, 1837).

In 1818 the Hathornes left Massachusetts and the Mannings for Maine, settling on family property in Raymond, while Hawthorne continued to attend school in Stroudwater, near Portland. The time spent at Raymond outside of term time would occasion the salad days of Hawthorne's youth: idyllic rambles in the wilderness and the exertions of fishing, hunting and skating were interspersed with first readings of Shakespeare and Bunyan, figures who would colour Hawthorne's oeuvre. Hawthorne was soon, however, forced to return to Salem and the Mannings for the benefit of his education; his mother, to

Hawthorne's great disturbance, remained in Raymond for a further two years while he prepared for college.

In 1821 Hawthorne would go up to Bowdoin College in *Bowdoin College* Brunswick, Maine. It was a small college of rusticated aspect, which had been founded in 1794, had only three buildings and five members of faculty at the time of Hawthorne's arrival, and which would be lovingly recreated in the early novella *Fanshawe*. Hawthorne did not excel academically, he would finish a solid eighteenth in a class of thirty-five, nor was he exceptionally gregarious as a student, though he would make and retain valuable friendships with his classmates, including future president Franklin Pierce, Horatio Bridge (who would do much to encourage and aid Hawthorne throughout his career) and Jonathan Cilley (for whom Hawthorne would write a memorial essay after his death in a duel in 1838). Uncle Robert funded Hawthorne's education, though not, in the writer's eyes at least, with any great generosity. Their correspondence is characterized in this period by Hawthorne's frequent requests for money and Manning's refusals. At least some of Hawthorne's allowance would be spent on gambling, as well as on the resultant fines imposed by the university authorities following the repeated detection of this crime.

Hawthorne's literary exertions would also begin at Bow- *Early Writings* doin. On his return to his family in Salem after graduation in 1825, he recommenced work on *Fanshawe*, which he had begun as an undergraduate. He completed this first novel in 1828 and published it privately in Boston. *Fanshawe*, in spite of its attractive milieu and wealth of romantic detail, is clearly the work of a tyro and by some distance the least satisfying of Hawthorne's novels. Hawthorne was commensurately displeased with this first effort: later in life he would disown the volume and refuse to discuss it, destroying his own copy and concealing its publication from his wife. It would not be reprinted until 1876, twelve years after its author's death. The period following *Fanshawe* represented something of a trial for Hawthorne's nascent literary skills, as the author began and abandoned a series of projects, and faced indifference and discouragement from those he asked to publish his works. A trio of short-story cycles were attempted and discarded during the late 1820s and 1830s: although portions of *Provincial Tales* and *The Story Teller* would survive and achieve publication as independent pieces, he would burn the manuscript of *Seven*

Tales of My Native Land after the collection's potential publishers made their lack of interest clear.

The first years of the 1830s marked the first of Hawthorne's forays into publication (and the arrival of his *w*). Short stories 'The Hollow of Three Hills' and 'An Old Woman's Tale' appeared alongside three biographical sketches in the *Salem Gazette* in 1830. The next year *The Token and Atlantic Souvenir* contained a selection of pieces by Hawthorne, as would future editions throughout the 1830s. Throughout this period Hawthorne, in contrast to his increasingly isolated mother and sisters, indulged an impulse to peregrination, exploring New England in an itinerant fashion and making occasional excursions further afield. Notably, in 1832 Hawthorne toured New Hampshire and Vermont for the whole of the summer, storing up a body of experience that would inform the structure of his projected volume *The Story Teller* and provide material for a number of short stories. Samuel Goodrich, publisher of *The Token and Atlantic Souvenir*, would finally reject *The Story Teller* in 1834, although some sections would attain publication through channels administered by Goodrich, and in other publications until 1837.

The second half of the 1830s marks the first full flowering of Hawthorne's literary career; this is the period of much of his classic short fiction, with publications including 'The Minister's Black Veil', 'The Maypole of Merry Mount' and 'Young Goodman Brown'. These piecemeal inclusions did not yet accrue to a career, and in 1836 Hawthorne began his first regular employment as editor of the *American Magazine of Useful and Entertaining Knowledge* in Boston. This position lasted from January until the publisher's bankruptcy in June, with Hawthorne receiving only $20 of the $500 of his contract, a professional disappointment that marked the beginning of a pattern in Hawthorne's attempts at non-literary employment.

1837 brought better news, however, with the publication of *Twice-Told Tales*. This volume was underwritten, without Hawthorne's knowledge, by old Bowdoin classmate Horatio Bridge, and received a commendatory review by fellow alumnus Henry W. Longfellow. *Twice-Told Tales* is made up of eighteen short stories culled from Hawthorne's periodical publications. 1837 would also herald important domestic changes, with the first encounter between Hawthorne and his future wife Sophia Amelia Peabody, third daughter of Nathaniel Peabody and

Elizabeth Palmer Peabody. Sophia's father was a dentist, while her mother was an associate of the Concord transcendentalists. Elizabeth would exert herself on behalf of Hawthorne – securing in 1839 a job for Hawthorne as weigher and gauger at Boston Custom House, the employment that would grant him the independence to propose marriage to Sophia and receive her acceptance. Sophia would remain devoted to Hawthorne throughout their life together, putting her own creative impulses second to supporting her husband's fragile emotions. Sophia provided illustrations for an edition of 'The Gentle Boy' and also wrote rich and extensive journals, though Hawthorne encouraged her not to publish these in his lifetime.

The 1840s marked somewhat of an intermezzo in Haw- *Brook Farm* thorne's literary career as the author began a series of re-evaluations of his way of life. He made some not particularly remunerative attempts at educational literature for children, resulting in *Famous Old People, Grandfather's Chair* and *Liberty Tree* (all 1841) and *Biographical Stories for Children* (1842). His lack of direction in this period resulted in his resigning from his work at the Boston Custom House and decamping to Brook Farm in 1841. This utopian community, based upon the ethic of shared work and intellectual communion, would find its fullest literary portrait in the elegiac satire of *The Blithedale Romance* in 1852. That book demonstrates the isolation and inadequacy the cripplingly shy Hawthorne felt in the midst of this progressive congregation, and his sojourn lasted only eight months – the diffident writer feeling he could not last the winter.

After his return Hawthorne promptly married Sophia (on the *Marriage* 9th of July 1842) and moved into the Old Manse in Concord, a property previously owned by the Emerson family. During his three and a half years in Concord, Hawthorne would become acquainted with the transcendentalist community, getting to know Emerson, Thoreau, Ellery Channing, Bronson Allcott and Margaret Fuller (rumoured to be the model for Zenobia in *The Blithedale Romance*). More stories were written and published and *Twice-Told Tales* expanded and republished, while 1844 would bring the Hawthornes a daughter, Una, named after the heroine of Spenser's *Fairie Queene*.

The next year the Hawthornes made way for the Emersons, *Salem Custom* as the ancestral heirs reclaimed the Old Manse and *House* Hawthorne and his young family moved in with the author's mother and sisters in Salem. This arrangement, however, was brief: the influence of Bridge and Pierce secured unchallenging part-time work for Hawthorne at the Salem Custom House from 1846, something which allowed the author sufficient financial independence to rent a house large enough for his mother and sisters to have their own apartments. Again, though, Hawthorne's bad professional fortune struck and he was removed from his near-sinecure in the aftermath of the election of Whig President Zachary Taylor, occasioning some scandal and the establishment of a subscription for the support of Hawthorne and his family. Hawthorne's professional misfortune was, however, the good luck of his readers, for it was in the period immediately following the ordeal of his dismissal that Hawthorne began *The Scarlet Letter*, his first real novel and greatest success.

Hawthorne's mother Elizabeth died in July 1848, an event that affected the writer greatly and influenced the direction his writing would soon take: the sombre tone of *The Scarlet Letter* and its treatment of isolated, suffering womanhood have been read as a tribute to the author's mother. The next few years were pivotal for Hawthorne. In 1850 he published *The Scarlet Letter*, and at the same time he found it necessary to vacate Salem once more, this time for Lenox in the Berkshire Mountains, the centre of a thriving intellectual summer colony, where Hawthorne would reside for a year and a half. The controversy over the loss of his position at the Custom House was partly to blame for this move, as well as the Salem townsfolk's unhappiness with his description of them in 'The Custom House'. This satirical introduction to *The Scarlet Letter* was purportedly written by a "decapitated surveyor", clearly a proxy for the sacked Hawthorne.

Friendship with Melville   While in Lenox, Hawthorne would make the acquaintance of Herman Melville, a writer fifteen years his junior, in possession of an expansive (though not untroubled) character much in contrast with Hawthorne's. The writers would know one another only briefly, but with an intensity that would colour both of their careers. They met on 5th August 1850, both writers being among a group of authors gathered together to climb Monument Mountain, and they bonded over a dinner at the home of David Dudley Field that night. Evert Duyckinck, Melville's friend and publisher, was also present on this sojourn and quickly commissioned work from Melville; an essay entitled 'Hawthorne and His Mosses', an ostensible review of the four-year-old work *Mosses from an Old Manse*, that would be published anonymously in *The Literary World*. Melville is embarrassingly fulsome in his praise, comparing Hawthorne with Spenser, and at length with Shakespeare: for Melville, Hawthorne needed "not a very great deal more, and Nathaniel were verily William". Hawthorne, not immediately realizing who had written the article, was most flattered.

The usually diffident Hawthorne quickly developed a relationship of uncharacteristic closeness with the intense young Melville. The authors visited one another regularly throughout their brief friendship, visits which occurred while Melville was working on the manuscript that would become *Moby Dick*, and appear to have been characterized by long and free speculation between the two writers, Melville describing their conversations at "ontological heroics".

After problems with his landlords and a growing disaffection with Lenox, Hawthorne left Berkshire on 21st November 1851, moving in with Sophia's parents in West Newton, and in effect ending the friendship with Melville. The significance of the Hawthorne-Melville friendship is not in its length, for it would continue with intensity for only fifteen months, but in the felicity of two such central figures in the American canon coming together at such crucial points in both of their careers. When they met in August 1850, Hawthorne had just published *The Scarlet Letter*, and when they parted in November 1851, Melville had just published *Moby Dick*. The two key works of the American mid-century, perhaps the two key works of American literature as a whole, were in place.

For all its importance, however, our record of this titanic meeting is scant. Hawthorne's letters to Melville were not retained, and only ten letters from Melville to the Hawthornes are extant: eight to Nathaniel, one to Sophia and one to Julian (Hawthorne's son, born in 1846). It has been suggested that Hawthorne's influence can be felt in the late and drastic redraftings of *Moby Dick*: though there is no first-hand evidence of Hawthorne's work, Melville's book would contain the famous dedication "In token of my admiration for his genius, This Book is Inscribed to Nathaniel Hawthorne". Melville's *Pierre* (1852) and his massive poem *Clarel: A Poem and Pilgrimage in the Holy Land* (1876) would echo the faintly homoerotically tinged relation between these men, while

259

the mismatch between the youthful Coverdale and senior Hollingsworth in Hawthorne's *The Blithedale Romance* tracks a similar dynamic.

Fired by the success of *The Scarlet Letter*, Hawthorne continued with his great literary spurt of the early 1850s and published *The House of the Seven Gables* and *The Blithedale Romance* in successive years, as well as another collection of short stories, *The Snow Image, and Other Twice-Told Tales*. He also published two books for children, *A Wonder Book for Boys and Girls* (1852) and *Tanglewood Tales* (1853), as well as *The Life of Franklin Pierce* (1852), the presidential candidate's campaign biography. In 1851 Hawthorne was for the first time able to support his expanding family (a second daughter, Rose, was born in May that year) through his literary work. In 1852 he was able to purchase The Wayside, Bronson Alcott's former house, and return to Concord with his family. Interestingly, it was his fiction for children that he produced so rapidly during this period that provided for Hawthorne and his family most handsomely: he made $2,460 from his children's writings compared with only $1,500 lifetime royalties from his most successful novel, *The Scarlet Letter*.

Support for Franklin Pierce At this time Hawthorne attracted the disapprobation of many of his New England associates by writing the campaign biography of his Bowdoin classmate Franklin Pierce in support of his bid for president. Hawthorne's apparent acceptance of the 1850 Compromise with the slave-owning states was implied by this action, and the cause of much consternation, along with some rather telling comments made by Hawthorne regarding slavery in that volume. The author, with a lack of concern that seems somewhat more than blasé, suggests that God will ensure that slavery "vanish like a dream" at the time that "all its uses have been fulfilled".

Pierce's successful campaign would secure Hawthorne the post of consul in Liverpool the following year, a post he would hold until 1857. Apparently the most lucrative position at Pierce's disposal, Hawthorne was able to put aside around $30,000 from his salary and the various commissions associated with the post, and therefore support the Hawthorne family through their European travels of the next few years. With his departure from the USA and his reintroduction into the workplace, Hawthorne's literary momentum slowed. He produced very little for publication in this period but for a series of essays about Britain which was begun at this time and published, with an appreciative dedication to Pierce, as *Our Old Home* in 1863. He worked on a series of richly descriptive English notebooks that would be published after his death and a number of stillborn manuscripts.

It was in November 1856 that Hawthorne had his next encounter with Melville, who was on his way to the Holy Land, via Greece and Italy. Hawthorne found Melville "a little paler, and perhaps a little sadder" than he had been in Lenox but, for this brief visit at least, much of their earlier intensity was rekindled. Melville, disheartened by both the lack of success of *Moby Dick* and the critical attacks upon *Pierre* (1852), and travelling on his in-laws' money for the sake of his health, spoke of "Providence and futurity, and of everything that lies beyond human ken, and informed [Hawthorne] that he had 'pretty much made up his mind to be annihilated'". Hawthorne had tried and failed to secure Melville a position in the Pierce administration, although this does not seem to have hindered their friendship during this reunion – the writers enjoying excursions to Southport and Chester Cathedral before Melville's departure. Melville briefly looked Hawthorne up on his return passage through Liverpool en route to America on 4th May 1857, though this meeting passed without comment by Hawthorne, and was commemorated with a journal entry of just two words by Melville: "Saw Hawthorne". They did not meet again.

With the Democratic Party's refusal to renominate Pierce as *Living in Europe* its presidential candidate in 1856 (after a disastrously divisive presidency) and the succession of James Buchanan, Hawthorne's consulship came to an end. As a result the family, with a significant accumulation of money, were soon moving in a different direction from Melville, heading from Liverpool to France and then to Italy, where they would spend five months enmeshed in the Roman expatriate colony and Hawthorne would begin his final novel, *The Marble Faun*. On leaving Italy the Hawthornes would settle in England for a year (in the quintessentially Victorian resorts of Leamington Spa and Redcar), and Hawthorne would finish *The Marble Faun* while Una recovered from an illness that developed during their Italian stay.

The early 1860s were a period of difficulty and depression *Final Works* for Hawthorne. *The Marble Faun*, his last complete novel, was published in America in February 1860 (and in Britain, as *The Transformation*, in March); after that Hawthorne returned to work on an English romance that he had been working on prior to *The Marble Faun*, although after two drafts he would set this aside once again. He then began work on a projected novel about an elixir of life (an obsession throughout Hawthorne's work, from 'Dr Heidegger's Experiment' (1837) onwards), but this would be broken off after the customary second draft in 1862.

The Civil War   The Civil War was troubling for Hawthorne, and in July 1862 he produced an essay for the *Atlantic Monthly* entitled 'Chiefly About War Matters By a Peaceable Man', from which a section on "Uncle Abe" Lincoln was blue-pencilled by the editors, who feared that it would upset the sensibilities of *Atlantic* readers. This article is ambiguous and Hawthorne was not thought of as having acquitted himself well by many who read him during the war years. More controversy would follow when Hawthorne dedicated a volume of English sketches, *Our Old Home*, to the pro-Southern Pierce in 1863. Through this period Hawthorne's health deteriorated, along with that of both his wife and his daughter Una – none was ever fully healthy after returning from Europe. The cause of Hawthorne's final illness is unknown, though his constant stomach pains have suggested to some biographers the possibility of some form of gastro-intestinal cancer.

Death   Hawthorne undertook a curative tour of the White Mountains with Pierce and died in his sleep on the 19th of May 1864 while staying at Pemigewasset House in Plymouth, New Hampshire. At midnight Pierce, with whom Hawthorne was sharing a room, awoke and noted that his companion was slumbering peacefully – when he woke again at around three o'clock the author was dead. He was buried in Sleepy Hollow Cemetery in Concord, Massachusetts. Portions of the novel on which Hawthorne had been working at the time of his death were published in the July 1864 issue of *Atlantic Monthly* as "Scenes from 'The Dolliver Romance'".

Nathaniel Hawthorne's Works

Hawthorne's tally of four full-fledged novels makes his literary career seem far less active than it actually was; Henry James, a far more productive author, detected "a strain of generous indolence in his composition". Until 1850 Hawthorne was primarily a short-story writer, and he produced a vast amount of fiction in this mode during his life. He also produced multiple volumes of literature for children, and voluminous notebooks detailing his experiences abroad would be published after his death. His relatively early death, and the interruptions to his work caused by his professional, familial and political interests, necessarily curtailed his production, but the fact that his three most widely read novels were produced in three successive years during one sustained burst of creativity speaks for his discipline as a writer.

Hawthorne began *Fanshawe* as an undergraduate at Bow- *Fanshawe* doin College, and this is reflected in both the novel's execution and setting. Published at Hawthorne's own expense in 1828, the writer would disown this early work, never allowing it to be republished during his lifetime and not revealing its existence to his wife. It would be twenty-two years before Hawthorne published another novel.

The novel tells, in a manner that recalls the soft irony of Washington Irving and the American Gothic of Charles Brockden Brown, the story of a young and ailing scholar, Fanshawe, who shares the morbidity, physical beauty and solitary nature of his creator, and who falls in love with the ward, Ellen Langton, of the rector, Dr Melmoth, at Harley College, a thinly veiled depiction of Bowdoin. After a leisurely start the novel soon picks up, with the kidnapping of the ward and the story's various characters fanning across New England in pursuit. After a denouement in which Fanshawe is allowed to display his latent heroism, Ellen offers marriage to the hero, but the scholar declines in favour of his more dashing competitor, Edward Walcott, and retires to study, and presently to die.

Like *Fanshawe*, *Twice-Told Tales* was published semi- *Twice-Told Tales* privately: its expenses underwritten, without Hawthorne's knowledge, by Horatio Bridge. The first edition appeared in 1837, and the second in 1842.

A handful of Hawthorne favourites were included in this volume, including 'The Gentle Boy', 'The Minister's Black Veil' and 'The Maypole of Merry Mount', setting out the contours of the psychological terrain of the rest of Hawthorne's work. However, these were not always the tales that were successful among Hawthorne's first readers – the sentimental and the allegorical were more to the taste of his mid-century audience: for instance, 'Little Annie's Ramble' was a great success upon publication, though it is to few readers' tastes today, and 'The Gentle Boy' was celebrated and reprinted regularly throughout the nineteenth century. It is perhaps Hawthorne's use of the "sketch" genre, adopted via Irving from the popular British literature of the eighteenth century, and displayed plentifully amongst these early volumes, that is least appealing to the modern reader. These pieces, with a conscious eye on publication, dispense with Hawthorne's troublingly exact notations on wayward psychologies in favour of a richly sauced conglomeration of sentimentality and local colour, coupled with what seems, when compared to the ubiquitous subtlety of Hawthorne's great fiction, ham-fisted symbolism and allegory. With *The Scarlet Letter* Hawthorne would create a new kind of novel catering for a new set of tastes, making his early successes obsolete and necessitating a re-evaluation of the other overlooked precursors to his masterwork.

Mosses from an Old Manse   Melville writes of Hawthorne's comic gift in this collection that "it is the very religion of mirth", and the extent to which Hawthorne's primary literary urge and skill is towards the comic is sometimes overlooked by those that come to his work via *The Scarlet Letter*. Melville emphasizes how essential the marriage of light and dark is to Hawthorne's work: "You may be witched by his sunlight – transported by the bright gildings in the skies he builds over you – but there is the blackness of darkness beyond; and even his bright gildings but fringe, and play upon the edges of the thunder clouds". As with much criticism by one author of another, this description seems to match more appositely the author of the nascent *Moby Dick* than the author of Hawthorne's many allegories and sketches. Melville is right, however, in emphasizing how closely comedy and tragedy are situated in Hawthorne: their interdependence is constant throughout the oeuvre.

It is in this volume, published in 1846, that we first meet 'Young Goodman Brown' – other classic tales include 'Rappaccini's Daughter', 'Egotism; or, The Bosom Serpent', 'The Birthmark' and 'Roger Malvin's Burial', stories which have been lauded in the twentieth and twenty-first centuries as psychological explorations to rival Edgar Allan Poe. The characteristic register is one of muted allegory shaded with the psychological terrors of repression: Goodman Brown faces and turns away from the sexuality of his own subconscious, which returns to consume its master in 'The Bosom Serpent', while Rappaccini is bound by the poisonous temptations of incest. 'Rappaccini's Daughter' and 'The Birthmark', with their related tales of the incarceration and sacrifice of beautiful women to the masculine pursuit of science, offer insights into Hawthorne's commitment to his work and to the emotional tenor of his marriage at this time.

The Scarlet Letter was published in 1850. The novel starts with a long introductory sketch of life in Salem Custom House, in which the narrator discovers an old faded scarlet "A" and the manuscript upon which the main narrative is based. *The Scarlet Letter*

The action of the novel begins with Hester Prynne emerging from prison with a baby in her arms, wearing a scarlet letter "A" as a symbol for her crime of adultery. Standing on a scaffold in front of a public crowd as a part of her punishment, she refuses to name the man with whom she committed the crime (and the father of her child, Pearl), despite a passionate appeal from the Reverend Arthur Dimmesdale. In a private conversation later, Hester refuses to reveal the identity of Pearl's father to her husband, Roger Chillingworth. Since they are strangers in the area, he makes her promise not to reveal his identity as her husband to the locals.

After her release from prison, Hester settles into the area, despite the vicious abuse heaped on her and her outcast status. She supports herself and her child by working as a seamstress.

Pearl grows up to be a sprightly and imaginative child, though also wayward and uncontrollable. In response to a rumour that Pearl might be taken away from her, Hester visits Governor Bellingham to try to plead her case. Bellingham is about to take Pearl away, but Dimmesdale appeals on Hester's behalf, and dissuades him.

Chillingworth, who is now the town's physician, becomes a close companion to Dimmesdale, whose health is failing. Rumours begin to circulate that Chillingworth is involved in the black arts. He becomes obsessed with discovering the identity of Pearl's father, and of uncovering the truth he believes is hidden in Dimmesdale's heart. One day, he finds Dimmesdale asleep in his chair, and sees something on his chest which provokes a "wild look of wonder, joy and horror".

Believing himself in full possession of Dimmesdale's secret, Chillingworth psychologically tortures him with comments specifically designed to cause him anguish. Dimmesdale's health declines further as a result, though at the same time his

265

popularity among his congregation grows. He practises self-flagellation, and speaks of his guilt in his sermons in a vague, unspecific way, which further increases his popularity, as it is taken as evidence of holiness.

In the middle of the night, Dimmesdale goes to the scaffold where Hester had to stand, overcome by self-hatred. Hester and Pearl, who are passing by, join him there. An enormous letter A appears in the sky. Hester notices the change in Dimmesdale, and talks with Chillingworth to try to help the minister. He confesses his wickedness, and releases her from her promise not to reveal his identity.

Hester and Dimmesdale happen to meet in the forest. She reveals Chillingworth's identity to him, and his evil manipulation. Dimmesdale is at first angry at her, but then they are reconciled. He decides to leave the Puritan colony, unable to live with his guilt, or confess his crime there, and Hester pledges to accompany him.

Dimmesdale, feeling liberated by his decision, delivers a sermon after the Election Day procession to rapturous acclaim, but soon afterwards almost collapses. He makes his way to the scaffold, accompanied by Hester and Pearl, and confesses his sin to the whole crowd, revealing the mark on his chest seen by Chillingworth earlier. He then dies. Afterwards, most people say there was a scarlet A on Dimmesdale's chest.

In his conclusion, Hawthorne tells us the characters' final fates: Chillingworth withers up and dies within a year. He leaves a fortune to Pearl, and she and her mother disappear. In their absence, the legend of the scarlet letter grows. Years later, Hester returns to the area, wearing the scarlet letter, but it is no longer a symbol of stigma. She becomes known for helping the needy, and appears at the end of the novel as the symbol of a hopeful future.

The manner in which the novel combines the portentousness of tragedy with a highly ironical narrative style, and the deeply personalized descriptions of the inner workings of its characters' motivations with a languidly distanced authorial voice, is one of its great innovations. *The Scarlet Letter* is also presciently open to a variety of issues pertaining to nineteenth-century women: the ramifications of a reform of the marriage bonds, working women (with particular concentration on the ubiquitous employment of seamstressing) and the position of the excommunicated "fallen" woman are all explored.

The House of the Seven Gables (1851) concerns the consequences of a historical feud between two New England families,
the Pyncheons and the Mauls. The grasping Pyncheons had in
the Puritan period taken from the Mauls the land upon which
the seven-gabled house was built, and had had its rightful owner
executed for witchcraft. In retaliation the Mauls cursed the
Pyncheons to die, generation after generation, of an explosive
apoplexy – or perhaps to be murdered. At the start of the
novel, the Pyncheon line is dying out, and the heir, Clifford,
is imprisoned. His sister Hepzibah, one of Hawthorne's most
charmingly drawn grotesques, is left to maintain the crumbling
Pyncheon mansion, alone but for a mysterious lodger. A
country cousin arrives to lighten Hepzibah's load, while
Clifford's release is imminent: however, Judge Pyncheon is the
embodiment of the accursed grasping Pyncheon spirit and will
stop at nothing to discover the secret which he believes is held by
Clifford and the house, and which he thinks will make him rich.

The difference between *The Scarlet Letter* and *The House of
the Seven Gables* could not be more marked. Where the earlier
work was taut and controlled, this new novel is sprawling and
digressive. Much of the effectiveness of *The Scarlet Letter*
stems from the careful detailing of its restricted cast of central
characters; in contrast, *The House of the Seven Gables* is an
ensemble piece that revels in the eccentricities of its players.

Many consider *The House of the Seven Gables* to be a failure, arguing that its diffuse focus and generic inconsistencies
undermine its gothic atmosphere. To come to this judgement,
however, is to approach this work from a set of preconceptions
that are not suited to it, that are not its own. Here Hawthorne
is attempting a very different exercise from *The Scarlet Letter*,
for while that book set out to underline the grim hypocrisies
of the Puritans, this new work sets out to offer an answer to
them. Like Hawthorne, the Pyncheons must do battle with
the wicked violence of their forebears in order to overcome
their Puritan inheritance and thereby remove the curse. The
dissonance, then, that some have found at the heart of this
novel between its broad comedy and ominous, gothic elements,
is integral to its project, for this is a novel that dramatizes the
need for both the Hawthornes and the Pyncheons to throw off
the weight of the past and replace the grey Puritan inheritance
with a comic joyfulness. This is shown most effectively in the
chapter 'Governor Pyncheon', in which the body of the recently

deceased Judge Pyncheon is described through a night alone in the Pyncheon house, the light irony with which Hawthorne treats his ghastly subject only adding to its ghoulishness. It is at this point in the novel that the Puritan past is overborne, the point at which the comic begins to hold sway.

The Blithedale Romance *The Scarlet Letter* and *The House of the Seven Gables* perhaps provided some kind of catharsis for Hawthorne, for in his next novel he switched his focus to the near-present and to a set of concerns that was fundamentally and unavoidably bound up with the nineteenth century. In *The Blithedale Romance* (1852) Hawthorne approached the various strands of nineteenth-century progressivism en masse, and explored, in a manner that is at once both conservative and progressive itself, their ramifications. According to Lawrence, "Hawthorne came nearest to actuality in the *Blithedale Romance*", considering the novel's acting out of the division between mental and physical labour a continuation of the dynamic that powered *The Scarlet Letter*.

Miles Coverdale narrates the novel with a detachment that recalls Hawthorne's own less than committed involvement with the Brook Farm project. Arriving at Blithedale in the midst of a New England snowstorm, Coverdale encounters, with an initial optimistic enthusiasm that is quickly replaced with ironic detachment, the community's central characters. Zenobia is the feminist matriarch of Blithedale, living in an uneasy and sexually charged truce with the misogynistic Hollingsworth. Later, a mysterious, impoverished young girl called Priscilla arrives from Boston, upsetting the precarious equilibrium of the collective.

The wilful, voluptuous, wild-flower-wearing Zenobia is rumoured to have been partly based on Margaret Fuller, an early campaigner for women's rights, with whom Hawthorne seems to have developed a connection approaching the romantic. Fuller and Brook Farm do not come off well in Hawthorne's romance: Zenobia and Hollingsworth's Utopianism is matched only by their insensitivity to the emotions of those around them. The bedraggled Priscilla is first rejected by Zenobia and then degraded to the role of performing clairvoyant. It is the blind belief of Hollingsworth in his grand schemes for prisoner reform that leads to his final act of betrayal and to Zenobia's demise. A direct correlation between the strength of the characters' belief in the project at Blithedale and the disarray of their lives develops: Hollingsworth and Zenobia are cruel *because* of their great kindness, their commitment to nineteenth-century reform not so far removed from the superstitions of the embattled Puritans.

As in all Hawthorne's writing, a healthy distance is maintained in *The Blithedale Romance* between the narrator's sensibility and his subject manner, though while the narrative style is ironic, this work is not pitched straightforwardly as satire – the characters' fates are too dark for that and Hawthorne's attitude towards the failed project too ambivalent for him to attack it outright. In *The Bostonians* (1886) James would approach a similar New England congregation to Hawthorne, though with sharper bitterness and less mercy, lampooning Hawthorne's sister-in-law Elizabeth Peabody as the doddering Miss Birdseye and puncturing the pretensions of those intellectuals that crowded around the transcendentalists with some rancour. Though Zenobia, Hollingsworth and the narrator are all made to appear ridiculous at various points in the novel, the overriding tone is an elegiac one, a muffled song of the abandoned dreams of Brook Farm and a farewell to Fuller, who died with her husband and son in 1850 off Fire Island, New York, when the ship in which they were travelling hit a sandbar.

Hawthorne's last completed novel, *The Marble Faun* (1860), *The Marble Faun* is of a markedly different design to his three "American" novels – *The Scarlet Letter*, *The House of the Seven Gables* and *The Blithedale Romance*. In this work the action is moved to the American expatriate community based in and around Rome, a milieu which James would make his own fifteen years later with *Roderick Hudson*. The novel is partly a travelogue of Hawthorne's own Italian excursion – a kind of Baedeker for American readers wishing to sample the corrupting fetor of old Europe: Hawthorne admits in its preface that "the Author was somewhat surprised to see the extent to which he had introduced descriptions of various Italian objects antique, pictorial and statuesque". The book stands beside James's *Italian Hours* as a still usable guide to Rome and Tuscany, replete with historical anecdote and local colour.

Its story is, however, significantly less readily resolved than the Jamesian realist novel (the Jamesian milieu of this later work notwithstanding, James preferred *The Scarlet Letter* to *The Marble Faun*): the slow dance of the characters' hallucinatory movement towards their doom is more symbolist than realist, and the key factors (and perhaps characters) in the novel are atmosphere and history: the timbre of nineteenth-century Italy. The lack of any real resolution in the novel caused such consternation that Hawthorne felt compelled to add a postscript to later editions of the novel, though this would offer precious little satisfaction to those who wanted to unpick the plot of *The Marble Faun*. The move to Europe allows Hawthorne a further reach into history than the Puritans who inhabit the prehistory of his other novels and short stories: soulless Romans capable of unspeakable wickednesses still haunt the catacombs and campagna of Hawthorne's Rome, and the dark happenings at the Palazzo Cenci, with its rumours of incest and rape, haunt the blithe Americans that intrude upon the city's summer vapours. Hawthorne tells the story of a group of three Americans in Rome: Marion, a talented painter of macabre scenes; Hilda, a copyist of great talent who struggles to reconcile her attraction towards Catholicism with her Puritan heritage; and Kenyon, an ironically detached sculptor who bears more than a passing resemblance to Hawthorne himself. The three move about Rome with Donatello, an Italian prince whose similarity to the carved faun of Praxiteles gives the novel its American name, and are shadowed by an outsider of mysterious origin whom Marion seems both repelled by and drawn towards. The novel charts the attacks of experience and history upon the innocence of Hilda (who reminds many readers of Hawthorne's wife Sophia) and Donatello, as well as the dangers of the exotic "other" to these Americans adrift in old Europe. The novel's drawn-out conclusion offers little hope for those characters that survive, its abiding timbre one of a fateful lost innocence. Hilda would become the model for James's Milly in *The Wings of the Dove* (1902), a character who "would have been a lady-copyist – it met so the case. The case was the case of escape, of living under water, of being at once impersonal and firm". This "living under water" is an apposite description of the atmosphere of *The Marble Faun*: the novel's concern with the unravelling fates of American artists submerged in an ancient and dangerous city. The dialogue between artistic creation, as manifested in the careers of Hawthorne's characters, and the artwork, symbolized by Donatello's proximity to Praxiteles's faun, is mirrored in the indeterminacies of the novel's texture.

The opening chapter of *The Dolliver Romance* (1864), his *The Dolliver* uncompleted last novel, is one of Hawthorne's masterworks *Romance* and approaches themes that are recognizable from numerous other locales in his work. It deals with Dr Dolliver, "a worthy personage of extreme antiquity", charged with the upbringing of his great-granddaughter Pansie, a reincarnation of Pearl and the many other impish little girls in Hawthorne's fiction. Dolliver, who appears to be upwards of a hundred years old, prolongs his life through secretive topes of a cordial invented by his deceased grandson. The depiction of Dolliver's ebbing and waning decrepitude is expert, while the doctor's domestic environment is drawn with great affection. The roughly sketched sections that follow do not match the quality of the opening, and the shape of the completed work can only be guessed at.

– Richard Parker

Select Bibliography

Biographies:
McFarland, Philip, *Hawthorne in Concord* (New York, NY: Grove Press, 2004)
Mellow, James R., *Nathaniel Hawthorne in His Times* (Boston, MS: Houghton Mifflin, 1980)
Miller, Edward Haviland, *Salem is my Dwelling Place* (Iowa City, IA: University of Iowa Press, 1992)
Stewart, Randall, *Nathaniel Hawthorne: A Biography* (New Haven, CT: Yale University Press, 1948)
Turner, Arlin, *Nathaniel Hawthorne: A Biography* (Oxford: Oxford University Press, 1980)

Additional Recommended Reading:
James, Henry, *Hawthorne*, ed. Dan McCall (Ithaca, NY: Cornell, 1966)
Lawrence, D.H., *Studies in Classic American Literature* (London: Penguin, 1971)
Millington, Richard H., ed., *The Cambridge Companion to Nathaniel Hawthorne* (Cambridge: Cambridge University Press, 2004)
Wilson, James C., *The Hawthorne and Melville Friendship* (Jefferson, NC: McFarland, 1999)

ALMA CLASSICS

ALMA CLASSICS aims to publish mainstream and lesser-known European classics in an innovative and striking way, while employing the highest editorial and production standards. By way of a unique approach the range offers much more, both visually and textually, than readers have come to expect from contemporary classics publishing.

~

To order any of our titles and for up-to-date information about our current and forthcoming publications, please visit our website on:

www.almaclassics.com